A KILLING CURE

A KILLING CURE

A JANE LAWLESS MYSTERY

ELLEN HART

SEAL PRESS

Copyright © 1993 Ellen Hart

Design by Clare Conrad
Cover art by Debbie Hanley

Library of Congress Cataloging-in-Publication Data

Hart, Ellen.
     A killing cure/by Ellen Hart.
        p.   cm.
     ISBN 1-878067-36-2
     I. Title.
     PS3558.A6775K55   1993
     813'.54—dc20   93-1009
                                                              CIP

This is a work of fiction and any resemblance to events or persons living or dead is unintentional and purely coincidental.

Printed in the United States of America
First printing, September 1993
10 9 8 7 6 5 4 3 2 1

Foreign Distribution:
In Canada: Raincoast Book Distribution, Vancouver, B.C.
In Great Britain and Europe: Airlift Book Company, London

For my very dear friend,
Chaz Merkel.
Long may he warble.

Cast of Characters

JANE LAWLESS: Owner, Lyme House Restaurant in Minneapolis.

CORDELIA THORN: Artistic Director, Allen Grimby Repertory theatre. Old friend of Jane's.

DORRIE HARRIS: Minneapolis City Council Representative.

ROSE GOWER: Granddaughter of Amelia Gower. Member of the Board of Directors of The Gower Foundation, resident at The Amelia Gower Women's Club of Minneapolis.

CHARLOTTE FORTNUM: Professor of German, University of Minnesota. Mother of Julia and Evie, Chair of the Board of Directors of The Gower Foundation.

MAE WILLIAMS: Poet, member of the Board of Directors of The Gower Foundation. Founder and editor of *Black Poetry Minnesota*.

MIRIAM CIPRIANI: Curator, Stroud Gallery of Art, member of the Board of Directors of The Gower Foundation.

JULIA LINDHURST: Daughter of Charlotte, wife of Freddy, sister of Evie. Art therapist.

EVANGELINE (EVIE) FORTNUM: Daughter of Charlotte, sister of Julia. Aspiring singer.

FREDDY LINDHURST: Husband of Julia. Doctoral candidate in German Literature, University of Minnesota. Teaching assistant in German Department.

DOYLE BENEDICT: Urban Studies major at the University of Minnesota, ROTC, part-time waiter at The Amelia Gower Women's Club.

EMERY GOWER: Nephew of Rose Gower.

RAYMOND LAWLESS: Jane's father, defense attorney in St. Paul.

BERYL CORNELIUS: Jane's aunt.

The man who goes up in a balloon does not feel as if he were ascending; he only sees the earth sinking deeper below him.

Schopenhauer

1

IT was just the kind of evening Charlotte Fortnum loved. Cloudy with a slight nip in the air and the faint hint of drizzle. The sculpture garden would be empty tonight. She would have it all to herself. The weather reminded her of the two years she'd spent in London. Those were good years—before the realities of adult life intruded. She'd been so certain of herself then. So sure of what she wanted. Lately, her life had taken a series of confusing turns. It depressed her to think about it, yet for weeks she'd been able to think of little else. To the outside world she probably still gave the impression of a woman who knew exactly what she wanted, who possessed an unfailing moral center. Unfortunately, Charlotte had a difficult decision to make. Probably the toughest decision of her life. And for the first time, even though she knew deep down what she had to do, her resolve was failing.

Opening her sensible black umbrella, she headed quickly into the garden. Hadn't people always said she walked like a woman with a purpose? Even on her weekly Sunday evening constitutional, Charlotte gave the impression of someone late for a class. But then again, she'd never wanted to keep her students waiting. Their time was as important as hers. Things had to be done correctly. Always in proportion. Life had to be *lived* that way. Charlotte knew people often saw this as rigidity, but whatever it was, she was too old to change. And, after all, wasn't that her answer? She'd known since the very first what her decision must be.

Passing the Cowles Conservatory, she stopped for a moment to look inside. Palm trees in Minnesota! Even after so many years, the sight still charmed her. She smiled inwardly. As depressed as she'd been, a brisk evening walk was always a tonic. Brooding had never been her way. She tipped her head back and took in the vast, slate sky. A fine mist bathed her face in coolness. September was her favorite month. The autumn made her feel so alive, so vital. Things would work out. She should simply stop worrying and do what she knew was right.

In the distance, Charlotte could see the steel and wood Irene Hixon Whitney footbridge. It looked like a pastel version of her brother's erector set. Perhaps a stroll over to Loring Park would do her good. The ducks might still be there. She felt in the pocket of her tweed raincoat for the small sack which contained the remains of this evening's cake. It would be at least an hour before it turned dark. She would be back to her club long before that.

With a last peek into the conservatory, Charlotte turned toward her favorite sculpture, the huge spoonbridge and cherry. It had become a landmark in Minneapolis. And why not? She was sick to death of traditional monuments. Men sitting on horses. Men standing with drawn swords. Men puffed with pride at the sight of some ghastly human slaughter.

"Psssst!"

Charlotte jumped.

"Over here," called a voice.

She squinted into a particularly lovely grouping of spruce next to the locked machine shed. She could barely make out a form standing behind one of the trees. "Who is it? Who's there?"

4

"Come over," said the voice.

Glancing around, Charlotte could see everything was quiet. The graveled garden paths were empty of visitors. She stepped hesitantly to the edge of the grass.

"Just talk to me for a minute," came a soft whisper.

"Oh," said Charlotte, putting her hand on her hip. "It's you. What are you doing out here?"

"Waiting for you."

"Why?"

"I saw you at dinner tonight. You looked like you'd made a decision."

Charlotte remained poker-faced. "I didn't see you."

"No. But I'm right, aren't I? You *have* decided."

Gravely, she nodded.

"I have to talk to you then. There are too many people milling around the club. We need some privacy."

"You're wasting your time. I've said everything I have to say."

The figure backed further into the trees. "But I haven't. Listen, just step in here for a moment. That way we won't be disturbed."

Charlotte hesitated.

"What's wrong?"

"I—" She cocked her head. "Why are you dressed like that?"

"Come on, you owe me this much. We were interrupted before. I never got to finish. I just want to talk to you for two quick minutes. If I can't change your mind in that time, I'll go. You're free to do what you want."

Charlotte closed her umbrella and lowered it to her side. It wasn't that she was afraid, it was just—all this tedious melodrama. Then again, it was so true to form. "All right," she said, marching into the dimness. "Say what you have to say." She stood about a foot away, her hand resting on a tree trunk.

"I'm sorry."

Her countenance became pure granite. "Is that all?"

"Isn't that ever enough? Your decision will ruin lives!"

"Don't you think—"

"That it's an overstatement?" The voice cracked with emotion. "No!"

Charlotte looked away.

"I'll do anything you want."

"I told you what I wanted weeks ago."

Silence. "Then it's useless, isn't it?"

"I'm afraid so." As Charlotte stood waiting for some clever new approach to this continuing argument, tiny hairs on the back of her neck began to prickle. An inner voice was beginning to sound an alarm. Could it be she'd misjudged? Involuntarily, she found herself inching backwards. "You look tired. Go home and go to bed. Besides—" She attempted an uneasy smile. "I need to get my walk in before dark. Doctor's orders."

"I hate you, do you know that? You're a machine. No feelings!"

Without warning, the figure flew at her. Strong hands gripped her neck, cutting off her breath. Charlotte tugged and clawed, struggling with all her might but almost instantly she felt a strange weakness.

"You're always so certain about what's right, so damn superior!" came the whispered voice. "Saint Charlotte. Our Mother Superior." The figure held on several seconds longer and then gave a shriek as Charlotte's body became limp. Released from the fierce grip, Charlotte slumped against a tree trunk and slipped to the ground.

The figure stood over her for a moment, paralyzed. In the distance a car horn sounded. The drizzle was turning to rain. After several more seconds, the figure carefully knelt down next to her, straightening her raincoat and smoothing back her hair. It seemed such a horrible place to leave her. So cold. So exposed. But then again, what did it matter? Charlotte Fortnum had ceased to care.

2

RAYMOND Lawless stuffed a stack of letters into his suit pocket and reached for the small box that someone had placed under his mailbox. It was an odd package. No return address. Nothing that even suggested it had been sent through the mail. Still, it had his name on it, and the correct address, 2046 Summit Avenue. The same house his father had bought when he'd moved the family from Illinois to Minnesota in the late forties. Raymond opened the screen door and entered the front foyer, setting the package on a rosewood credenza under the stairway. Then, slipping out the letters, he leafed through them until he came to one addressed to his housemate, Marilyn. It was from her best friend, Irene, who was currently on a month-long cruise with her new husband. For some reason, the letter rankled. It wasn't the cruise part. Raymond and Marilyn had been on several cruises together. No, it was definitely the husband part. And wasn't that the kicker? After all these years of living together, Raymond was beginning to think that marriage was what he wanted after all.

He could trace this growing realization to the marriage of his son, Peter, five months ago. It had been such a wonderful day, full of young love and high spirits. Why was it then, when Peter could jump into this kind of commitment with total trust, did Raymond feel the need to hang back? After all, he'd been living with Marilyn for almost thirteen years. He loved her dearly, couldn't imagine a life without her. Perhaps, at least initially, he'd felt that a second marriage might in some way be a betrayal of his first wife. But surely that was no longer the case. What had really kept him away from the altar all these years? It was a question he had to think about.

As he stacked the mail neatly next to his briefcase, the phone began to ring. Loosening his tie, he popped a Peppermint Lifesaver into his mouth and headed for the kitchen.

He grabbed the receiver. "Hello."

"Ray, it's Norm. I'm still at the office. We got a call from Al Bennett a few minutes ago. He said Emery Gower's arraignment is set for Monday morning, 9 A.M."

Raymond leaned back against the counter, running a hand through his shaggy silver hair. "Is that right? The county attorney isn't going to let this one get away from her. Ok, you better call Brad Lewis and cancel our morning appointment."

"Will do."

"Oh, and Norm, are you positive we've got all the paperwork on this one? We're going to have to act fast."

"We'll have everything by Monday morning."

"Good. If you need me, I'll be here pretty much all weekend."

"Fine. Later, Ray." The line clicked.

Less than a week ago, Raymond Lawless had been retained by Rose Gower, Emery Gower's great aunt, to defend him against murder charges stemming from the recent death of Charlotte Fortnum. It had already become a *cause célèbre* in the Twin Cities. In addition to her position as professor of German at the University of Minnesota, Ms. Fortnum had been chair of the board of The Gower Foundation for the last twelve years. This foundation, founded in the late 1920s by Amelia Gower—Emery Gower's great great grandmother—was one of the largest philanthropic foundations in the Midwest. Public opinion was already at a pitch. The citizens of Hennepin County wanted this murder solved, the murderer punished.

When Emery Gower was arrested, Raymond knew the press smelled blood. Day by day, he watched them turn it into a public lynching. Adding fuel to the fire, several weeks before Charlotte Fortnum's murder, Emery had been fired from his position as field assistant in the foundation's outreach program. This had been his fifth job within the organization in less than a year. After composing a venomous opinion piece about the inner workings of the foundation—which he hand delivered to the *Star Tribune* and which they had been only too happy to print—Emery stormed into The Amelia Gower Women's Club and dropped the newspaper on top of Charlotte Fortnum's half-eaten meat loaf, threatening her with a law suit, (and some said bodily harm) if she didn't reconsider his employment status *on the spot*. Needless to say, he was quickly shown the door. This had become the much discussed motive for her murder.

Right from the start, Raymond knew they were in for a fight. The police had found fibers from one of Emery's jackets all over Charlotte's raincoat. Charlotte's hair had been found embedded in the same jacket. The physical evidence was mounting. Still, after talking to Emery at great length earlier in the day, Raymond felt certain a defense could be made. Emery was so adamant about wanting this to go to trial. No plea bargains. Raymond had never met anyone who was more persuasive about his own innocence. Not that it necessarily meant anything. Over the years, he'd defended all sorts of people. Most maintained their innocence to the very end. Yet, there was something different about Emery. Raymond suggested a lie detector test, explaining that it would probably not be admissible in court. Still, if Emery passed, he might be able to get that into evidence at some point. Emery jumped at the idea. He wanted to do it right away. Raymond promised he'd set it up.

Yet, even though he felt he could work with Emery, there was something distinctly arrogant about the kid. If that came across in court, it was only going to make things more difficult. After the arraignment on Monday, he would have to file for an extension. Ninety days was not going to be enough time to gather all the evidence in the case.

Raymond checked his watch. It was nearly six. Marilyn would be home soon and he'd promised to get dinner started. Oh well, another few minutes wouldn't matter. Passing through the foyer on the way into the living room, he picked up the package he'd just received and carried it with him. He made himself comfortable on the sofa and then began to unwrap it. It was heavy for such a small bundle. Under the brown paper he found a cardboard box. Marilyn often bought cosmetics from a woman on the next block. But then, his name was on it, not hers. It must be something else. He opened one end and pulled out some papers from around a long metal object. He eyed it for a moment before the catastrophe sank in.

It was a pipe bomb.

His hand froze. Why hadn't it gone off? Perhaps there was something wrong with it. Or maybe it was on a timer. No, they didn't usually work that way. As an officer of the court, he'd seen several over the years. Normally, simple movement set them off. So why was he still alive? He had to get out. Ever so carefully, he eased the object onto the coffee table. So far so good. He didn't even want to breath. Slowly, he began to inch off the couch. The fact that any second could be his last didn't help his concentration. His movements had to be kept smooth—fluid. Instead, they were graceless and jerky. Keeping his eyes fixed on the metal pipe, he backed out of the room. When he got to the kitchen door, he closed it behind him and then turned and raced out through the patio just in time to find Marilyn pulling into the drive.

He jumped in the front seat of her Honda. "Back up!" he ordered.

"What?" She blinked at him as if he were a madman.

"Do what I say! There's a bomb in the house!"

Marilyn didn't need any more explanations. She backed out of the drive and burned rubber. "What are we going to do?"

"Drive to that convenience store on Cleveland and Grand. I'll call 911 from there."

She stole a peek at him before reaching for his hand. His face was ashen.

3

JANE Lawless stepped out of her restaurant into the cool September evening, feeling a bit like a prisoner just let out of jail. It had been a hectic day. Three cases of fresh head lettuce had been delivered early in the morning, all designated for a function the Lyme House was catering at the State Capitol at noon, all of them rusted clear to the core. No one in the kitchen had thought to check the quality, they were simply lifted into the cooler. On top of that, one of the two gas-fired trunnion kettles used to hold the evening's soups had cut out about two hours before dinner. By the time it was discovered, the soup, a cream of fresh asparagus, was ruined. And to make matters worse, one of the sous chefs had become so angry at a waiter during lunch he'd tossed a casaba melon at his head. After half an hour of frantic arbitration, Jane felt like a dish rag. Such were the joys of restaurant ownership. And all this wonderful, job-related excitement on her thirty-ninth birthday.

As she headed for the walk which circled Lake Harriet, Jane was glad her family had minimized the celebration this year. It wasn't that she hated birthdays, she just never felt entirely comfortable being the center of attention. No, this year she'd gotten off with a brunch invitation on Sunday. Tonight she and Dorrie Harris, the woman she'd been dating for the past seven months, were getting together for a little private party. Since Dorrie was a notoriously lousy cook, Jane had suggested just a bit of brie, some fresh fruit, and a loaf of crusty French bread. Oh, and a nice bottle of domestic champagne. No use breaking the bank. On further thought, Jane decided being the center of attention was sometimes all right, as long as it was one special person doing the attending.

Dorrie lived less than a mile from the restaurant. On nice evenings, Jane liked to walk the eight blocks instead of taking her car. Tonight the lake was as smooth as glass, the canopy of trees surrounding the water already bright crimson and yellow. Another few days and the leaves would be at their peak. Jane felt almost jubilant as she strolled along, glad to be finished with the duties of the day and ready for a pleasant, relaxing evening. In part her mood was due to Dorrie Harris. Jane had come to care about this woman a great deal over the summer. After Christine's death—Jane's partner of some ten years—she had felt for the longest time that she would never again know any kind of deep personal happiness. Yet now, all of that had changed. Dorrie had become an important part of her life. No one knew for sure what the future held, but at least Jane had come to terms with Christine's death, enough to let another person in. For now, that was enough.

Jane headed up the hill to Lake Harriet Parkway. Attached to Dorrie's condo was a comfortable deck overlooking the lake. In just a few short minutes she would be able to put her feet up and sip champagne, the general chaos of the day forgotten. This just might turn out to be a great birthday after all.

After being buzzed into the building, Jane took the elevator to the third floor. It was a short walk to number 317. She knocked softly.

Dorrie opened the door, a welcoming grin on her face. "You made it!"

Over and over again, Jane was struck by the warmth

of this sweet-spirited woman. Dorrie could be as tough as necessary in her everyday work life, but it was her gentleness and humor Jane had come to trust. "Was there ever any doubt?" She stepped into a small hallway which led into the dining room. "What? No brass band? No birthday kiss?"

"My, aren't we frisky tonight." Dorrie slid her arm around Jane's shoulders. "Come in first." She led the way into the living room. All the drapes and shades were pulled and only one very dim light burned next to the sofa.

"Kind of dark in here," said Jane, looking around. "Were you planning on showing home movies?"

"Cute." Dorrie moved a few paces away.

"What's going on?"

Suddenly, from the bedroom, the kitchen and the balcony a cacophony of voices shouted "SURPRISE!!!" A second later a solid mass of people emerged into the living room, all wearing silly colored hats and blowing paper horns.

Jane was stunned.

"The brass band," smirked Dorrie, waving to the assembled crowd.

Cordelia, Jane's oldest and dearest friend, leapt out of the throng and crushed her with a bear hug. Since Cordelia was the approximate size of a bear, the image was not lost on Jane. "Happy Birthday, dearheart," proclaimed Cordelia. "We surprised you, didn't we?"

Jane gave Dorrie a steely glance. "That's . . . an accurate statement."

"Great! Everyone should have a surprise party at some point in her life. It's a rite of passage!" Cordelia beamed triumphantly.

"Should they?" Jane swallowed hard. So much for her quiet evening sipping champagne on the deck. Realizing this approach was going to get her in big trouble, she plastered on what she hoped was her most winning smile.

"A toast!" shouted Cordelia.

Everyone scurried into the dining room and began setting out food and breaking out bottles of beer and sparkling water.

Dorrie walked up behind Jane and put her hand on her shoulder, turning her around. "Are we still pals?"

This time, Jane's grin was genuine. "You're pretty sneaky."

"Well, it was partially your family—and Cordelia, of course. Actually, it was mostly Cordelia."

"It figures," muttered Jane.

"The food is going to be a lot better than what I had planned."

"This is silly. You don't have to apologize. This is all terribly sweet."

Dorrie touched Jane's face. "I know how you feel about large, noisy parties."

"I don't mind large parties. I just...prefer small ones." She squeezed Dorrie's hand, giving her a small wink.

"Your point is taken." She winked back.

"Janey," called her brother Peter. "Get over here! You've got some presents to open. And Aunt Beryl made the cake. Your favorite. Amaretto!"

With a resigned but pleased shrug, Jane left Dorrie standing in the center of the living room. A moment later a whoop exploded in the dining room as Jane entered. "Speech," someone shouted.

Several hours of boisterous partying later, Jane and Cordelia sprawled on the deck, waiting for Dorrie to bring out a fresh pot of decaf. It was nearly midnight. Everyone had finally left. The moon sat high in the sky, its reflection a bright yellow party ribbon across the inky blackness of the lake.

"I don't understand what happened to my father and Marilyn," said Jane.

15

"They said they were going to be here," called Dorrie from the kitchen. "Marilyn confirmed with me this morning."

Jane shook her head. "I tried calling their house, but I didn't get an answer. Their machine wasn't even on."

"If I know your father, he probably got involved in a Perry Mason rerun and simply lost track of time." Cordelia smirked between blasts on her paper horn. Her entire body was draped with crumpled crepe paper. "For my next birthday I intend to rent a 747 and stage a suitably decadent bash while orbiting the IDS building in downtown Minneapolis. What do you think?"

"Just the simple pleasures," observed Jane.

Dorrie opened the screen and stepped onto the deck. She set the tray on a low table and then dumped herself into a chair. "I'm getting too old for this."

Cordelia leaned back into her chaise lounge, her auburn curls spread out like a Medusa. "Why children, the day has barely begun. You old poops would never make it in the theatre. By the way, you *are* coming to the opening of my new play next month?" She sniffed. "If I do say so myself, my artistic direction this time out is typically brilliant."

Jane sipped her coffee. "We have our tickets."

"Good. I need to make sure my club has access to several rows of good seats, if not the opening night, then at least sometime in the first week."

"Your club?" repeated Jane, arching an eyebrow.

Lazily, Cordelia fluffed her hair, her smile indulgent. "Now that I have attained a certain *mythic* status in this community, dearhearts, I felt it incumbent upon me to become a member of one of the oldest and most prestigious women's clubs in the Twin Cities."

Jane knew Dorrie had joined The Amelia Gower Women's Club shortly after her election to the city council last year. She'd explained how important it was to network with other women. Even the new mayor of Minneapolis,

16

Phoebe Atwater-St. John, belonged. "You're not saying—" said Jane.

"She is," nodded Dorrie. "I sponsored her and she was drummed into the corps last night."

In the semi-darkness, Cordelia's smug look made her face look like a pleased pumpkin. "You could join too, you know, Janey." She tapped a thoughtful finger against her chin. "Sure! *I* could sponsor you."

Jane shook her head. "I doubt they'd be very interested in someone with the last name of *Lawless* right now. That is, since Dad is defending the man who supposedly murdered Charlotte Fortnum—I assume you know who she is?"

Cordelia's indignation was just short of heroic. "Of course I do! Don't be tedious. Dorrie and I had dinner with her not less than a week before she . . . bought the farm, so to speak." She flailed her arms at a mosquito buzzing around her head.

Jane shot Dorrie a questioning look.

"I think you're probably right," said Dorrie, stirring some cream into her coffee. "This wouldn't be a very auspicious time to join. Frankly, I never thought you'd be that interested."

"I'm not," said Jane. "But I am curious. Tell me, is the consensus over there right now that Emery Gower is actually guilty?"

"I'd have to say yes," said Dorrie, noticing Cordelia flick an ant off her rather remarkable décolletage. "Emery Gower is the grand nephew of Rose Gower. She's one of the four members of the board of directors of The Gower Foundation. Well, really three members now that Charlotte is gone. Anyway, he came to town about a year ago. From what I understand, the Gower clan is rather large. I think he grew up somewhere in North Carolina. Rose had never met him before. He'd gotten his MBA from Northwestern several months before he arrived. He pretty much camped out on her doorstep until he convinced her to give him a job with the Foundation. Rose firmly believes he's innocent. Unfortunately for her, I think she's a majority of one. Charlotte Fortnum was well-loved. It must be doubly hard for Rose right now because she and Charlotte were very close. Emotions are running pretty high."

"In other words," said Cordelia, "your father's face is no doubt being used as a dartboard in more than one rec room around town."

Dorrie got up as the phone in the kitchen began to ring. "I'll get it," she said, frowning slightly. "Kind of late for a phone call."

"Not at my house," countered Cordelia, readjusting the crepe paper around her neck before it strangled her. "Why, just last night—"

"Jane," called Dorrie, "it's for you. Your father."

With a sense of relief, Jane got up and crossed into the kitchen.

Dorrie resumed her seat out on the deck. Several minutes later, Jane rejoined them.

"Are you all right?" asked Cordelia. "You look . . . kind of funny."

Stiffly, Jane sat down. "That was Dad."

"We already know that," declared Cordelia.

"Oh." Jane gave a weak smile. "Right."

"So give."

"Well, it seems this afternoon someone sent him . . . a pipe bomb. Except . . . there was no bomb in it. It was empty."

Cordelia and Dorrie exchanged glances.

"Is he all right?" asked Dorrie.

"Do they know who sent it?" asked Cordelia.

Jane rubbed her neck. "See, Dad had no way of knowing it was a hoax. Somehow he and Marilyn got to a convenience store and called 911. The bomb squad came. They took it away and did whatever they do to set it off, but it was a dud. Just a pipe made to look like a bomb."

"Jesus," said Dorrie under her breath.

"One of the policemen found some of the papers it'd been wrapped in. It was just some pages torn from a magazine. A trade magazine, I think he said. Except—"

"Except what?" asked Cordelia, a little too eagerly for good taste.

"Well, one of the pages had a mailing label on it. It had been sent to The Amelia Gower Women's Club. By the time the police discovered this, Dad had been taken to the hospital. He just called me from there. He wasn't sure . . . I mean, his heart started feeling funny."

"God!" Cordelia's hand flew to her mouth. "Is he all right?"

"They want to keep him overnight for observation. I guess he checked out fine. He *assured* me he was fine." Jane could feel her own heart rise into her throat. "I wanted to drive over right now but he said he was going to try to get some sleep. He made Marilyn promise not to call here earlier because he didn't want to ruin the festivities."

"Ninny," muttered Cordelia.

"Marilyn is with him," continued Jane. "I'll go over first thing in the morning."

Cordelia drummed her fingers on the chaise. "Do you realize what this could mean? Someone at *my* women's club may have been responsible!"

Dorrie remained silent, her eyes fixed on her coffee cup.

"I suppose," observed Jane, "it's possible someone is so furious with him for defending this Emery Gower that they wanted to get back at him. A fake pipe bomb was an easy trick."

After a long minute Dorrie asked, "Do you think your father will quit the case?"

"Pish. Not Perry Mason!" Cordelia's nose wrinkled at the idea. "He has to make sure the real killer starts sniveling in some quiet corner of the courtroom so that the rest of us morons will know who did it. Right Janey?"

"Unfortunately, I don't think my father would even

consider dropping the case. He's been the subject of harassment before. It didn't stop him then, and from the tone of his voice tonight, it won't stop him now." She hesitated for a moment. "Listen, you two know the people over at that club. Are any of them capable of something like this?"

"Of course not," said Cordelia, her protest simply a reflex.

Dorrie folded her arms protectively over her chest. "Nobody knows what's in another person's mind."

"What do you mean?" asked Cordelia.

Dorrie finished her coffee but said nothing more.

"Well," said Jane, stretching her limbs to relieve some of her tension, "I think I might just have to make a visit over there after all. How 'bout it, Cordelia? Invite me for lunch?"

Dorrie gave Jane an uneasy look. "Do you think that's wise?"

"Wise?" repeated Jane. "Only one way to find out."

4

Rose Gower hunched next to her dressing table, intently watching a candle flame flicker in the darkness. She usually set the white taper in front of her triptych mirror, that way the reflections made strange patterns on the walls of her bedroom. Whenever she had trouble thinking something through, she waited until after midnight and then lit a candle. Perhaps it was simple superstition, but Rose felt certain her mental energy was more focused at this time of night. Sometimes she even saw things in the mirror. Once, she thought she saw her grandmother, Amelia Gower. The vision had frightened her at first, but then a feeling of warmth, of absolute safety rushed over her. She'd been so confused about a problem she was having with a co-worker. That night, a perfect solution occurred to her. Ever since, when Rose had a particularly knotty problem, she hoped to see that vision again.

Tonight, she not only hoped, but she prayed to her favorite picture of Jesus hanging over her bed. Such a kind face the artist had given him. *Please, Dear Lord, let me talk to my Grandmother just one more time before I die. She'll know what to do. I'm an old woman. I'll be with you soon. Have mercy on me this one last time.*

Rose waited and watched, the silence in the old mansion was like a friend who had waited and watched with her so many times before. The problem she was wrestling with tonight was the worst in many years. Her great nephew, Emery Gower, had been accused of murdering one of her dearest friends. It seemed inconceivable to Rose that such a serious, thoughtful boy could have anything to do with something so horrible. She'd found the best defense attorney money could buy. She'd insisted to everyone who would listen that he was innocent. Of course she felt terrible that Charlotte had been murdered so brutally, but Emery had nothing to do with it. Deep in her bones, she knew it was true. But what should she do? Everyone was so angry with her! And The Chamber? What would happen now? Who would they get to replace Charlotte? Could decisions be made with only three members? No, that didn't seem right. *Oh, Grandmother, why don't you come and talk to me? Surely you'll know what to do. After all, you started all this. It's your responsibility! You can't leave us alone when everything is so confused. Emery and I need you. The Chamber needs you!*

Rose rubbed her sore eyes. Her glasses were on the nightstand next to her bed. Unfortunately, she could see very little without them. Her own mother had gone blind long before her seventy-fifth year. At seventy-four, Rose dreaded the idea of losing her sight. Yet, there were times when she felt a strange sense of connection to the world without those glasses. It was almost as if her other senses were heightened by her inability to see. No, that wasn't it exactly. It was more like her other senses came together to form something new. Something beyond the normal range. She often wondered if other people experienced this.

It was getting awfully late. Perhaps it was best to call it a night. But before she could blow out the candle and get up, that same inner sense came over her again. Even though Rose knew she had the third floor of the club all to herself, she felt a presence. Grabbing her cane, she crossed into the living room. "Grandmother?" she said softly.

The room was silent.

Feeling her way to the door, she opened it and glanced into the hall. Here, she could feel the presence even more strongly. "Grandmother, is it you? I'm not afraid. I called for you!"

Near the stairway to the attic chamber, Rose heard a low rustle. She turned. Yes! There it was. It was indistinct, merely a form standing in the shadows. But it was there!

"Please," pleaded Rose. "I have to talk to you."

"You do?" came the whispered reply.

"Of course. That's why you're here." She stepped further into the hallway.

"No, don't come any closer! I mean . . . there has to be a certain distance between us."

"I understand," nodded Rose. She didn't really, but she wanted to be cooperative. This was much better than the vision in the mirror. This vision actually talked back! "But is it you, Grandmother? I was such a small girl when you left us. I hardly even remember your voice." She waited.

"Yes, Rose. It's me."

Rose could feel her heart jump inside her chest. "I knew it. Won't you come in?" She motioned to her doorway. "I could make us some tea. I do so need to talk to you. Emery is so upset. Charlotte is dead, you know."

"I . . . know."

That was interesting. The voice sounded sad. But of course a spirit could be sad. Rose had always assumed her grandmother was watching over them from heaven. Charlotte Fortnum had been a member of The Chamber for almost twenty years. Almost as long as Rose. In that time, Amelia must have gotten to know her well. And for her to actually make an appearance now, this must be a very grave time indeed. "Shall I put the kettle on?"

"No." The reply came swiftly. "Not tonight."

"But when then?"

"I . . . you see . . . I'm just here to make sure you're

taking care of *the treasure*."

Rose cocked her head. "The treasure?" She frowned and looked down. What did her grandmother mean by that? It was no doubt some kind of test. Something she must figure out. "I assure you, we've been good stewards."

"Good! Where is it?"

"Where is what?"

"The treasure."

Now the voice sounded impatient. Rose would simply have to try harder. She thought for a moment. Deciding to take a chance, she said, "I'll show you."

From downstairs came the sound of a door closing. The figure of Amelia seemed to jump. "I have to go."

"No!" insisted Rose. "We haven't had time to talk yet."

"You go back into your rooms. I'll come again. But I'll want to see the treasure when I come back."

Rose was heartsick. "What about Emery? Have I done the right thing in hiring that lawyer?"

"Sure. Why not. That deadhead can use all the help he can get."

"What?" Rose didn't think this sounded like something her grandmother would say. Then again, it was that huge oil painting over the fireplace down in the dining room which had formed much of her physical impression of the woman. Amelia Gower had died when Rose was only six.

"Yes, you did the right thing. I'll help Emery, don't worry."

"I won't worry, Grandmother. I promise. But when will I see you again? Tomorrow night?"

"No."

"When?"

"Soon, Rose. I can't say exactly."

"All right."

"Now go to your room!"

Yes, that imperiousness was correct. Rose remembered that much. Without further comment, she turned and closed the door behind her.

Quickly, the figure stumbled into the stairway. "Shit," muttered the spirit of Amelia Gower, realizing an expensive spiked heel had just broken off.

5

JANE pulled her car over to the curb in front of the women's club and sat for a moment looking up at the huge Prairie Gothic mansion. The three-story brownstone rested high on a hill behind The Walker Art Center. From its rounded turrets Jane imagined you could see for miles. Directly down a steep street was the famous Tyrone Guthrie Theatre. This was no doubt the route Charlotte Fortnum had taken the night of her death. From what the newspapers said, Charlotte had recently moved out of her home in south Minneapolis and had taken up residence at the club. Jane wondered what the rooms must look like. Probably old but elegant. She'd heard that the kitchen was also excellent. Well, at least lunch was going to be pleasant. Other than that, she wasn't sure what she hoped to find. Perhaps it was nothing more than curiosity. Still, when Dorrie had called yesterday morning and tried to talk her out of going, she had remained adamant. If a member of that organization had tried to frighten her father into an early grave, she had to at least take a look. She checked her watch. Nearly noon. Hopefully, Cordelia had remembered to make reservations.

Jane parked her car in the rear lot and then stepped under a dark green canopy which covered the walk to the front of the building. The front double doors were made of a rich brown, highly polished wood. Opening one of them, she was immediately struck by the gorgeous wine-colored oriental carpets and the general magnificence of the grand foyer. To the left, a rounded arch led into a large parlor which contained many small sitting areas. That same rich brown wood was everywhere. Women sat talking, laughing, having a glass of wine or cup of tea before being summoned into the dining room. The wonderful aroma of fresh brewed coffee wafted through the crowd, lending an unmistakable air of coziness to the friendly scene.

Backing out of the room, Jane decided to do a little more snooping. The central hallway led further into the bowels of the building, giving her the sensation of moving deep inside an impenetrable fortress. She felt dwarfed by the oversized doorways. The massive, metal chandeliers. The broadly carved wooden ceilings.

"Oh, I am sorry!" said a young man rushing around a corner and bumping right into her. He was carrying three large bags overflowing with boxes and cans of food. Several items fell out and dropped to the floor as he juggled the unwieldy load. "Are you all right? Sometimes I just don't watch where I'm going." He leaned down to grab a cereal box and several more items slipped out. "Damn!"

Jane bent down to help. "You've really got your arms full," she said, chasing a rolling soup can across the floor. "Where are you headed?"

"To the food shelf room. It's just through here." He led the way.

Jane followed, picking up more groceries as they dropped out.

Exhausted and slightly disgusted, the man set the bags on a table just inside a large utility room. Metal shelves filled with foodstuffs lined the walls. A frail, white-haired woman sat behind a desk in the back, writing furiously on a clipboard. She was wearing a Minnesota Twins cap turned backwards, and a navy blue sweat shirt and matching sweat pants. She looked up as they entered. "Freddy," she smiled. "That's great. Who brought this over?"

"Julia and I," he answered, brushing off his light blue polo shirt. He turned and nodded his thanks to Jane, taking some of the cans from her arms. "Just set them all down here. Rose will stock it." He held out his hand. "My name is Freddy Lindhurst. You probably know my wife, Julia." He smiled sheepishly. "I'm really sorry about running into you like that. I guess I was in too much of a hurry."

As Jane shook his hand, she studied him for a moment. Freddy was a sensitive looking young man, probably in his late twenties, with soft, corn silk hair curling gently around his thin face. The eyes were his most striking feature, deep set and very light blue. He seemed to possess the kind of weary gracefulness reminiscent of a figure by Botticelli. Except for a somewhat weak chin, his face was distinctly handsome. It was a face you could trust. On principle, Jane distrusted such faces.

"I'm afraid I don't know Julia," said Jane. "I've never been here before. I'm a guest of Cordelia Thorn's. We're having lunch."

"Ah," said Freddy. "Cordelia...yes. We just met. She's going to be quite an addition around here."

"And I'm Rose Gower," said the woman behind the desk. She stood and walked toward them, a cane held firmly in one hand, the clipboard tucked under her arm. "I don't really need this," she said, holding up the cane. "But once in a while it comes in handy." She poked Freddy in the stomach.

He grimaced playfully and then glanced at the door as a very pregnant woman entered carrying another bag of groceries. Quickly, he snatched it from her and set it on the counter. "Honey, I told you I'd get that! I don't want you carrying something so heavy."

"Julia Lindhurst," said the woman, smiling at Jane. Physically, she was the antithesis of her husband. Short and square, with dark brown hair and eyes. "Freddy worries too much." She patted her stomach. "I'm due next month."

Jane smiled pleasantly. "Nice to meet you. I'm Jane Lawless."

Freddy turned from the table, a surprised look on his face. "Lawless? Any relation to Raymond Lawless?"

"Yes, he's my father."

An awkward silence followed.

Finally, Rose pushed Freddy aside with her cane and held out her hand. "I'm so very delighted to meet you, Ms. Lawless. I hired your father to represent my great nephew."

Julia's jaw tightened. Her smile had evaporated. "I'm afraid you've come to the wrong place, Ms. Lawless. Charlotte Fortnum was my mother. I can't say any of us think very highly of someone who would defend a man so clearly guilty."

"You don't know that!" insisted Rose. Her paper thin skin flushed with anger. "Everyone around here's already got him strapped to the electric chair!"

Freddy cleared his throat. "Honey, I think we should be going." He put his arm behind Julia's back and gently nudged her toward the door.

Rose waited until they were gone and then shook her head. "I don't know anymore. I'm just trying to do what's right. The boy has a right to a defense. Why can't anyone see that?" She fussed absently with an errant wisp of hair. "I'm very sorry about what happened to your father last Friday night, Ms. Lawless. The police were here on Saturday. They seemed to think one of us was responsible."

"You mean the fake pipe bomb?" said Jane.

"A terrible business. You must tell him how upset I was to hear about it. But I can't believe one of our members had anything to do with it."

Jane waited, but she didn't go on. "I'll tell him."

"Good. You do that." She started unpacking one of

the bags Freddy had brought in. "Of all people, I'm sorry you had to run into Julia. She's understandably upset right now. I'm afraid your presence here is just one more reminder of what's happened. She and her mother were very close, you know. If you ask me, this whole thing is tearing us up! Why, Julia and her sister are like my own grandchildren. I used to babysit them when they were little."

"Julia has a sister?"

"Yes. Charlotte was married very briefly when she was in her mid-twenties. Julia is the oldest. Her younger sister, Evangeline—we call her Evie—just turned twenty-five last week. It wasn't much of a birthday I'm afraid. Actually, you may know Evie. Your father represented her several years ago. That's when I was first introduced to him. Another bad business, Ms. Lawless. Evie got herself mixed up with some terrible people. Even your father wasn't able to get her off. She spent nearly two years in jail. She was just released three months ago."

"I don't believe we've ever met. I don't generally get involved in my father's cases."

"No, of course not. Well." She adjusted her harlequin glasses and moved back to her desk. "Unfortunately, Evie's still a wild one." Rose lowered her head. She seemed to be talking to herself now as she stared at her hands. "Poor child. She didn't get along with her mother. Charlotte, God rest her soul, was sometimes a bit too... controlling with her kids. Not that Evie didn't need some controlling. It's just...they never saw eye to eye on anything. On the other hand, Julia seems to have weathered the storms of childhood quite well. Yes. She's so much like Charlotte. Practical. Liberal in her social values, yet personally rather conservative."

Down the hall came the sound of sandals slapping against the polished wood floor. A second later, Cordelia burst into the room wearing a black and gold striped caftan with bright purple fringe running diagonally from the neck to the bottom hem.

Jane turned to her. "Cordelia. What a surprise." She

eyed the outfit, raising a thin eyebrow. "New bowling duds?"

Cordelia cast a disdainful glance in Jane's direction, giving a regal sniff. Her eyes fell to the older woman seated behind the desk. "Oh, hello Rose. Nice to see you again."

Rose stood and walked closer, regarding Cordelia's attire with open amazement. She touched a bit of the fringe.

Cordelia glared at Jane, daring her to say something more.

"You know Cordelia," smiled Jane, "that outfit makes you look like..." She knew better than to elaborate.

"Like what?" Cordelia wasn't going to let it drop.

"Well...ah...you know. Like someone from a foreign country." There.

"Really?" Cordelia seemed pleased. "What country?"

Jane decided it would be impolitic to suggest Mars. "Oh, well, I was thinking some place like...Montana."

Cordelia rolled her eyes. "Janey, not to change the subject too quickly, but *this*," she waved her hand to the shelves, "is a *storage room!* I think you must have taken a wrong turn. The dining room is across from the main hall. You know, dearheart, contrary to rumor, we do not eat out of tin cans." Suddenly, her eyes locked on a box of Captain Crunch. "Hum," she said fingering the unopened top, "someone had the taste to donate my favorite cereal."

Rose banged her on the hand with the cane. "I think I'll just take this and put it on the shelf." She set down her clipboard and picked up the box, crossing to a rear shelf.

Jane glanced at a note written haphazardly in red ink on the bottom of an inventory sheet. "Chamber meeting, Monday, 11 P.M." It had been underlined several times and then circled. She looked up as Rose returned.

Rose's eyes fell to the note. With a nervous jerk she picked up the board, slipping it back under her arm. "Well, I wish you two a good lunch. I've got a lot of work to do in here."

"In other words," said Cordelia cheerfully, "get lost."

31

She grabbed Jane's arm. "Come on, sweety. Salt and cholesterol await."

Jane found herself being dragged down the hallway at break-neck speed. "I'm not interested in eating salt and cholesterol."

"Sure you are. Don't be disagreeable."

"Listen, Cordelia, I have to talk to you for a moment."

"Talk away."

Jane yanked her to a stop. "What's a *Chamber meeting*?"

"Excuse me?"

"Look, I know clubs have all sorts of small groups—bridge groups, gardening groups, literary groups, speakers who come in to talk about various topics. You must have been given a list."

"Of course I was. I am the owner of several lists. As a matter of fact, I even suggested a new group. Friday night poker. Cigars on me."

"You're such a prince."

"Queen," smiled Cordelia, fluttering her eyes.

"But what about this Chamber? There's a meeting tonight at eleven."

"Never heard of it. Besides, the club closes at ten-thirty. Except for those staying here of course."

"Of course." Jane thought for a moment. "All right, then tell me this. How well do you know Rose Gower?"

"Rose? Oh Janey, she's a peach. She's the granddaughter of Amelia Gower, our illustrious founder. Aren't those harlequin glasses just a hoot! I want a pair just like them—mother-of-pearl inlay and all. She lives all by herself on the third floor. I've haven't yet been invited up, but I hear it's very posh. Oodles of the old Gower antiques. The rest of the guest rooms are on the second floor. The dining room, library, billiards room, some small private meeting rooms and the assembly hall are on the first. I'll show you around after lunch."

"Does Rose get out much? Do you know if she belongs to any other organizations?"

"From what I've seen, she sticks around here most of the time. She doesn't drive anymore. Her eyesight is bad."

"Interesting," said Jane.

"What? Come on Janey, give. Something's going on in that brain of yours."

"It's probably nothing."

"Well, I realize *that*."

"Cordelia." Jane put a hand on her hip. "If we didn't have such a long and involved history together—"

"Oh, come on. I was only teasing. Besides, I do *not* like being told I dress like a member of a Montana bowling team." She closed her eyes and attempted a hurt look.

"Is Dorrie here yet? She thought she might join us."

Cordelia recovered immediately. "We walked in together but I doubt she'll be having lunch with us."

"Really? Why?"

"Well, Miriam Cipriani—*the* Miriam Cipriani, curator of art acquisitions at The Stroud Gallery of Art and also on the board of directors of The Gower Foundation—tackled her just as she walked in the front door. Miriam insisted on speaking with her. It sounded pretty important. Dorrie didn't look pleased, but she agreed. If you ask me, the entire interaction was weird, weird, *weird*."

"What do you mean?"

"Oh, I don't know. Dorrie kept looking over her shoulder while they were talking. She seemed jumpy. You know, nervous about something."

"Dorrie? That doesn't sound like her."

"I know." Cordelia sniffed the air. "Janey, my body grows weak. I need sustenance. I will have to be *carried* into the dining room if we don't—"

"All right. I'm sorry. Please," she held out her hand, "after you."

"Good." Cordelia hoisted up her caftan. "Now. Last one to the table buys lunch!" She bolted down the hallway, skirts flying, leaving Jane standing alone, listening to the echo of flapping sandals. Jane wondered if this entire morning hadn't been a wild goose chase, with Cordelia epitomizing the goose.

6

It was almost 1 A.M. The Chamber meeting had gone long tonight. Too much to discuss. Too many strong emotions. Feeling exhausted, Rose picked up her cane and walked to the door, taking one last look at the round, oak table where she had presided for over twenty years. She remembered her first meeting, so long ago now. The high spirits, the intense feelings of sisterhood, of getting a necessary job done. It was nothing like tonight's fiasco. Sighing deeply, she switched off the overhead light and began her descent down the narrow, carpeted stairs which led to the third floor. She locked the attic door behind her and trudged across the hall to her own apartment.

Once inside, she eased herself into a comfortable chair and tried to think. Tonight, the act of lighting the candle in her bedroom seemed overwhelming. She was tired. Not just physically, but weary of all the strife. If only Amelia would come again soon. Rose hadn't told anyone about the first visitation. What hurt most was the realization that not even the two people closest to her, Miriam Cipriani and Mae Williams, would understand. Yet Rose had been close to the spirit world all her life. Her grandmother *had* appeared to her two nights ago—she was the very same women who, in the spring of 1922, had set everything in motion. She'd insisted from the very first, and rightly so, on absolute secrecy. Now was no time to become faint-hearted.

Rose was still upset with herself for allowing Jane Lawless to see that notation she'd made at the bottom of her inventory sheet earlier in the morning. Miriam had just been in to give her the meeting time, and without thinking, she'd jotted it down on the first available piece of paper. By grabbing the clipboard off the table so quickly, Rose had perhaps made too much of it. Unfortunately, Jane had noticed. Oh well. Nothing could be done about it now. Rose heaved a weary sigh and took off her glasses. She leaned her head back against the chair and closed her eyes. Outside in the hall, she heard the sound of footsteps. Then came a soft knock. Who on earth would come to see her at this time of night?

Rising with some difficulty, she made her way across the room and cracked open the door. The hall outside was completely empty. For a moment she stood perfectly still.

"Hello child," came a soft whisper.

Rose could feel herself gasp. "Grandmother?" For some reason, she'd gotten it into her head that the next time Amelia appeared, it would be at the foot of her bed. Obviously, she'd been wrong. She glanced into the same shadowy corner as the other night. A deep sense of relief overwhelmed her. "Is it really you?"

"Yes. It's me."

This was too good to be true. She had so much she wanted to talk over—especially after tonight.

"Now, Rose. I've come to see the treasure."

Oh drat. She'd hoped her grandmother would've forgotten about that. Of course, she'd given it some thought, but she still hadn't come up with an answer. If she asked Amelia to be more specific, she'd only sound obtuse. No, she had to think fast.

"I'm waiting, Rose."

"Let me just get my cane and glasses. I'll just be a minute."

"No glasses!" came the quick response. "My form would only frighten you."

"Of course." She backed into her apartment and felt along the wall until she came to her chair. The cane was leaning against it. As she picked it up, she realized she was still wearing her old sweatshirt and sweat pants. How could she entertain her grandmother in something so... so informal? Passing the wall closet, she reached inside and found her best silk shawl, the one she wore only on special occasions. She quickly wrapped it around her shoulders. "I'm coming," she called, her voice cracking with the strain of trying to rush. Returning to the hall, she waited.

"You lead the way."

Resolutely, Rose straightened her back and turned to the attic stairway. She unlocked the door and started up to the chamber room. "I think you're going to be pleased. As I told you the other night, we've been very good stewards." But of course her grandmother must know that. This didn't make a lot of sense. On the other hand, maybe Amelia *hadn't* been able to keep track of what was happening here on earth. How could Rose be expected to know what went on in heaven?

Reaching the landing, she switched on the light and walked inside. Instantly, the light was switched back off. She could make out the pointed beam of a flashlight as it washed over her face.

"This is better," announced the spirit of Amelia Gower. "The light hurts my eyes."

"But I can't see a thing."

"Isn't there another lamp up here? One that's not so bright."

Rose thought for a moment. Well, there was that oil lamp she sometimes used in the summer if there was a storm and the power went out. Last time she'd seen it, it was on top of one of the file cabinets. "Over against the far wall," she said. She could hear the figure rustle away. "It's an oil lamp. Do you have a match?"

The room was suddenly suffused with a soft glow. If

37

only she had her glasses. She felt her way to the center table and stood for a moment getting her bearings. The main cabinets had to be directly to her left.

"So, where is it, Rose? I'm waiting."

"But couldn't we talk for a few minutes, first? I've got so many things I need to ask you."

"No, first the treasure."

Rose used her cane to guide her to the right spot. The bottom cabinet was unlocked. She bent down and pulled open the drawer, reaching inside for the ledger.

"What's that?"

"It's in code," said Rose eagerly. "We've been working on it for nearly five years."

A hand snatched it from her.

Rose could hear pages being turned.

Suddenly, the book slammed shut. "That's great. But surely you don't think I came for *that*?"

Rose could hear the ledger drop on the table. "I . . . I'm not sure." She could sense the figure moving around restlessly.

"What's this?"

Rose watched a blurry hand pick up the red and black lacquered box which sat in the center of the table. After the meeting tonight, she'd forgotten to put it away. By the sudden, thrilled intake of breath, she knew her grandmother had found something she liked. Rose smiled. "Those always were your favorites, weren't they?"

"These must be worth a fortune!"

"Probably. We've never had them appraised. I don't know what we'd do without them."

"What do you mean?"

Rose hesitated. What a strange question. "Grandmother, you left those jewels for *us*. A perfectly cut emerald and a matching ruby. If we ever get deadlocked on an issue, we use them to break the tie. Don't you remember? Before your death, The Chamber had five members. After you were gone, the number was left at four. Those jewels were the fifth voice. *Your* voice."

"But I'm here now, Rose. I can answer your questions in person."

Without returning the box to the table, the figure retreated further into the darkness.

"You mustn't take those!"

"But Rose, they're already mine."

The voice was mocking her now. She couldn't stand it. She covered her ears with her hands and shut her eyes. "But I don't understand. Why would you do this? Why would you come—"

The truth hit her with the force of a blow.

Rose looked up, her face filled with amazement. "You're not my grandmother! This is a trick!" She backed up several steps, tripping on the edge of a rug. She was beginning to panic. She had to get out. Find some help. This was disaster! The security of the room had been breached. Where was her cane? Oh God—she felt herself stumbling. *Falling.* Dear Lord, the stairway! There was nothing to hold on to. Nothing in front of her but emptiness.

7

JANE and her Aunt Beryl carried their after-dinner coffee into the screened porch and sat down. In the backyard, Jane's two little terriers busied themselves sniffing the bushes.

"The garden is a masterpiece," said Jane, stretching her arms over her head expansively. "It's never looked this good. Calendula, asters, zinnias, nasturtiums. Even snapdragons."

"Next year if I'm still around, I'd like to concentrate on the perennials. I wanted to get the feel of the ground first." Beryl patted her cottony white hair into place.

"Your garden in Lyme Regis must be horribly neglected by now."

"I certainly hope not. I took great pains to make sure one of my neighbors tends it regularly. Hadley McNeil? Did you ever meet him? He fancies himself a great horticulturist."

Jane shook her head. It had been many years since she last visited England. Her aunt's neighbors had no doubt changed many times in the interim. "Do you think you'll stay a while longer then? I heard you telling Evelyn Bratrude you were thinking of going back." Jane tried to keep her voice neutral. She didn't want to pressure her aunt in any way. Nevertheless, she was hoping her aunt's visit to Minnesota would be permanent. Beryl was a great companion. After Christine's death, Jane had been lonely living in a large house all by herself. The other half of the coin was that since her husband's death, Beryl was also lonely kicking around her empty cottage on the southwestern coast of England. Granted, she had a son living in London. But Tony was involved in his own life. He only saw his mother a few times a year.

Beryl sighed. "I do find that I miss some of the old friends. Even the cottage. Then again, if I went back, it wouldn't be the same. Jimmy's gone. It never felt right without him there." She turned to her niece. "Would I be a burden if I did stay?"

"Are you serious? That's what I want! What I said to you the night you first arrived still goes. This is your home. For as long as you want it."

With a plump hand, Beryl patted Jane on the knee. "You know, it's odd. Your father and I still don't get on very well. But it seems that in our old age, we've come to appreciate our shared history. We both loved your mother. I think in a way, it has formed a bond between us." She lifted her chin and raised an eyebrow. "Not that we'll ever be friends. Don't misunderstand."

"Of course not." Jane nodded politely. This whole situation between her father and Beryl had become so incredibly amusing. Neither would admit a growing fondness for the other, though it was becoming clear to everyone *else* that their pokes and jabs, once so potent, had now become simple tradition. After all, it was the way everyone *expected* them to behave. How could they disappoint their public?

"Oh, by the way, a woman phoned you shortly before you got home. I asked to take a message but she said she'd ring you later."

"Did she leave a name?"

"Sorry." Beryl took a final sip of coffee. "Now, I'd better get that casserole ready."

"Casserole?"

41

"Didn't I tell you? Evelyn and I are driving over to St. Paul with it. It's for your father. After that scare in the hospital last Friday night, I told him he needs to take better care of his health. Marilyn always works late on Wednesdays and you know, left to his own devices, he'll probably eat something disastrous. I can't allow that. The man needs proper nutrition." She slapped her knees and got up.

"And you're going to make sure he gets it."

Beryl cocked her head. "I'm sure there's a hidden meaning in that, Jane dear, but I don't have time to play." She turned and marched into the kitchen.

Jane could hear her banging pots and pans. Well, so much for their after dinner game of Scrabble.

At the sound of a door closing downstairs, Jane blinked open her eyes. She'd fallen asleep on the sofa in the upstairs sun room while reading the newspaper. Beryl must just be getting home. Since she'd taken the dogs with her, Jane didn't have her normal sentries standing guard. She checked her watch. Nearly nine-thirty. It was already pitch dark out. Beryl and Evelyn had probably stayed to keep her father company until Marilyn got home.

Brushing some cookie crumbs off her red, rag wool sweater, she got up and crossed to a window overlooking the driveway. That was funny. The drive was empty.

She started downstairs. As soon as she reached the landing, she glanced into the living room. A long shadow fell across the Turkish oriental rug, giving Jane a start. "Beryl?" she called. She walked a few paces into the room.

There, sitting motionless in a rocking chair by the fireplace was a woman. Even though the dim light behind her was enough to obscure her face, Jane knew she was in the presence of a stranger. "What's going on?" she asked, feeling the hairs on the back of her neck prickle. "Who let you in here?"

The woman rose, her face moving into the light. "My

name is Mae Williams. I knocked on the door, but no one answered. I saw the lights on upstairs so I thought maybe someone would be home soon. Your back door was unlocked." The woman dropped her voice to its deepest register. "I need to talk to you, Jane. Privately. I called earlier but you were out. It's very important. I know it was unorthodox, but I decided to let myself in and wait."

Jane was aghast. As she stood glaring, not sure what to do, a faint recognition dawned. "You look familiar. Sure. You're the poet. I went to one of your readings last winter."

"I'm flattered."

Jane took a moment to size up her unexpected guest. Mae Williams was a tall, African-American woman, probably in her early forties. She had short-cropped, slightly graying hair, an intense, somewhat imperial manner and an imposing voice. From her limited experience of the woman, Jane knew she was not only a dynamic speaker, but outspoken. She had single-handedly started *Black Writers Minnesota*, a small periodical which, in the last few years, had gained a national forum.

"Please," said Mae. "Won't you sit down?"

How nice, thought Jane. Inviting me to sit in my own living room.

"Look, I can see you're upset. I'll grant you, this is an unusual way to be introduced."

"It's a damn sight more than that! Try breaking and entering. Well . . . at least entering."

"Please, if you'll just give me a few minutes, I think I'll be able to explain my reasons for being here."

Jane could feel her anger waging war with her curiosity. In the end, she knew which would win. "All right." She sat down on the arm of the couch. "I'm listening."

Mae resumed her chair by the fireplace. Measuring her words carefully, she said, "I've come here tonight to ask a favor, Jane. You don't have to respond right away, but think about what I'm saying. You see, since taking a posi-

43

tion on the board of directors of The Gower Foundation—"

"You're part of *that*?"

Mae nodded.

"Then you must be aware that my father is defending Emery Gower for the murder of Charlotte Fortnum."

"Yes. But that's not what I came to talk to you about. Two days ago, my dear friend Rose Gower died. Miriam Cipriani, another member of the board, found her body. After a brief investigation, the police ruled the death accidental. Rose had fallen down the attic stairs sometime Monday night. Death was instantaneous."

Jane already knew most of this. It had made the front page of today's *Star Tribune*. She'd been shocked and saddened when she'd read it. To think that she had just met Rose on Monday. "What does this have to do with me?"

Mae sat quietly for a moment. She seemed to be scrutinizing Jane's face as if to confirm something. Finally, she said, "We have reason to believe the death was not accidental."

Jane was thrown. "I don't understand. Why don't you tell that to the police?"

"We can't." She paused for several seconds. "What I'm about to tell you must remain strictly between us. Is that understood?"

Oh no, thought Jane. I'm not playing that game. Besides, she didn't care for one-sided demands. "I won't make any promises until I know what this is all about."

"All right. That's...fair enough." Mae rearranged herself in the chair, giving herself a moment to regroup. "The night Rose died, something was stolen from the attic room directly above her third floor apartment. Rose would never have removed these items herself, therefore we suspect she wasn't alone. Also, strangely, she was wearing her favorite shawl that night, the one she wore *only* on special occasions. Whoever she was entertaining must have held some importance for her. When Miriam found her body the next morning, she noticed that Rose wasn't wearing her glasses. Rose always wore glasses. She couldn't see a thing without them. Later, I found them on a table in her living room."

"That is strange. What was stolen?"

"A small lacquered box containing two jewels. An emerald and a ruby. And," she hesitated, "a ledger."

"What was in the ledger?"

"I'm afraid I can't tell you that. It's in code, so it wouldn't make sense to you anyway. But it's brown leather, with a gold 'C' stamped on the front."

"Is that why you can't talk to the police? There's something in the ledger you don't want them to see?"

Mae nodded. "It's not information The Gower Foundation would want made public. We simply can't have the police snooping around. Nevertheless, something awful occurred the other night, Jane. Something which seems inexplicable. We've got to find out what happened. We must get our property back. Lives may depend on it."

"I don't understand."

"No, I'm sure you don't, but for now, that's all I can tell you."

Jane could feel the woman's eyes boring into her. Mae William's intensity was beginning to border on the frightening. "All right, then why are you here? What do you want from me?"

"We need your help. Your friend Cordelia Thorn happened to mention to Miriam one evening that you'd been instrumental in solving several local crimes. One at a sorority at the U of M, and one up in Repentance River. So, yesterday, Miriam and I had you checked out."

"Did you now? And did I pass?"

For the first time, Mae smiled. "You got an A."

Lucky me, thought Jane. "I don't suppose you'd care to be more specific?"

"Specific?" She gave Jane another amused smile. "Of course. We found that you were honest, hard-working, what some people might call a pillar of the community.

45

You have one brother, Peter, who's a cameraman for WDPC and who recently got married. No other siblings. Your father is a defense attorney in St. Paul. Your closest friend is Cordelia Thorn, artistic director for the Allen Grimby Repertory Theatre in St. Paul. You're politically liberal, you make charitable contributions to causes in which you believe, you're well-read—have a degree in American Literature from the University of Minnesota—you're a feminist, a dog-lover, somewhat of a loner, a gourmet chef, a restaurant owner, and you're a lesbian. Your lover, Christine, died five years ago. You drive a rattle-trap Saab and seem to be rather conservative—someone suggested the word *cheap*—with your personal finances. You own a home approximately four blocks from your restaurant where you live with your English aunt. I believe her name is Bell."

"Beryl."

"Pardon me. And, most importantly, I believe you're a woman we can trust. Will you help us?"

Jane felt her head spinning. "Quite a dossier."

"You have an open life. Nothing there was a secret."

She nodded. "All right, but by *us* do you mean The Gower Foundation?"

"Yes, in a manner of speaking. Primarily, Miriam Cipriani and I would like to hire you. We're all that's left of the board of directors now that Rose and Charlotte are gone. Oh and yes, we do intend to pay you for your services."

Jane couldn't help but register surprise. She gave this all a moment to sink in. "You want me to find out who was with Rose in the attic the night she died?"

"We do."

"And you want me to find and return the ledger and the two jewels."

"Exactly. We're desperate to recover our property."

"Then why do I feel like you're not telling me everything?"

Mae returned Jane's stern gaze. "Because Jane, I'm not. But I'm telling you everything you need to know. Both Miriam and I will assist you in every way possible."

"I can't promise anything."

"We understand that."

"And there are two people I would need to take into my confidence. First, Cordelia. You can consider her . . . my partner."

Mae considered it a moment. "All right. Agreed. I thought you might insist on that. From what Cordelia told us, it did seem she was an important part of your previous investigations."

"You make me sound like some kind of professional."

Again, Mae allowed herself a small smile. "Maybe you should be. Who's the other person?"

"Dorrie Harris."

"No. Absolutely not."

"Why?" Mae's response had been so swift and unconditional, Jane wondered what was behind it.

"She's too public a personage. Too political, with too high of a profile. If you insist on telling her, I'm afraid our deal is off."

What deal, thought Jane? She hadn't agreed to anything. Still, she couldn't help but be intrigued. "Ok, but before I accept your offer, I'd like an honest answer to one question."

"And that would be?"

"Who might benefit most from the theft of the jewels?"

Mae sat forward, her hands knotted into a single fist. "Well, I would. So would Miriam."

"I see."

"I don't think you do. But for now, that's all I can tell you."

"So you want me to investigate Miriam."

"That's a possibility."

Jane shook her head. "Neither of you trusts the other?"

"Not entirely."

"Did you take them, Mae?" Jane hoped her directness would catch her off guard.

"No. I didn't."

"Do you think Miriam did?"

"I don't know."

"There's no one else who might have had a motive?"

"I've tried and tried to come up with an answer to that. I suppose it could be a common thief. Someone who took the jewels simply for the money."

"What about the ledger. Who might benefit from its disappearance?"

"Again . . . I don't know."

"But Miriam thinks you took it?"

"Actually, no. The ledger is something entirely different. Neither of us would have taken that."

"I see." She didn't really. "All right, one more question. Do you think Rose and Charlotte Fortnum's deaths are related?"

Mae sighed and leaned back in her chair. "I don't know. If they are, then I suppose that means Emery Gower is innocent."

"But *you* don't see any connection?"

She shook her head. "It's very complex. I can think of certain things that might link them—" Her voice trailed off.

"Like?"

She gave a shudder. "Maybe someone is out to murder the entire board of directors of The Gower Foundation."

Jane found this a suitably chilling response. She stared quietly into the cold fireplace for a moment and thought. What would it hurt if she did do a bit of snooping? She might uncover something important. Then again, the potential danger couldn't be overlooked. It seemed more than probable that a killer and a thief were on the loose at that club. Perhaps one in the same person. Even as she considered the matter, Jane knew what her answer would be.

"All right, but as I said before, I can't promise anything. If things get too nasty, you may *have* to call in the police."

Mae stood and extended her hand. "Good. Now, I have a check here for five hundred dollars." She bent down and retrieved it from a heavy cloth bag filled with books.

"I don't know," said Jane, hesitating.

"Look, if you don't want the money, give it to one of your charities. But please, take it." She waited.

Jane folded it and put it in her pocket. She could think about that part later. "I'll need to see the attic room where the death occurred. And I'll want to have free access to the club."

"Of course." Mae handed Jane several keys. "One of them is the front door key. The club closes at ten-thirty. The other two are for Rose's apartment on the third floor, and the door to the attic which is right across the hall. We'll simply tell everyone you've become a member. That I sponsored you."

"Fine." She walked Mae into the front hall. "By the way, in that little dossier of yours—"

"Yes?"

"Who referred to me as cheap?" Jane could feel her teeth begin to grind.

"I'm afraid all our sources must remain confidential."

Jane stuck her hands deep into the pockets of her jeans. "Somehow I figured you'd say that. Ok, but one last thing. No more surprise late night visits, all right?"

"You should lock your doors. You never know who might be lurking around."

Something about the comment made Jane shiver. She would have to have a little chat with Beryl. Since her aunt had never locked her doors in Lyme Regis, she was having trouble remembering to do it now. Jane didn't want to be an ogre, but she also didn't want to have any repeat performances of this evening.

"I'll probably see you sometime tomorrow," said Jane.

"Good. I'll tell Miriam. And Jane...thanks." She turned and headed down the walk, disappearing quickly across the street.

8

"I don't see why you can't just give me the money now," insisted Evie Fortnum, stuffing the last bite of an English muffin into her heavily lipsticked mouth. She was seated at a linen covered table under the large oil painting of Amelia Gower.

This morning, the club's dining room was filled with the soft buzz of voices and the tinkling of breakfast dishes. Miriam Cipriani sat across from her, grimacing inwardly at the magenta hue Evie's hair had acquired in the past few days. Well, at least the haircut was reasonable. And no matter what Evie did to herself, she would always remain a lovely young woman.

Evie examined a chipped nail. "Look, I know my mother didn't trust me with money. Maybe she was right ...*once*. But that was when I was a kid. I've matured, Miriam, in case you haven't noticed. I also know what she left Julia and me isn't going to make us rich. I just want the chance to do something with my life. That money would help."

Miriam chewed her melon and tried to look sympathetic. Not that she was. She and Charlotte had discussed at some length the necessity—should anything ever happen to Charlotte—of keeping Evie's inheritance safe until the young woman turned thirty. Back when the will was first written, Miriam never imagined the twists and turns their lives would take. For one thing, she thought she and Charlotte would be together forever. Miriam had raised Julia and Evie as if they were her own daughters. Yet now, three months after Evie had been released from prison, Charlotte was dead. Miriam knew that both Julia and Evie were having a terrible time coming to terms with their mother's death. Each for different reasons. She also knew Evie's insistence on talking hard, cold money was in no way a negation of her genuine sadness. It was just the way Evie was. Basically a good kid. A little headstrong, perhaps. On occasion, prone to bad judgment.

"Well," said Evie, propping her chin on her hand and glaring at Miriam. "Am I going to be favored with a response, or do I follow you over to your office at the Stroud, shouting in your ear? Art museums hate loud voices, Miriam. It might irritate the clientele. Or, I suppose I could pour honey all over your desk to get your attention. You could tell everyone it was an installation piece."

Miriam patted her mouth with the napkin and then laid it carefully in her lap. "You know I have no power to change the will, Evie. It's what your mother wanted."

"What *mother* wanted. Mother knows best. *Saint Charlotte*."

"She hated it when you called her that."

Evie gave her a withering stare. "And I hated it when she tried to run my life."

Miriam had had enough. "Listen, you little idiot. Your mother loved you. Fiercely! She only wanted what was best for both you and Julia. Ok, so you disagreed. Big deal. But you've got to get on with your life, whether it pleases people or not. You'll get the money, but not now. It's not possible." She took a deep breath. "Look, I'm the last person to sit here and tell you Charlotte was easy to live with."

Evie snorted, then turned her head away.

"We had our problems too. I can't tell you we would ever have gotten back together. But that's the way life is sometimes. You can't count on things. You have to count on *yourself*." She knew if she kept on with this, she would start crying. Charlotte's death had hit her every bit as hard as it had the two children. Sometimes she felt like she would never recover. There were so many things left unresolved. Still, she refused to show her emotions in public. She mustn't lose control.

"But...god, Miriam, that money could make all the difference. This gig we're playing right now, it could be my first real break. Do you know who came in the other night? Prince! He heard me sing one of my *own* songs. I could see him sitting out there. He was really listening! I'm good, Miriam. I could make it in this businesses, I know it. But I'm just scraping right now. They're going to kick me out of my mother's room upstairs at the end of the month. Then what? This day job I've got wandering around in a gorilla suit singing 'Happy Birthday' to zombie assholes in corporate America doesn't pay shit. Where am I going to live on so little? I'm too tired in the morning to deal with an eight-to-five. And even if I wasn't dead tired, I couldn't stand to moo into the office every day with the rest of the cattle. Can you see me standing around the water cooler, snapping my gum and talking about how my boyfriend and I spent a thrilling weekend at The Mall? They might as well shoot me right now!"

Such passion, thought Miriam wearily. Watching Evie was like watching a home movie of herself at that age. Every emotion was an exaggeration. Every situation was the end of the world. "You can move back home with me. You know you didn't have to leave when your mother did. Just because we were having problems didn't mean you were part of it."

"I was always part of it," said Evie dejectedly.

Out of the corner of her eye, Miriam noticed Doyle Benedict, one of the young club stewards, trying to get

Evie's attention. Evie must have noticed it too because she closed her eyes and gave an exasperated "ugh."

"Love in bloom?" asked Miriam.

Evie rolled her eyes. "Men with snouts and pug faces do not turn me on. Besides, he's a militarist. ROTC at the university. Oh god no, he's coming over." She started to slide under the table.

"Evie! Get back up here."

"Hi," said Doyle, sidling up to the table. "Can I get you ladies more coffee?"

"Good, Doyle." Evie mimicked a smile. "That was an improvement. You didn't say *girls* this time. I suppose it proves you can learn. An important quality for a university student."

He cocked his head. "Was that a compliment?"

She ignored the question, pretending to look carefully at his face. "And no traces of powder or blush. But some-one needs to talk to you about astringents. Your pores are a mess."

Doyle blushed. "Cut it out."

"If you weren't several sizes too big, I'd ask to borrow that little red number you were wearing the other night. Did that guy ever actually go home with you?"

"Excuse me?" asked Miriam. She wanted to be let in on the joke.

Doyle yanked at his tight collar. "Look Evie, you know why I was dressed like that. Come on. Cut me some slack." He cleared his throat. "I was just wondering... are you free tonight?"

Evie grinned. "You wanna hit the bars together and first you need to borrow some of my make-up. Right?"

A woman at another table waved to him. He shifted his feet impatiently and muttered, "Wrong. Look, I gotta go. I'll catch you later."

As he walked away Miriam asked, "What was all that about?"

Evie leaned back in her chair and shook her head.

"He's a nerd's nerd. I saw him in a bar last Friday night in total drag. Actually, he looked pretty good. I didn't recognize him at first. When he saw me, he came over to my table. He goes, "I finally got around to pledging a fraternity, Evie. This is just a prank. Yuck yuck." He laughs like a cartoon gopher. He's a senior in Urban Studies this year. Thinks he needs a good fraternity network for his business future. Anyway, so as part of the initiation for this fleabag joint, he had to spend the evening in a bar hustling other guys. Seriously dumb, right? *So* juvenile." She fluffed her hair.

Miriam finished her coffee as she watched Doyle charm a group of older women at a table near the door. No doubt he made good tips. Pushing the cup away, she returned her gaze to Evie. "So, what do you say? Would you like to come back home?"

Evie lowered her eyes. "Actually, I kind of would." She looked up. "I could give you some money . . . but only occasionally, Ok? I'm desperate for clothes right now. I can't be expected to sing on stage looking like a rag woman!"

"I understand," said Miriam.

Evie nodded. "If it hadn't been for that damn prison sentence . . . "

"You did the deed, darlin', so you did the time."

She shook her head. "Any other lawyer would have gotten me off. It was that Lawless creep. He had too many other *important* matters on his plate to give much time to me."

Miriam frowned. She was terribly concerned that Evie still blamed a lawyer for her problems. It was a bad sign.

"Well, I gotta hit the bricks." Evie rose from the table and tossed her napkin over the remains of her omelet. "Thanks for breakfast. I'll move my stuff back in tonight."

"Great."

"And Miriam . . . thanks."

9

"You're *suffering*, dearheart! Remember? You've had a tough life. Callouses from playing racquetball with the Ambassador's son. A clumsy waiter spilled a Long Island Iced Tea on you last night at dinner. Your children think you dress like a K-Mart floor manager...your wife, sadly, agrees. *Nothing* is going right. Now. Try it again from the top of page five. And this time, give me *angst!*"

Cordelia flopped back down on her theatre seat. She hated the first days of rehearsals for a new play. Other than a few inspired moments, nothing decent would emerge for several weeks. Dramatically, she held the back of her hand to her forehead. Fevered exhaustion. That's what it was. The entire morning had been an hallucination. Either that or it was the result of last night's midnight egg roll run. One never truly knew. Ah, the mystery of life, she thought to herself as she watched two actors bump into each other. A vase of flowers was sent crashing to the floor. "Barnie!" she shrieked, throwing her arms in the air. "Damage control! Get in here with that mop and broom. And while you're at it, bring the Pledge. This set is a freaking pit."

"Do I hear a bit of directorial hyperbole?" asked Jane, easing into the seat next to her.

Cordelia turned, lifting her chin and raising a skeptical eyebrow. "I *never* exaggerate."

"May I assume this new play is a comedy?"

"A tragedy," muttered Cordelia, heaving herself up. "In every sense of the word. Everybody," she called, trying to sound cheerful, "take five. No, make it ten." As if trying to hide, she oozed back into her seat and shielded her face from the stage. "Do you suppose they think I meant *minutes*? Silly people. I meant years. I don't want to see any of them back here for *ten years*!"

"What is it you always say? It's only art."

Cordelia quietly seethed.

"I need to talk to you about something."

"You have exactly nine years. And counting."

For a moment, Jane glanced up at the empty balcony. She didn't want to be overheard. Then, huddling close, she said, "This is going to sound kind of strange, but I had a visitor last night. You probably know her. Mae Williams?"

Cordelia lowered her voice to a sinister basso. "Let me guess. A private poetry reading?"

"Cordelia, this is no joke. She came to me in sort of an official, unofficial capacity as a member of the board of The Gower Foundation. It seems she and Miriam Cipriani think Rose Gower's death wasn't accidental."

"Do tell? Why don't they talk to the police? Unless, of course, they want you to cater the murder investigation."

"Just listen!"

"I am!"

Jane tugged on her sweater. "There were some... items stolen the night Rose died. Two jewels and a ledger. All were taken from the attic room just above her apartment. It seems the ledger contains some rather private information the foundation doesn't want the police to know about."

"Like what?"

"Mae wouldn't tell me. But she wants me to find the

stolen property. She actually *hired* me."

"I knew it! I knew it would come to this. Don't you re-member? I predicted this years ago." She buried her head in her hands—but continued talking. "I can see it all now. You're going to sell your lovely restaurant, move to some scummy rat-infested office downtown, start smoking ciga-rillos . . . "

"Cordelia?"

"You'll begin talking out of the side of your mouth. Calling women *dolls. Babes!* The only light in your office will seep from cracks in the dusty Venetian blinds. It'll throw weird shadows over your clients' faces. You'll rent a seedy trench coat . . . what am I thinking? You already *have* a seedy trench coat!"

"Cordelia?"

"*What!*"

"May I continue?" She waited, exaggerating her pa-tient expression.

"Oh . . . if you must."

"As you might well imagine, I have certain misgivings about trying to help them. First of all, someone at that women's club might have been responsible for sending my father that pipe bomb. Second, I don't like working in the dark. Mae said there were things she simply couldn't tell me. But then she countered by insisting I would be told ev-erything I *needed* to know."

"How kind of her. Why all the secrecy?"

"Beats me. And get this. Apparently, both Miriam and Mae have a motive for stealing the jewels—but not the led-ger."

"And that motive would be?"

"Another one of their secrets."

"They're *sure* Rose was murdered?"

"No, but it's a possibility. She may have been enter-taining someone late Monday night in the attic room above her apartment. She was wearing her best shawl, but oddly, no glasses. Oh, by the way, anything I tell you has to be kept in the strictest confidence. None of the particulars of her death have been given out. The press only got the essentials. I talked to Mae earlier this morning and she stressed that *no* one at the club was allowed up on the third floor after Rose's body was found. They're keeping all of this very quiet."

"Mmm," said Cordelia. She appeared to be lost in thought.

"The thing is, last Monday was the day we had lunch at the club. Remember that note I saw?"

"What note?"

"The one on Rose's clipboard. It said, 'Chamber meeting, Monday, 11 P.M.' She got kind of nervous when she saw I'd noticed it. Don't you find that strange? If she was going to be at a meeting that night, maybe it had something to do with her death. The paper said the death occurred around midnight, but they can't pin it any closer than that."

"I was at the club Monday night. Since the theatre is closed, I decided to have dinner with a couple of friends. See if I could interest them in a game of bridge."

"Did you run into Rose?"

Cordelia put a finger to her chin. "Actually, I did. Several times. The first was around four-thirty. The dining room doesn't open until five, but Rose was sitting in there, all alone, just staring up at the picture of Amelia Gower hanging over the mantle. She seemed completely lost in thought. I figured it was best not to disturb her. After all, that painting *is* the club icon. Maybe she was praying."

"And then you saw her later?"

"She was leaving with Freddy Lindhurst. He's married to Charlotte Fortnum's daughter, Julia."

"We've met. Do you know where they were going?"

"Well, Rose mentioned something about a choir practice. Freddy sings in the choir over at St. Mark's. I guess she loved choral music and sat in on their practice fairly often. Since Rose didn't see well enough for a nighttime stroll, I'm sure they drove."

Jane shook her head. "I need to find out what she was doing later that evening. Maybe somebody else knows about this Chamber meeting. Look, what are you doing tonight for dinner?"

Cordelia swallowed hard. "I don't suppose you'd believe me if I told you I was fasting?"

"I'll meet you at my house at six."

"Why do *I* have to get mixed up in this?"

"You're my official partner, *dearheart*."

"I am?"

"Besides, you wouldn't want me to eat alone."

"I could cope with my guilt."

"Six sharp," said Jane.

10

FREDDY drove his Mustang into a parking space behind the club and sat for a moment watching his wife search for a comb in her purse. One thing he knew for certain, a strong, bulldog face like hers would never appear on the cover of *Vogue*. Yet to him, everything about Julia was beautiful. She'd brought an emotional dimension to his life that, even two years ago, he never could have imagined.

Freddy was raised in a family that valued learning above everything else. From the time he was a child, he knew he would go to college, get his masters, and then go on for a doctorate. Since his own inclinations had been quiet and bookish, it hadn't been hard to follow family orders. But the day he met Julia Fortnum, everything changed. The world, once seen only in blacks and whites, suddenly burst forth with all the colors of the rainbow. The subtlety and complexity dazzled him. Julia quickly taught him that feelings were just as important as ideas. To a young man steeped in the importance of educational achievement, it had come with the force of an epiphany.

At first, his parents resisted their marriage plans. Julia would only stand in his way. Why didn't he establish himself as a professor first and then marry? It was only after his father had met Charlotte Fortnum, a revered name at the University of Minnesota, that both parents relented.

Good old Charlotte. At least she'd been useful for something. Not that Freddy himself hadn't been somewhat awed by the idea of marrying the daughter of such a famous woman. Then again, Charlotte had never been thrilled with the idea of having Freddy Lindhurst, doctoral candidate in German Literature, as a son-in-law.

For one thing, she disapproved of his thesis. Other people might laugh at something so picayunishly academic being taken so seriously, but between them, it became a prime source of contention. Charlotte was not a fan of Herman Hesse, telling him privately that—given a bit of time and maturity—he would outgrow his attraction to the man's writings. Freddy saw this as pure condescension. Charlotte insisted Hesse's early works were too simplistic and romantic. The later works unintelligible and self-indulgent. Hesse believed only in the individual. No use trying to change the world. No mass struggle would ever benefit mankind. Clearly, this philosophy went against everything Charlotte believed. Freddy knew Charlotte took his decision to translate one of Hesse's lesser known works, *Die Kunst des Müssiggangs* (*The Art of Indolence*) as a personal slap in the face. Perhaps he'd even intended it that way. Charlotte and all her political concerns drove him crazy! She got under his skin the way no one else could. He knew others revered her as some kind of moral giant, while he saw her as merely exhausting and opinionated.

As Freddy turned off the motor, he noticed that Julia had finished combing her hair and was now sitting mutely, staring at a faint, dispiriting drizzle which formed droplets on the windshield. Lately, she had begun to have moods where she shut him out completely. It left a sinking feeling deep in his stomach. Charlotte's death had hit Julia hard. "Are you all right?" he asked gently. He placed his hand on the back of her neck, feeling her body stiffen at his touch.

"I'm fine." She attempted a smile. "I suppose we'd better get in to dinner. Evie said she'd be ready around seven. It's too bad the evening's so dreary. Bad luck seems to be the order of the day."

"You're *not* coming, Julia. Is that understood? I want you to stay at the club while I help your sister move her things back to Miriam's. Don't you think I can see how tired you are? Lifting a bunch of boxes is not what you and the baby need. You're not getting enough rest, honey. Every night—tossing and turning."

For a moment, she didn't say a thing. Freddy waited anxiously, feeling a film of sweat form on his forehead.

"I have a lot to think about right now, Freddy. But don't worry, our baby is going to be fine. *Everything* is going to be fine."

The sudden fierceness with which she looked at him melted all his anxiety. "I believe you," he said tenderly.

As she took his hand, her expression softened and then turned wistful. "You and mother were more alike than you ever realized, did you know that? Ideas were everything to her. They ruled the world. You're exactly the same way. Except, you never could agree on which ideas were the right ones. Me, I'm not even particularly interested in the argument. I know what seems right. I don't care if I tie all those feelings into some kind of logical philosophical premise or not." She looked down into her lap. "But...I miss her, you know?" She began to cry, turning her face to the window.

"I know, honey." Freddy slid over and took her in his arms. The utter desolation in her sobs touched something deep inside him. He held her tight. Nothing was ever going to separate them. *Nothing*.

"She'll never even meet her grandchild. She would've been a terrific grandmother, I'm sure of it. I don't care what she said, she would've spoiled our children rotten." She sniffed back her tears.

Freddy could feel the muscles in his neck tighten.

Lovingly, Julia smoothed the soft blond curls around his forehead, leaning her head on his chest. "It's just going to take me some time, ok? And now with Rose gone too, I feel like a huge chunk of my life is missing. All I have left are you, Evie and Miriam. We have to take care of each other."

"We will," he said gently. He hesitated for a moment. "Julia?"

"Yes?"

"Well . . . I mean, I suppose it's not really the best time to bring this up, but you've been so . . . distant lately. I haven't wanted to press you about it."

Julia sat up.

"There's nothing wrong, is there? I mean . . . with us?"

"There's nothing wrong, Freddy."

"Because if there was, you'd tell me, wouldn't you? We could handle anything as long as we're committed to each other. I believe that with all my heart."

Julia glanced over her shoulder as a rusty green Saab rattled into the parking lot. A second later Jane and Cordelia got out and dashed for the side canopy. "Damn," she said under her breath.

Freddy looked up, frustrated at the interruption. "Back again so soon? That Lawless woman is turning into a pest."

"What do you suppose she wants? She's spying for her father, Freddy. I *know* it."

Freddy watched Julia's face flush with anger. "Look, let's just forget about her. Emery is so clearly guilty, no jury would acquit him. I know how much it means to you to see the murderer of your mother caught and punished. But that's going to happen. Emery's an arrogant ass. He'll get what's coming to him. Just because that woman is snooping around—I mean, it doesn't mean a thing. What could she possibly find?"

Freddy could see Julia relax a bit. That was good. She

had her mother's quick temper. Still, everyone knew Emery's guilt was beyond question. Nothing was going to change the final verdict.

"You're right," said Julia, giving him a peck on his cheek. She snapped her purse shut. "Let's go eat. Evie's probably performing later tonight at that new bar. What's the name?"

"Wizards."

"Right. You wouldn't want to hold her up."

He smiled and nodded but hesitated before getting out, shivering inwardly as the worst possible scenario occurred to him once again. Did she suspect? He and Evie would be alone together for at least an hour tonight. That was good. He needed the time to relax. Unwind. Perhaps Evie had a better sense of what was going on with her sister. Then again, if she did know, would she tell him?

11

"I am not entering the dining room with you while you've got that silly hump strapped to your body." Cordelia stood statue-like next to the coat room, pointing at Jane's backpack. A young woman peered curiously at them from behind the counter. "Do you want to go camping, Janey, or do you want to have dinner in a civilized manner? Take your pick." She tapped her foot impatiently.

Jane handed over the offending hump. "I would have left it in the car, but you know the driver's side lock doesn't always work and—"

"I do not care to discuss the inexorable disintegration of that horrific vehicle. Now. On to brighter matters." She turned, sucked in her stomach, charged down the hall and sailed into the dining room. After Jane was seated, Cordelia picked up the menu and said, *sotto voce*, "I could be having dinner with Andromeda tonight."

"Really? Did your crystal ball break down?"

Cordelia cast her eyes to the heavens before returning them to the menu. "In case you didn't know, Andromeda is no longer selling New Age . . . paraphernalia."

"No?"

"No. She's now selling used cars."

Jane stifled a giggle. That was quite an occupational

leap . . . of faith. "Better watch out, Cordelia. She'll have you trading in your 1988 Buick Le Sabre for a 1978 Pinto—in mint condition, of course." She looked up as a young man arrived to take their order.

"Ah, Doyle," said Cordelia, flapping her napkin and stuffing it in her sweater. "Bring me a Brandy Alexander. Make it a double. Oh, and ask the bartender to put one of those little paper umbrellas in it." She batted her eyes innocently at Jane. "Well, *you're* driving, dearheart. I might as well enjoy the evening."

Jane ordered a cup of tea.

A few minutes later Doyle returned with their drinks.

"It's too bad Rose isn't here to read your tea leaves, Janey," said Cordelia, saluting the oil painting of Amelia Gower before taking a sip of her creamy, lethal-looking concoction. Amelia gazed benevolently at the diners, her eyes alert, watching. "Isn't that right, Doyle? I'm told she used to read yours once in a while."

With just the right hint of regret in his solid face, Doyle nodded. "She liked doing it. At first I thought I was simply humoring her, but you know, turns out she had a gift. About a month ago she said I'd be coming into some serious money soon. I thought she was just fooling around, but, now I find out, she was right."

Jane looked up. For some reason, Doyle seemed agitated, rocking back and forth on the balls of his feet. "Is that right?" she said pleasantly. "An inheritance?"

"I suppose you could say that," he smiled. "I can always use the extra cash. My parents pay my tuition over at the U, but I have to earn my spending money. Life is going to be a lot easier this quarter," he grinned, taking out his pad and pencil. "Can I take your orders now?"

After watching Cordelia devour the last bite of her rum chocolate torte and finish her fourth cup of coffee, Jane excused herself and went to fetch her keys out of the backpack she'd left in the coat room. She needed them to unlock the attic door. She might even take a peek inside Rose's apartment while she was at it.

As she walked quickly down the main hallway, she tried to shake the vague sense that someone had been watching her. To be honest, all during dinner she'd felt it. She hated this kind of unfocused apprehension. Under other circumstances, she might have left. Tonight, however, she had a mission. No shadowy impression was going to chase her off.

As she approached the coat room, Jane noticed the young woman who'd been in charge earlier was gone. A small sign near the door said, "Back in fifteen minutes." She moved around behind the counter and began her search. On a shelf in the back of the room she finally found her backpack. Quickly, she unzipped the side pocket and reached inside. That was funny. She felt inside again, but the pouch was empty. She always kept her keys in exactly the same place. Where could they be?

Cordelia lumbered up to the front desk, patting her stomach. "One of the women on the fall lecture committee wants to speak with me about giving a short talk." She stopped when she saw Jane's puzzled expression. "What's up?"

"I can't find my keys. I'm sure I put them in my backpack, but they're not here."

"Maybe you dropped them."

"I fail to see how I could have dropped them if they were zipped in this pocket."

"Don't bite. It was just a suggestion."

Jane hated it when she misplaced things. It set her off like nothing else could.

"Maybe you left them in the car."

Attempting to reign in her frustration, Jane headed outside with Cordelia hot on her heels.

"There," said Cordelia, beating her to the spot. "Still in the ignition."

Jane put a hand on her hip and shook her head. "How could I have done that?"

"Simple stupidity?"

Jane clenched her teeth. "Why don't you go talk to your friend about giving that talk. I'm heading up to Rose's apartment."

"Fine," said Cordelia, slamming the door and tossing Jane the keys. "And when I finally rejoin you, may your mood have altered *substantially*."

Jane took the elevator to the third floor. By the time she got to Rose's door, some of her frustration had dissipated. She would have to apologize to Cordelia. Using a friend as a punching bag was generally not her style. She slipped one of the keys Mae had given her into the lock and was surprised to find it already open.

"Hello?" she called softly, moving cautiously inside. The interior was dark. No lights were on. As she crossed through a small hall into the living room she stopped. There, lying on an antique chesterfield couch, seemingly asleep, was a young woman. A half empty bottle of brandy rested next to her on the floor. She didn't appear to have heard Jane come in.

Jane cleared her throat. From outside came a rumble of thunder. A second later rain began to pelt the windows.

Slowly, the young woman opened her eyes. "Who the hell are you?" She ran a hand over her face.

Jane hadn't expected to find anyone in Rose's rooms. How was she going to explain her presence? "My name is Jane."

"What do you want?" The woman reached around on the floor until she found the bottle.

"Well . . . I've just joined the club. Someone said there were rooms upstairs for members to rent. I thought I'd check it out."

"This is a private residence. Members aren't allowed."

Instead of letting the woman chase her off, Jane stood her ground, glancing for a moment at the furnishings. A pair of green brocade Queen Anne chairs. A beautifully polished, mahogany highboy. Several Chinese rugs. A tasteful collection of cloisonné vases. "This is a very beautiful room. Have you lived here long?" She decided to play dumb.

Raising her head off the pillow, the young woman took a sip from the bottle and then said, "I don't live here. My . . . grandmother did. Before she died. Rose Gower."

"Of course. But—I didn't know she had children." It suddenly dawned on her who this woman must be.

"Ok. I lied. She wasn't my grandmother." The voice was slurred. "But my sister and I always called her that. She was a bosom buddy of our mother's. I'm Evie Fortnum." There was a flash of lightning.

Jane wondered if the twilight was playing tricks with her eyes. The woman's hair looked decidedly magenta. She also appeared to have been crying. "I was very sorry to hear about your mother's death. And Rose's. It's a lot to handle."

Wearily, Evie dropped her head back on the pillow. "Yeah."

"My mother died when I was thirteen. It took me years to come to terms with it, if I ever really did. I still miss her. For a long time I felt like this protective shield was gone. It was scary facing the world without it. It leaves you so vulnerable. So opened up. It's like, you don't just lose the person you loved, you lose your own history. The chronicler who was always there to remember your life for you. It's all gone."

Evie took another sip of brandy. She pointed to a chair. "Have a seat."

Jane wondered how drunk the woman was—if anything she said had made sense. Since she'd been invited to stay, perhaps it had.

"My grand and glorious mummy and I never got

along. I'm the black sheep," she added, hoisting the bottle high over her head. "Actually, I was a blond sheep for a while. Now I'm a crimson sheep." She touched her hair. "I'm a singer. Have you ever heard of *Fusion*?"

Jane had. "You mean the band?"

"Yup. I'm lead singer. *Evangeline*. I just go by my first name."

Jane had heard them perform several times. If she remembered correctly, Evie Fortnum had the husky kind of singing voice she liked. She sounded a bit like Stevie Nicks. "I'm impressed."

"You are? Announce it over the loudspeaker then. I could use a vote of confidence."

Jane made herself a bit more comfortable. "Your mother didn't approve of your singing?"

Evie laughed. "Oh, I suppose the singing was ok—as long as I got my little tush over to that fucking University and took the requisite courses in *mind screwing*. She also didn't like my friends much. It's how I got in trouble last time." She raised her head off the pillow and smiled serenely. "Cocaine *issues*, as my mother's friends would say. What did you say your name was?"

"Jane."

"Well, I'm a jail bird, Jane. Attempting to sell crack to a cop. Pretty bright, huh?"

"Really bright."

"Yeah, well, I served my time. And I'm clean now."

"Except for the booze."

Evie grinned. "I gotta have some fun, don't I? And besides." Her expression turned dark. "I can't sleep without it."

"Because of your mother's death? And Rose's?"

"Maybe."

"I'm curious. Did you ever know Emery Gower?"

"Emery? Sure. A real jerk. He deserves everything he's going to get."

"Rose seemed to like him."

"Rose was . . . an old woman. She tried to help him. That was her first mistake."

"What was her second?"

"Introducing us."

"Really? Did you date?"

"Who wants to know?" Evie sat up. "You're awfully nosey."

"Sorry."

"Yeah. Well." She ran a hand through her hair. "My life would have been just fine if I'd never met that muscley little turd. Everyone warned me. Mom. Julia. Even Miriam."

"You're pretty close to Miriam Cipriani, aren't you?"

"Julia and I grew up with her. She and Mom—" She hesitated. "My mother was a lesbian. You got any problem with that?"

"None."

"Good. She and Miriam have been together since Julia and I were kids. Well, I mean they *were* together . . . until recently. And Julia's married now. Marriage is such a crock. Don't get me started. But I moved back in with Mom and Miriam after I got out of the slammer." Her lip curled. "That is, until Mom left a couple months ago."

"Do you know why they separated?"

Evie took another swig of brandy. "I don't know. They were arguing all the time. I'm not sure what it was about cause every time I walked into the room they'd stop talking. For a while I figured it was me. But it wasn't. It had to do with the foundation. That's all I know. Miriam's invited me back to the house to live with her. She's all right, really. Kind of hard-headed sometimes—" Evie stopped. It was beginning to dawn on her that she was telling some rather intimate things to a complete stranger. "Say, who are you again?"

"My name's Jane."

"Last name, sweetie."

The jig was up. "Lawless. Jane Lawless."

A look of surprise grew on Evie's face. "You related to that millionaire smartass lawyer who defended me?"

"He's not a millionaire."

"Do you think I care?" She stood, flailing her arms in the air. "Fuck that bastard. If it wasn't for him, I'd never have gone to jail. He didn't have the time to give me a real defense. It wasn't my fault. I was the fucking *victim!*" She crumpled into a chair and began to cry.

In spite of all her anger, Jane felt sorry for Evie. Her life was obviously a mess. If she didn't stop drinking and get some help, nothing was going to get better.

"Anybody in here?" came a strong tenor voice. A second later Freddy appeared in the doorway. "What's going on?" He glared at Jane. "Evie, are you all right?"

Evie wiped her sleeve across her eyes. "Of course I'm not all right! Give me one reason why I should be."

He stepped further into the room. "Why are you talking to her?" he demanded. "Evie? Answer me!"

"Go to hell." She got up and bumped past him into the bathroom, splashing water in her face.

"You better leave," said Freddy, turning to Jane.

"Of course."

Evie erupted into the hall and headed for the door.

"Stay put," he ordered. "I'm here to help you move."

"I'm going downstairs," she sniffed. "I'll be in my room."

Freddy stood in the center of the floor rubbing the back of his neck, clearly not knowing what to do. Something about him seemed tightly strung. Almost frightened.

"So, I guess I'll be going," said Jane pleasantly, standing up and backing toward the door. For some reason, she was afraid he was going to stop her. Instead, he bolted into the hall and disappeared. Jane waited until she could no longer hear footsteps and then released her breath, heaving a sigh of relief. Thank god that was over. She moved slowly and somewhat uncertainly to the window which overlooked the sculpture garden. Well, at least she'd finally shaken the feeling of being watched. In this room, she felt totally cut off. It gave her the creeps. She dug in her pocket for her keys. The attic room was next on the evening's agenda.

Resolutely, she left the apartment and approached the door to the attic stairway. It was the only other door in the darkened hall. She slipped one of the keys into the lock. The first one didn't work. She tried the second. To her dismay, this one wouldn't even fit into the lock. The third was also too large. She tried the first again, but no luck. Standing back, she gazed uncomprehendingly down the hall. What was going on? Had she mistakenly been given the wrong keys? If Mae and Miriam wanted Rose's death investigated and they were committed to helping, this was no way to prove it.

She stood a moment longer deciding what her next move should be. As her eyes swept the scene, she noticed a faint light coming from under the bottom of the door. She pressed her ear hard against it and listened. Sure enough, upstairs she could hear the soft hum of some kind of motor. Strange. She wondered what it could be. Whatever the case, someone was obviously up there. She knocked several times, waiting for at least a minute before knocking again, this time even harder. Still, there was no response. Once more she leaned close and listened. The motor had stopped. She glanced down at her feet and noticed that the light had also been turned off. "Great," she muttered to herself as she gave the door a kick. So much for cooperation. She waited one more minute, her ear pressed against the wood, before completely giving up and heading for the elevator. She didn't want to jump to conclusions, but if someone was playing games, she wasn't amused. She'd been hired to do a job and she was damn well going to do it.

12

JANE splashed her way up the front walk to Dorrie's condo and rang the number. After being buzzed in, she took the elevator to the third floor. She was grateful to see Dorrie's smiling face when she got to the door.

"Still raining out?" asked Dorrie, noticing Jane's damp hair.

"Miserable night." Jane moved into the living room and removed her jacket and wet boots. "I'm glad you're home. I knew you had a meeting with some group tonight. I didn't know how long it would go."

Dorrie passed into the kitchen and returned a moment later with two steaming mugs of coffee. She joined Jane on the couch. "Great minds think alike. I was hoping you'd come over tonight. I haven't seen you since the party." She leaned close and nuzzled Jane's hair. "By the way, how did your lunch go at the club? I was sorry I had to miss it."

Jane was glad to finally be somewhere comfortable and sane. Dorrie looked so beautiful in the soft lamp light. She'd even taken off her ever-present horn-rimmed glasses which always gave Jane the feeling of being in a business meeting. The room smelled of sandalwood and pine. All she wanted to do was relax. "It was fine."

"Cordelia said you met Rose Gower."

"I did." She hated having to keep secrets from Dorrie. Her natural inclination was to tell her everything, but she'd made that promise to Mae. She couldn't break it.

Dorrie took a sip of coffee. "So, come on Jane. Tell me. Did you find a connection between that fake pipe bomb and anyone at the club?"

"Hardly." They both leaned back into the soft cushions, their arms entwined. "Cordelia introduced me to a few people. All by myself I managed to run into Charlotte Fortnum's daughter, Julia, and her husband, the one who looks like the Botticelli angel."

Dorrie laughed. "Freddy. That's so true."

"Tonight I met the other daughter, Evie. She's really a mess. I think she could use some help. If nothing else, someone needs to take that bottle of brandy away from her."

"Tonight? You were over there again?"

Damn, thought Jane. She was saying too much. Best to simply get off the subject. "Yup. Say, what are you doing Friday night? There's a new restaurant that's just opened up downtown. You know me, I always like to check out the competition. Would you like to go? My treat. I could make reservations. We could even go to a movie afterwards."

"Why did you go to the club again tonight?" She wasn't going to let it drop.

Jane swallowed hard. "I like the food?"

"I already told you how I feel about your being over there. I thought I made myself clear. Don't my wishes count for anything?"

"Sure they do." Jane wasn't used to Dorrie being quite so directive. It was out of character. "You think I should stay out of it. Let my father handle his own investigation."

"Exactly. But you went anyway."

"Look, what's the big deal? You took off with that Miriam Cipriani on Monday before I even had a chance to say hello. We had a date, Dorrie. I'm the one who should be pissed."

"What do you mean by that?"

"What do I mean by *what*?"

Slowly, Dorrie got up. She took a seat a few feet away.

"Are we having a fight?" asked Jane.

"I think so."

Jane set her mug down. "Look, I don't care about any of this. I came tonight because I missed you. Can't we drop the subject of the club?"

"Will you promise me something first?"

"What?"

"That you won't go back. You'll leave it all alone."

Jane took a deep breath. This was getting stickier by the minute. "Why is it so important to you?"

"It just is."

"And you can't tell me why?" All this reticence was beginning to annoy her. "Does it have anything to do with that urgent conversation you needed to have with Miriam Cipriani on Monday?"

Dorrie got up and walked into the kitchen.

Jane followed. "Well?"

"I think I'm going to be asked to join the board. With Charlotte gone, and now Rose, there are two openings." She stood in front of the sink, squeezing every drop of water she could out of a dish rag.

"You know this for a fact?"

"No, but I think I'm right."

It was Jane's turn to be upset. The current attrition rate in Gower Foundation board members frightened her. It was definitely a high risk occupation. "Why don't you just get a job as night cashier at a 7-11 on Nicollet and Lake Street!"

"Pardon me?"

"Two of the four board members are dead, Dorrie. Doesn't that suggest something to you?"

"What are you saying?"

Good question, thought Jane. What *was* she saying? Unfortunately, she'd spoken again without thinking. It had been a long day. "I don't know," she said, returning to the living room. "It just doesn't seem like it's something you should do." She dumped herself into a chair.

Dorrie stood in the doorway. "Why?"

"Well...for one thing, you're too busy on the city council. How could you possibly fit in so many new responsibilities?"

"I could manage. But what did you mean about Rose and Charlotte? Rose's death was accidental. And the murderer of Charlotte Fortnum has already been caught—at least theoretically. There's no connection, Jane. Why would you say something like that?"

Jane squeezed the bridge of her nose. "Look, what do you know about Miriam Cipriani? Or that other member of the board, Mae Williams?"

"I know they are honest, deeply committed women."

"Ok. I would never suggest otherwise. But, I mean, is it really something you want?"

Dorrie stood very still. In a voice barely audible, she said, "I don't know."

Jane got up and went to her, taking her in her arms. "I'm not trying to tell you what to do, any more than you are with me. Can we just drop this for now."

Dorrie rested her head on Jane's shoulder. "I love you."

"And I love you."

"You believe me, don't you?"

"Of course I believe you. What a silly question."

"Because...I'm not always a good person, Jane. Sometimes I get very confused."

Jane led her back to the couch. "Come on. No more talking in circles tonight. My brain can't stand it."

Dorrie held Jane's face in her hands for a moment. "You're too good for me."

"Oh, just stick a sock in it, will you?"

Dorrie smiled. "You'll stay the night?"

Jane grinned. They resumed their positions, arms intertwined.

For the first time, it struck Jane what sad eyes Dorrie had. When her face was animated with its usual blend of mischief and intelligence, it was all hidden. Tonight, the every-day veil had lifted. The vulnerability it revealed was like a magnet. Jane truly loved this woman. It was as if a magic genie had suddenly appeared and granted her that one fateful wish. *Find me someone to love.* Dorrie was everything she'd hoped for. So, that being true, why couldn't she just relax and enjoy it? But maybe she hadn't asked the genie for the right thing. Or perhaps the request had been incomplete. She tried to shake off the overpowering feeling that she would spend the rest of her life trying to stuff that genie back into its bottle.

13

IT was time to meet Miriam Cipriani. Jane left her restaurant early the next afternoon and drove over to the Stroud Museum of Art in St. Paul. She had called the curator's office and found that Miriam would be there most of the day, hanging a new show. That particular gallery was closed to the public, but Jane would be able to gain admittance simply by taking the elevator to the fourth floor.

Miriam held the prestigious title of Senior Curator. The receptionist had said her special interest was in emerging American artists. The new show was a collection of works on paper which included prints, etchings, charcoal and pencil drawings and even some photographs. Jane had always enjoyed the Stroud. Last year she'd even bought a membership for herself and Beryl.

Riding up on the elevator, Jane wondered again how she should approach the problem of the keys. It was probably best not to make an outright accusation of stonewalling. Perhaps Mae had made an honest mistake. The bottom line was, why would she be hired to investigate a matter and then not be allowed to see the scene of the crime?

Jane stepped off the elevator and immediately spotted a tall, raven-haired woman standing in front of a large portrait—a beautifully done serigraph. A man on a ladder was adjusting the height. Most of the stark white walls were still empty. As the woman turned to see who had arrived, Jane was struck by her elegance. Her clothing, tan silk slacks and a cream silk blouse, and her jewelry and make-up were impeccable. She looked like someone who belonged in an art museum—she almost looked like one of the works of art. Her olive skin was flawless, her expression serious and shrewd. Jane judged her to be in her early forties. So this had been Charlotte Fortnum's lover. Over the years, Jane had read about the two of them often in *Equal Time*, a local gay and lesbian newspaper. From the photos she'd recently seen of Charlotte on the front page of the *Star Tribune*—a pudding-faced woman in a nondescript brown suit, hair pulled back into a matronly bun—they had been an odd couple indeed.

"May I help you?" asked Miriam, walking over to several unframed photographs resting against the wall. She ignored Jane as she paged through them until finding the one she wanted. "The gallery is closed today."

"I know. I came to talk to you."

Miriam gave her a distracted nod. "Yes?"

"I'm Jane Lawless."

For a moment, Miriam didn't move. Then, her eyes finding Jane's and holding them for several seconds too long, she said, "Of course. Come with me." Quickly, she led the way to a small conference room at the back of the gallery, her low heels echoing in the empty hall. She waited until Jane was seated on the other side of a long table and then shut the door.

Jane felt ill at ease under Miriam's scrutinizing gaze. For a moment it seemed so intense, she wondered if she should simply give her name, rank and serial number, and get the hell out.

"I suppose you've come about the keys," said Miriam, sitting down uneasily on the other side of the table. She didn't smile. "Mae tried to get in touch with you last night at your house, but you were gone. It seems she got mixed up. Gave you the wrong set."

"Really?" said Jane.

"I have two here you can use. The one for the front door is still fine." She drew out a key ring from her pocket and removed the keys. "Just throw the others away." She pushed them across the table.

"Thanks."

"Was there something else you wanted to talk to me about?"

Jane was put off by her *in charge* manner. As Senior Curator, she was no doubt used to being in command. Then again, so was Jane, though she knew she never projected her power with such obvious relish. This wasn't going to be a totally amiable conversation. She'd bet on it. "I'd like to know what your reasons are for suspecting Mae Williams of taking those two jewels?"

"Who told you I suspected her?"

"Mae."

Miriam drummed her fingers on the table. "Well, that's simply not true."

"Look," said Jane, hoping this wasn't going to be a complete waste of time, "I can't find something when I don't have any idea why it might have been taken. That also goes for the ledger."

"I realize—"

"I don't think you do. I'm not a magician. I'd like a few straight answers."

"All right." She adjusted her jade beads. "I'll try to oblige."

"Good." Jane decided to try another approach. "Did you see Rose the night she died?"

"At dinner for a few minutes. But then she left with Freddy Lindhurst, he's Julia Fortnum's husband, to drive over to a choir practice. I was told he brought her back around ten."

"What do you know about a Chamber meeting that night?"

Miriam tried to hide her surprise but Jane had caught it. If she lied now, it would be obvious.

Miriam cleared her throat. "Chamber meeting? What's that?"

"There was a meeting at eleven that night. I think Rose was part of it. Where was it, Miriam? In that attic room? Were you there? Was Mae?" She knew she was leaping to some rather large conclusions, but she hoped it would pay off.

"Except for dinner, I was at my home the entire evening. I have no idea where Mae was. But it doesn't matter. Surely you must realize that neither of us would hurt Rose! Someone else was with her that night. You weren't hired to accuse us, for god's sake. You were hired to find out what happened!"

"Then quit lying to me." She held Miriam's gaze. "Do you think there's any connection between Charlotte Fortnum's death and Rose's?"

"No."

"Why did Charlotte move out? I've heard you were having a great many arguments before she died."

"That was . . . personal. I didn't kill her, if that's what you're suggesting."

Jane folded her hands on the table. "You still loved her, then?"

Miriam regarded her from a chilly distance. "Personal relationships don't always work out. We'd been together for eighteen years. People grow apart. Love *can* die, you know. It happens." She shrugged. "Charlotte was a wonderful woman. Strong. Competent. Very funny. Did you ever meet her?"

Jane shook her head.

"That's too bad. You would've liked her. Most people did. But our relationship was over. It wasn't easy, but the break had been made. I had no motive to want to hurt her. Or Rose. As far as I know, Rose had no enemies. As for Charlotte, I think the motive for her murder is a matter of public record. My sense tells me that the reason Rose was killed had to do with those jewels and that ledger. Other than simple monetary value, there is no reason I can think of for the theft. I find it hard to believe a stranger could have gotten in without setting off an alarm. The jewels originally belonged to Amelia Gower. Rose owned them legally and I would imagine she left them to the foundation in her will. Now, I suggest you start earning that five hundred dollars and stop bothering me. That's all the help I can give you."

Jane knew she was being dismissed. "What about Dorrie?" By the look on Miriam's face, she knew she'd hit another nerve.

"What about Dorrie?"

"Are you going to ask her to join the board of directors?"

"Who told you that?"

"Would you believe a little bird?"

Miriam gave her a disgusted look. "We have made no official decisions on that."

"An unofficial decision then?"

Miriam leaned back in her chair. "Why are you so interested?"

"She's a friend."

"Well, dammit, she's a friend of mine too."

Jane cocked her head. "Really? From the club you mean?"

"For your information, I've known Dorian Nesbitt Harris since we were in college."

Something about her tone angered Jane. Perhaps it was the insinuation that Jane was merely a newcomer in Dorrie's life and therefore of little consequence. Or, more likely, Miriam was simply irritated by this entire interaction and Jane was being overly sensitive. "She's never mentioned you."

"No? Well, perhaps there are other things she's never mentioned either." Miriam glanced at her watch. "I've given you all the time I can spare. If you have any more

84

questions, please contact Mae. She's the one handling this."

They each stood. Jane could feel Miriam bristle as she crossed to the door. Why had this entire conversation seemed so unnecessarily adversarial? There was the obvious fact that Jane was frustrated by being kept in the dark on some important issues, but could that have created so much negative electricity? "Thank you for your help," she said, walking around the table and moving into the gallery. She followed Miriam to the elevator.

"I'm sorry if I seem...distracted today," said Miriam. "I've got a lot on my mind."

"I understand," said Jane, pleasantly. She didn't really, but she also didn't want to end the discussion on a totally sour note.

"I hope you can help us." Miriam, waited as the elevator doors opened and Jane got on. "Then again, perhaps we're not meant to find out the truth."

"It's too early to tell. Well, see you around. I'll say hi to Dorrie for you."

As the elevator doors closed, the edges of Miriam's lips curled into a smile. "You do that, Jane."

14

"MIRIAM has always been utterly charming every time I've spoken with her," said Cordelia. She was sprawled on the couch in front of Jane's fireplace, a quilt covering everything but her head. A fake fur tam was pulled down tightly over her auburn hair, making her normally attractive face look a bit like a squashed mushroom.

Jane entered the room carrying a large bowl of popcorn and two mugs of hot chocolate. She set everything down on the mahogany coffee table.

"And while you're at it, toss another log on that fire. It takes longer every year for my old bones to get used to this autumn chill." She lifted her head to look at the bowl. "You did put extra butter on that, didn't you?"

"*Some* butter." Jane stoked the fire. "Getting back to the subject, Cordelia—"

"What subject?"

"My visit this afternoon with Miriam Cipriani. The only conclusion I can come to is that, for whatever reason, she simply doesn't like me. Maybe it's my personality. Or the way I dress."

"Definitely the second."

"I beg your pardon?"

"Well, face it Janey, jeans and a ski sweater are hardly her cup of tea. Add the two-year-old—less than immaculately white—high tops and you have a fashion disaster. By her standards, of course."

"Of course." Jane grabbed a handful of popcorn and sat down in the rocking chair. "Did you know she was an old friend of Dorrie's?"

"No. Then again, it doesn't surprise me. Everyone's an old friend of Dorrie's. She's in politics, Janey. It's the way of the world. Actually, come to think of it, I saw them together last night."

"You did? When?"

"Well, it was after you'd gone upstairs to explore strange new worlds in the attic room. I was standing in the main hall having a conversation with Alberta Epps about giving that talk. I happened to glance out the front window and there was Miriam waiting under the canopy. She was only there a minute or two before Dorrie drove up. Miriam got in the car and they left together."

"Really? I knew Dorrie had a meeting last night. I thought it had something to do with the city council."

"I rather doubt it."

Jane rubbed the back of her neck. "I hate this. Dorrie thinks I'm a busybody. She's upset that I'm still snooping around over at the club. How can I explain the truth to her when I made that promise to Mae? It's driving me nuts."

"The path of true love is never easy."

Jane grimaced at the soap opera cliche. "Look, let's forget about all that for a moment. I want to think something through tonight. You can help. Are you listening, Cordelia?"

"My synapses are standing at attention, Janey. They're even wagging their tails to prove they love you."

"Good. Now." She popped some kernels into her mouth. "What do we know for sure about the night Rose died?"

"I lost my shirt in a bridge game."

Jane stopped chewing. "Cordelia, please don't be frivolous. This is serious."

"Of course, dearheart. Forgive me. It just leaked out."

She sat up and lifted the bowl into her lap, eyeing it suspiciously. "A little abstemious with the butter, Jane, but I forgive you. Now, my turn. I'll start the ball rolling. First, Rose spent a good while before dinner last Monday night staring at the portrait of her grandmother in the dining room. Perhaps it was simple catatonia. Who can know? That's where I came in. Later, I saw her leave with Baron von Lindhurst."

"And we know Freddy brought her back around ten. You saw her go up to her rooms."

"I did."

"Then, earlier that same day I saw a notation she'd made about a Chamber meeting at eleven that evening. I think we can assume it had to be somewhere in the house since she didn't like to go out after dark."

"I detect a small problem here, Janey. You don't even know what a Chamber meeting *is*. Or if she attended."

"No, you're right. But when I mentioned it to Miriam, she lied. Said she didn't know anything about it. But she couldn't hide her surprise, Cordelia. And she *was* surprised."

"Ok, but what does it mean? It's probably just some private group she doesn't want you to know about. Nothing you or the CIA would be interested in."

"But why was Rose secretive about it too? When she saw I'd noticed that notation on her clipboard, she whisked it away. What could this Chamber meeting be about?"

"Well, let me think." Cordelia tapped a finger against her chin. "Hey! I got it." Eagerly, she sat forward and thrust her arms in the air, attempting to frame the scene she was picturing in her mind. "See, Rose plays tuba. Miriam the French horn. And Mae the oboe. They're secretly practicing a gavotte by Boismortier."

Jane sat absolutely still, staring straight ahead in utter disbelief. "Chamber music?"

"Precisely."

"You know, I don't know why I even talk to you sometimes."

"You're just jealous of my finely honed imaginative powers." Cordelia heaved a deep sigh. "Oh come on, Janey, don't be so grim. I know we're talking about a death here, but sometimes you need to lighten up. Let your mind play a little. Besides, I've spent every day this week over at the Allen Grimby directing a farce. It's hard to change gears. And forgive me, but doesn't some of this seem like a farce to you?"

Jane swallowed a gulp of cocoa. "Maybe."

"If you really want my opinion, the strangest part of this whole thing was finding Rose without her glasses— and wearing some fancy shawl over an old sweatshirt. If there's a key to anything, that's it."

Jane hesitated and then got up, plopping down on the couch next to Cordelia. "I agree. But your little scenario doesn't really help. And...you're hogging the popcorn." She yanked the bowl into her own lap. "Now, if you will just bear with me for another minute. Where was I?"

Cordelia sighed, banging Jane on the head with a small couch pillow. "Nowhere, Janey. You're absolutely nowhere."

Jane grabbed it away before she could do further damage, but she knew Cordelia was right. "I don't get it. Why would Mae come all the way over here to ask me to find out the truth about Rose's death, and then stonewall me? She won't tell me what's in the ledger. She won't tell me why she suspects Miriam of stealing the jewels, but she obviously does. She even hints that she has a motive herself, but she won't elaborate. And then she goes and gives me the wrong keys."

"Maybe she and Miriam are just using you to assuage their guilty consciences."

"What do you mean?"

"Well, maybe they don't really care if Rose's murderer is found, but since they can't contact the police—for whatever reason—they need to feel they've done *something*. You're the something."

"I never thought of that."

Cordelia leaned over and selected the kernels with the most butter, stuffing them into her mouth all at once. "They probably don't care if they ever recover the loot."

"No," said Jane, shaking her head, "I think you're wrong there. They want that ledger badly." She finished her cocoa. "You know what?"

"What?"

"We have to try to get into that attic again."

"We?"

"And when we're done, if I don't find anything that will help me solve this, I'm going to call Mae and tell her I've torn up her check. I don't need this kind of aggravation. I've got my own business to run. Dorrie thinks I'm a meddler. You've pretty much told me I've lost my sense of humor. I think you're right, Cordelia. This *is* a farce. Now, finish your cocoa."

Before Cordelia could respond, two little terriers bounded into the living room and jumped up on the couch.

"Beryl must be home," said Jane, getting up and stretching. "She took them for a walk."

"Ugh," shivered Cordelia. "Their noses are so cold! Get away from that bowl you little runt. Scram!" Gulliver snuggled close, putting his head in her lap. "Janey," she whined pathetically, "they're *all wet*. Wretched beasts! You never have to put up with this when you have cats."

"I prefer it to fur balls," smirked Jane. She grabbed Bean and nuzzled him with her nose.

"Do I smell popcorn?" asked Beryl, entering the room and walking briskly to the fireplace. She removed her hat and hat pin, setting them on the mantle, and then patted her hair back into place. "Cordelia, you look like a mummy. Are you cold?"

Cordelia pulled the quilt up over her head.

"We were just leaving," said Jane.

"Oh?" Beryl warmed her hands next to the fire. "Will you be late? It's already close to ten."

"I shouldn't be more than an hour," said Jane. She yanked the quilt off Cordelia and swept her hand to the door. "After you?"

"All I wanted was a quiet evening. As far as I'm concerned, this is kidnapping."

"Don't grit your teeth, Cordelia dear." Beryl lifted the bowl off the couch. "You wouldn't want to damage your molars."

15

"IF I come down with pneumonia," complained Cordelia, following Jane up the steps to the club's front door, "I'm sending you the bill."

Jane turned to find her friend standing rigidly by the wrought iron rail, her eyes squeezed shut. She was shivering. "The kitchen doesn't close until ten-thirty, Cordelia. We'll get something to warm you up."

"Sure. A trivet and a can of sterno."

Jane held the door.

As soon as they were inside, Jane noticed Doyle Benedict, the young club steward she'd met the other night, clearing tables in the dining room. Except for a cracking fire in the main hall, the club seemed quiet and deserted. Doyle looked up when he saw them standing in the foyer. He came out immediately.

"Good evening, Ms. Lawless. Ms. Thorn. Can I help you? The kitchen closes in fifteen minutes. If you'd like something, I should put your orders in now."

Cordelia adjusted her fake fur tam. "Splendid. We'd like two glasses of Port and a large scoop of that Stilton I saw earlier. Can you serve us in the hall? I want to sit by the fire. Oh, and put it on Ms. Lawless's bill, Doyle. And don't forget to give yourself a nice gratuity." She gave Jane a satisfied smirk.

"Cordelia and I will just be a few minutes," added Jane. "We have to go upstairs to talk to someone first."

"Of course. I'll have it ready for you when you come down."

Jane grabbed Cordelia's arm and dragged her over to the elevator before she could think of anything else to order. She pushed the button and waited for the door to open.

Doyle continued to stand and stare.

"Chop chop," called Cordelia, scowling at him. "Time is of the essence."

Jane gave him a little wave as they got on.

"He seems a bit overly interested in our activities," said Cordelia, lunging for the hand rail as soon as the elevator began its upward climb. "Is this thing safe?"

"Perfectly."

After rattling to a stop they both got off and approached the attic door.

While Jane searched for the right key, Cordelia examined her fingernails. "Did you happen to notice that guy's biceps? It's the first time I've ever seen him in a short sleeved shirt. With a few more pounds on him, he could pass for a wrestler." She raised a thoughtful eyebrow. "Doyle the Destroyer."

"I didn't notice. Now. One of these new keys should work." On the first try the door opened.

"Let's make this fast," said Cordelia. She pushed past Jane and bounded up the steps. "I'm starving. I hardly ate *any* of that popcorn."

Jane stuffed the key ring into her pocket and followed. At the top of the stairs she found a light switch and flipped it on.

"Well," said Cordelia, taking in the cluttered, utilitarian-looking room, "not exactly what I expected."

"What did you expect?"

"Oh, I don't know. Taste, for one thing. This place is a

dump. Or perhaps . . . a press for printing hundred dollar bills. Something that would justify all the fuss about the key."

Jane had to agree. The room was a disappointment. For one thing, it looked like it had been recently cleaned. Even the oriental carpet had been vacuumed. That must have been the sound she'd heard last night. A vacuum cleaner! If she was supposed to examine the scene of the crime for clues, she'd once again been effectively thwarted. Everything had been sanitized beyond recognition.

Glumly, she stood with her hands on her hips, taking in the dispiriting sight. One wall was completely covered with a built-in book case. Directly in front of it, preventing anyone from getting to the books, stood four metal filing cabinets. A round antique table and four ladder-back chairs dominated the center of the room. The lack of windows or breathable air made her nose itch.

Cordelia trudged over to one of the filing cabinets and drew open a drawer. "Not locked," she said, trying to sound cheerful. "Also, sad to say, not used. It's empty." She tried each succeeding drawer and found exactly the same thing. Nothing. "What do you make of it?"

"What *can* I make of it? It's obvious every shred of evidence I might have found has been cleaned away. This is a waste of time Cordelia." She knelt down and examined the carpet along the far wall. "Someone even moved those files. You can see by the indentation in the rug that they used to be here."

Cordelia was busily engaged in moving several of the filing cabinets away from the book case. "These are some interesting volumes, Janey. Some of them are quite old."

"Really." Jane couldn't work up much interest. Lethargically, she opened one of the bottom drawers. "Hey? Look here. Something the cleaning crew missed."

"What?"

"It's a piece of paper caught in the back. Can you reach in and get it? Your arms are longer than mine."

Cordelia bent down and pulled it free. She handed it to Jane. "What is it?"

"It's handwritten. Something about . . . it's about AIDS, Cordelia. Two lists of drugs." She turned the paper over. "And will you look at this? It's written on a piece of Charlotte Fortnum's personal stationery."

"No kidding. Maybe it's Charlotte's handwriting." She leaned against the bookcase. "I wonder what it means?"

"I don't know." Jane reread it. "But it's a start. Why would something like this be up here in a filing cabinet? We need to find out if The Gower Foundation funds anything to do with AIDS." She looked up. The room was empty. Cordelia had vanished. "Cordelia?"

No answer.

Jane didn't want to raise her voice. She was afraid someone might hear. "Cordelia!" she barked, as loud as she dared.

"Yes?" The voice was muted, barely audible.

"Where are you?"

"I don't know."

This was too much. "Quit playing games and come back here!"

"I'll try."

Jane watched in amazement as the bookcase moved outward and Cordelia reappeared.

"Just look at that, Janey. It's part of the wall. If you push right here," she showed her where she'd been leaning, "it opens."

"I'll be damned." Jane moved around the files and took a closer look. "Where does it lead?"

"I couldn't tell. It was dark. I was so surprised to be on the other side, I just stood there."

Jane tapped a finger against the side of her face. "I don't suppose you have a flashlight."

"Oh sure. I always carry one in my bra."

Jane spied an oil lamp sitting on a small table. Next to

it rested a matchbook. Quickly, she lit it and then returned to the bookcase. "Let's take a look."

Cordelia hesitated. "What about our Port? And the Stilton? Doyle the Destroyer seemed awfully interested in what we were doing, Janey. If we're gone too long, he may come looking for us."

Jane knew she was right. She checked her watch. It was a quarter to eleven. "Look, you go downstairs and make some excuse for me."

"Oh, no. I'm not letting you go back in there all by yourself. It could be dangerous."

Jane faltered for a moment. "Then come with me."

Cordelia folded her arms over her chest and drew herself up to her full six-foot height. "Jane, this is not the time. The club closes at ten-thirty. We're already past the witching hour. We have no business being here this late. It's only going to make us look suspicious. Do you want that?"

"You just don't want to be thrown out before we get a chance to eat that cheese."

"Don't forget the Port." She gave Jane a friendly chuck under the chin.

Reluctantly, Jane conceded. "All right. For once you represent the voice of reason." Still, she was disappointed. She was aching to get behind the wall. "We have to come back tomorrow, Cordelia. This can't wait." She blew out the lamp.

"I believe my dance card is filled for the next several weeks." Cordelia pushed the filing cabinets back in front of the bookcase. "Sorry."

"Well, I'm coming back—with or without you."

Cordelia put a hand on her hip, giving an exasperated snort. "How does that poem go, dearheart? Shall I compare thee to . . . a mule?"

16

EVIE Fortnum sat on a stool in front of a long work table, watching her sister knead the bubbles out of a hefty chunk of red clay. Julia pressed and pounded with a zest Evie found entirely too energetic for so early on a Friday morning. As usual, she had a hangover. This one wasn't as bad as some she'd had lately, but it was bad enough. She massaged her temples.

"I'm sorry Freddy and I didn't make it over to Wizards last night to hear you sing. We both wanted to come, but I just crashed on the couch. Couldn't get up. Pregnancy really takes it out of you."

Evie played dispiritedly with a wisp of scarlet hair. She felt like a good pout. "That's all right. It doesn't matter."

"Oh, come on. That glum routine hasn't worked on me since fifth grade." Julia gave her a little nudge. "And besides, I can't believe you don't understand."

"No, I do."

"Then what is it?"

"I don't know. Quit pressing me all the time, will you? What do you expect me to say?"

Julia covered the first piece of clay with plastic wrap and drew out a second lump from a bucket.

"Well, I mean...I suppose it's mom's death. And

Rose's." Evie got up and moved to a window overlooking a parking lot. Colored leaves were scattered like confetti over the blacktop. She didn't want to talk about that part of it—at least not to Julia. Julia had always been more verbal, more able to express herself. It made Evie feel stupid. Tongue-tied. The words flowed easily only when she got mad and didn't care what other people thought—or when she was drunk. "I can't . . . oh, you know what I mean. I'm just having all these weird reactions. I go to sleep at night and I hear the two of them whispering about me. It never seems to stop. I'm always the bad kid. I'm always doing something dumb." She turned around. "Look, I didn't come here to talk about that."

"No? Sometimes it helps."

"And don't treat me like one of your clients. It makes my skin crawl."

Julia glanced at her sister for a moment, and then went on working the clay.

"God, you're so fucking together. Then again, why shouldn't you be? Mom always loved you best." She gave her sister a smirk. This had been a game between them since they were kids. It felt comfortable to kick such an old saw around for a while. It was solid ground. Evie had been grasping at solid ground for weeks.

"Here we go."

"I know. It's the running joke, right?"

"It's not true, Evie. You know it and I know it."

Julia clearly wasn't going to play. Still, Evie had never let that stop her before. "No? You're the one who went to college. You did everything right—just the way Mom wanted it. A masters degree. A good job. An active, responsible life. You're an important therapist in Minneapolis, Julia. You work with disturbed youth. An *art* therapist, no less. Whatever the hell that is."

"I didn't do everything right," said Julia under her breath.

"What?"

"Nothing."

"And *me*, on the other hand...all I do is mess things up. And I'm selfish. I don't give a damn about any of Mom's causes. I want to live the one life I've got for *myself*—not others. All I love is music. I want to write, to perform. I want people to listen. I'm the bad sheep, Julia. You're the good."

"You're not a sheep, Evie. You're a horse's ass." She didn't smile.

Interesting, thought Evie, picking up a piece of clay. She must have hit a nerve. "Thanks for the vote of confidence."

"Oh, come on. You think you're the only one who ever disagreed strongly with Mother?"

"No, I know better than that. But I don't remember any huge fights you ever had."

"It was our styles that differed, Evie. That's all. You always wanted to confront. To start an argument. I intellectualized everything. She loved that. And I was more subversive about my dissent. Quieter." She stopped kneading and looked away. "Except once."

"Yeah, well, whatever."

Julia pulled over the stool and sat down. "Look, I want to try to explain something to you and I hope you'll listen. I think it will help." She paused, picking up a towel and wiping her hands. "I have this theory. See, I think the world is divided into—for want of a better term—the dark and the light. Most therapists base their ideas on what I call the heroic standard. They attempt to move people out of the dark and into the light—forever. I suppose you could say that in a way, this has been the primary mission of all religions as well. Psychological theory may just be the modern equivalent. But I not only believe this process to be wrong, I think it's naive. Life is a continuum, Evie. We all move back and forth freely between the light and the dark. Not only is it natural, it's necessary. With the kids I try to help, I don't set myself up as all knowing. I flow with them. I try to discover, through their art, the shadows in their lives. I want them to *feel*. To explore their own images and dreams. I want them to *think* about the permitted and the forbidden. Do you see what I'm saying?"

"I . . . suppose so." Evie could feel her head pounding. She hated lectures. She also had to find some aspirin before she drove over to the club to meet Freddy.

Julia shook her head. "Well, give it some thought."

"Uh . . . sure. I will."

Julia stood, leaning hard on the clay once again. "Are you all moved back into the house with Miriam?"

Evie stretched. "I am. Thanks to your husband."

"Yeah. He's always there for everyone. Ready and willing to help." She banged the clay on the table, picked it up, and banged it again.

"Do I detect a note of annoyance?"

"Me? Annoyed? What did I just get through telling you, Evie? I'm perfect. Always on top of things."

Evie shifted uncomfortably. She knew that hadn't been the point of Julia's little speech. If it hadn't been for this damn hangover, she might have listened more carefully. "Yeah," she laughed.

"You two have certainly been spending a lot of time together lately."

"I guess we have. I've needed a friend."

"And Freddy's willing to oblige."

Evie stood up straight. "What are you saying?"

"Me? Why nothing. Just an observation."

Evie poked her finger into the side of a clay lump.

"You dating anybody right now?"

"Nope."

"I suppose you miss Emery now that he's in the slammer."

Was Julia baiting her? Freddy was supposed to be the only one who knew the truth about that. "Hardly."

"I hear he may be getting out on bail."

Evie could feel her body tense. "Who told you?"

"Mae Williams. Oh, and it seems Rose told her she'd signed something that said, in case of her death, a large part of her estate would go to his defense."

"I didn't know."

"Yup. Say, what about that...what's his name? The steward at the club."

"What?" Evie was having trouble concentrating.

"Doyle? Yeah, that's it. He has a thing for you."

"Lucky me."

"Really?"

"Look, why all this interest in my personal life? What are you getting at?"

Julia rubbed her hands on her heavy canvas apron. "All right. I suppose that *is* the adult thing to do. Just come out and say it. So...are you sleeping with my husband, Evie?"

She hadn't expected that. For some reason, it struck her as terribly funny.

"Why are you laughing?"

"You know, Julia, we both have our blind spots. I think you're smarter than me and I've always envied that. Sometimes I feel so dumb around you. But you think, since I'm better looking, that every guy you've ever dated has really wanted me. That includes Freddy."

"*This* is a denial?"

"Yeah. It is. If you don't trust your husband, that's your problem." She could tell by the look on Julia's pug face that her last comment had hurt. God, why did she always have to do that? It wasn't what she wanted. It just happened.

"Fine." Julia undid her apron and laid it on the table.

Evie watched her sister retreat into a closet. She reappeared a moment later carrying a stack of magazines.

"I'm afraid I've got a class in ten minutes. I have to run down to the office and grab the registration list."

"Sure." Evie moved slowly toward the door. What a bust. The conversation hadn't gone the way she'd hoped.

She'd wanted to talk to her sister about their childhood. About the times they'd sat in the dark behind that attic bookcase and listened to their mother and Rose talk. She wanted her sister to interpret things for her, just as she always had. To make sense of the senseless. She desperately needed to be reassured. Her mother *had* loved her... hadn't she? She wasn't all bad. Still, Evie knew the nightly whisperings wouldn't go away. Rose and Charlotte. They grumbled and muttered—and always, Evie was the subject. Deep in her bones, Evie knew that even six feet under, they were not at rest.

17

JANE rushed down the hall to her office and picked up the phone. Since it was early morning and the restaurant was still closed, she'd been able to hear it ringing as soon as she'd stepped inside the back door. "Lyme House," she said into the receiver. "This is Jane Lawless."

"Jane!" It was her father. "I'm glad I caught you."

"Hi. How are you feeling?"

"Absolutely top shape. Really. Had the doctors check me over again yesterday and everything looks fine."

Jane hadn't talked to him for a couple of days. After the pipe bomb incident last Friday night, he'd gone back to work bright and early on Monday morning. It had been against her advice. And to be honest, it had worried her. He needed to take a few days off. "I was hoping Marilyn had tied you up. Either that, or talked you into a short vacation." She could hear him laugh.

"Listen honey, could you stop over to my office for a few minutes this morning? What do you say? Does your busy schedule permit?"

"Sure, I could do that. But what's up?"

"Well, that's what I'd like to talk to you about in person. Why don't we say, eleven o'clock?"

"Fine. I'll be there." She hung up the phone and sat

down behind her desk, trying to determine if her father's tone of voice gave anything away. He sounded happy. Even buoyant. Whatever he wanted to discuss, it didn't seem like bad news.

Several hours later Jane found herself on I-94 heading for St. Paul. Her father's office was in a 1920s downtown brownstone, very close to the Cathedral. As she changed lanes in preparation for making an exit, her car phone began to beep. She picked it up.

"Good morning, stranger," came a familiar voice.

"Dorrie! I'm glad you called. I figured you'd be in meetings all day."

"Just about. I've only got a minute."

"And you decided to spend that minute with me. That's what I call devotion." Jane began to joke. Normally, Dorrie would play along. Today, she was silent. "Dorrie? Did we get cut off?"

"No...someone is waving at me, Jane. I'm going to have to go. Listen, I was hoping we could get together tonight. I've got some good news. You're going to absolutely love it."

"Define *love it*."

"I'm not kidding. I know you'll be very excited."

Dorrie sounded distracted, not the least bit genuine. Still, she was probably just busy. "What time?"

"Say around nine? I should be home by then."

"It's a date. Should I bring anything?"

"No. Well...on second thought, how about some of those Cornish pasties from your restaurant. That would be easy enough. And you know I can't resist them."

"No pickled onions?"

"You can skip those, thanks."

"English mustard?"

"Sure. Extra mustard."

"And a bit of salad with our new ginger and lime dressing?"

"Stop! I'm not even going to get lunch today until after two."

"Poor baby."

"So I'll see you tonight, right?" There it was again. That hesitation.

"I'll be there. If not with bells on, then with a suitable alternative."

"Great. Gotta go."

Jane put down the receiver and took the Marion Street exit. Dorrie sounded stressed. Whatever this great news *was*, Jane wasn't so sure she wanted to hear it.

She found her father sitting in front of the round, spoked window in his office, feet up on the massive oak desk. He was talking on the phone. Gone were his impeccably cut suit and tie. Today, he was wearing a pair of comfortable jeans, and a red corduroy shirt. He looked more relaxed than she'd seen him in years. Between bursts of conversation, he waved her to a chair.

"Well," he grinned, after hanging up, "that's my daughter. Right on time. It's a good thing too, since I've got a plane to catch." He nodded to several suitcases standing near the door.

"Where are you going?"

"Stresa. It's on Lake Maggiore in Northern Italy. I've only been there once before, but I've always wanted to go back. Marilyn and I will be gone five days. Unfortunately, that's all I can spare away from the office right now."

"Any particular reason for the trip?"

Still grinning, he got up and closed the door. "Actually, yes. That's what I wanted to talk to you about. I've already spoken with your brother. We had dinner last night."

"Oh?"

"I wanted to talk to him first. Sort of man to man. You understand."

"I'm not sure I do."

He sat down on the edge of his desk and folded his arms over his chest. "Honey, I'm going to ask Marilyn to marry me."

Jane's eyes widened. "Does she know?"

He shook his head. "Actually, I thought *she* was going to ask *me* a few months ago. It was right after Peter and Sigrid's wedding. I think the whole affair struck a chord in both of us. But then she didn't. It got me to thinking. What would I have said if she had asked?"

"And? What was your conclusion?"

The grin returned. "I want this, Jane. More than I've wanted just about anything in my whole life. I need to make sure you understand. I think one of the reasons I've resisted the idea of marriage for so many years was because I felt it might be a negation of what your mother and I had. I loved her very much."

"I know."

"But I also love Marilyn. I'm just glad I don't have to make a choice between them." He shivered at the thought. "I want to make a commitment to Marilyn in front of the people who mean the most to me. My family and friends. I'd like to do it the same way Sigrid and Peter did."

"In my backyard garden."

"Yes!" He stood, throwing his head back and laughing. "With all of Beryl's wonderful flowers. And Cordelia in her best tux, crying like a baby. Oh, and lots of those silly little canapés."

"Don't forget the hideous champagne punch."

"Right!" He looked down. "And most importantly, with you and Peter there by my side." His eyes began to tear. "What do you say?"

Jane could feel herself being swept up in his dream. She stood and gave him a hug. "I'd suggest you find out what Marilyn thinks."

He wiggled his eyebrows and dashed behind the desk. "Look at this." He lifted a small ring box out of the top desk drawer. He opened it and handed it to her.

Jane whistled. "Not too shabby."

"It's an emerald. Marilyn hates diamonds. She thinks they're pretentious."

"Oh, this emerald isn't the least bit pretentious, Dad. Don't worry."

"Good. I was hoping you'd say that." He fidgeted with his watch. "She'll be here any minute. Peter's going to drive us to the airport."

Jane handed the ring back.

"Why don't you keep me company until they get here? Oh, and one more thing. Don't tell Beryl any of this. I want to break the news to her myself—in person. But I don't have time to do it before we leave."

"Sure. No problem."

He sat down behind his desk. "So, what's new with you?" Even that simple question made him giggle.

Jane was so happy for him. She didn't have a doubt in the world that Marilyn would say yes. "Well, same old stuff, I guess. Nothing really new." She couldn't tell him about her investigation of Rose Gower's death. Still, she was curious about one thing. "How's Emery Gower's defense going?"

He took a deep breath and sighed. "Slow. I was finally able to get the judge to set bail. He should be out early this afternoon."

"Really?" That surprised her. She hadn't thought he'd be released. "How did you manage that?"

"Well, after all, the guy has never even had a parking ticket. He's totally clean. I argued his case for almost an hour. I will say the judge set the bail unreasonably high, but there was nothing I could do. Thanks to a codicil in Rose Gower's will, part of her estate is at the disposal of his defense."

Jane had an idea. "You know, this might sound strange, but I'd like to talk to him."

"Why?"

"Well...see, it's kind of a long story." She gave him

her most innocent smile.

"Cordelia said you went over to that club and did a bit of snooping."

"I did."

"Does this have something to do with that pipe bomb incident? Because if it does, for god's sake Jane, let the police handle it."

"I will. But there's something else. It would take too long to explain right now. I promise I'll tell you all about it...soon." She paused. "Do you know where Emery is going to be staying?"

Ray hesitated. "Telling you is against my better judgment."

"So noted."

"Don't act like a lawyer."

"Sorry."

Restlessly, Ray flipped through some papers. After a few moments he said, "I advised him not to go back to his apartment. The press would eat him alive. We got him a room at the Maxfield Plaza, in downtown St. Paul. Room 1127. He's under the name Ted Johnson."

"Thanks."

"Don't mention it. You better be careful, Janey." He narrowed one eye. "This whole case has me worried."

"I thought you were almost positive he was innocent."

He shook his head. "I don't know. The only person who knows for sure is Emery. And he's a clever kid—sometimes too clever for his own good. He could easily have done it. Nevertheless, he has a right to a defense and I'm going to give him one." He leaned back in his leather chair and closed his eyes. "But the next five days are mine, Janey. And Marilyn's. I'm not going to think about *anything* but us." Slowly, his grin returned.

18

JANE spent the rest of the day at her restaurant working on the new fall menu. The soups and deserts needed some last minute fine-tuning before the copy could be sent to the printer. Cordelia called around two to make sure their dinner date at the club was still on. For perhaps the second time in recorded history, Cordelia noted that *dinner* was merely peripheral to something more important. The central reason for visiting the club again tonight was to see what really lay behind the attic bookcase. Jane promised to meet her there at six.

Since it was now nearly four, she decided to see if Emery had been released as promised. She picked up the phone and dialed the Maxfield Plaza.

After several rings, a man answered. "Maxfield," he said in a pleasant, relaxed tone.

"Hi. I wonder if you could tell me if a Ted Johnson has checked into the hotel yet? He's in room 1127."

"Just a moment." A few seconds later the man came back on the line. "Yes. Just a few minutes ago. Would you like me to ring his room?"

"No, that's ok. Thanks." She hung up.

So, Emery was there. If she was going to see him today, she'd better get a move on. Quickly, she picked up her keys and switched off the lights. After a short trip through the kitchen, she ducked out the back door and headed for her car.

I-94 was a madhouse at rush hour. Highway construction was also a perennial problem. Nevertheless, Jane made it to the hotel in good time, parked her car in the lot across the street, and was standing in front of his door by a quarter of five. She knocked softly.

"Just bring it in," shouted a deep voice.

She tried the door and found it open. Stepping inside, she took a brief look around. This was not a simple hotel room, it was a luxurious suite, complete with two bedrooms and a large, comfortable sitting area. The furnishings, like everything else at the Maxfield, were understated and classic. All the windows had been opened and the sheers were flapping in the breeze.

Jane turned as a muscular, sandy-haired young man appeared in one of the doorways. He had a towel wrapped tightly around his waist while drying his hair with another. "Who are you?" he asked, coming to a dead stop.

"My name is Jane Lawless."

"Lawless?" He cocked his head. "There's more than one of you?"

"Raymond Lawless is my father."

"Ah," he said, a smile forming. "Well, I mustn't be inhospitable then." He nodded to a chair. "I'm expecting room service. I thought they'd arrived awfully fast. Please, make yourself comfortable. I'll just be a second." He disappeared into one of the bedrooms.

Jane was a bit surprised by the southern drawl. As she thought about it, she did remember something in the newspaper about Emery growing up in North Carolina. He was obviously a man used to living by his charm, the accent and the smiles flowing as sweetly and easily as honey.

She sat in one of the wing chairs to wait. It wasn't long before he reappeared, this time dressed in a pair of stone-washed jeans and a white t-shirt. In one hand he was holding a pair of white socks. His wet hair was combed straight back, revealing a pair of deep-set brown eyes. Actually, he was quite good looking, with strong, rather pointed features and an eager, wolf-like expression.

He flopped down on the couch and stretched his long legs. "Lordy, *lordy* it feels good to be out. Your daddy's a miracle worker—what did you say your name was?"

"Jane."

"Of course. Jane." He leaned down to put on the socks. "Did he send you over here to check up on me? Don't worry, I'm being a good boy. Only ordered two beers with my burger." He grinned as he checked his watch. "Room service is sometimes slow in places like this. But I'd say we've got a good fifteen minutes before it arrives."

Jane made herself more comfortable. She was glad he was in a talkative mood. It would make things easier. "What are your plans now that you're out?"

His face turned thoughtful. "Well, I'm not sure. Try to prove my innocence, I guess. That's number one."

"You know, I don't really have all the details about what happened the night Charlotte died. My father only said there was a lot of circumstantial evidence against you. I don't suppose you'd be willing to go through it with me? It might help." Jane knew she hadn't exactly been up front about the reason for her visit. Apparently Emery thought she'd come to check up on him. For now, it might be best to leave it at that.

"Sure, I suppose. What do you want to know?"

"Well, first of all, where were you that night?"

He grunted. "You knew Charlotte had fired me, didn't you? If you ask me, she was afraid of my influence on Rose. That Gower Foundation needs a man's input. Too many women running the show. I'm not a chauvinist, Jane, don't get me wrong, but enough's enough. Every time I'd get a foothold in one of the departments, she'd switch me to someplace else. It was a plot. Anyone could see it. For pete's sake, I'm a Gower! My great great grandmama started the whole thing. There hasn't been a real Gower in charge since 1927. I came to Minneapolis to remedy that and it stuck in Charlotte's craw. Mark my words, she was out to ruin my career."

That was interesting. Emery clearly felt running The Gower Foundation was his birthright. Jane was pretty sure that *had* stuck in Charlotte's craw. "But what about the night she died?"

"Yeah, see that's the problem. I didn't have any money so I had to take a shitty job at an answering service about two blocks from my apartment. It was all I could find. I live close to the club, Jane. I needed to stay there so I could visit Rose more easily. We were getting pretty friendly. Lord, I was so sorry to hear about her death." He paused for a suitable length of time and then went on. "Anyway, I was at work that night. This is where it gets sticky. I got a phone call about eight. A voice says that someone is messing with my motorcycle which I always park behind my apartment building. Now, nobody messes with my bike. *Nobody*. Since there was another guy answering phones that evening, I figured I'd just go take a look. He could handle things until I got back. When I got home, sure enough someone had knocked the bike over. Man, was I steamed. I checked it over carefully, but everything seemed Ok. I spent a few minutes looking around, but I didn't see a soul. On my way back I ran into the guy who owns the answering service. My bad luck, right? Well, needless to say, he got all hot and bothered that I'd left in the middle of my shift."

"Did you tell him about the call? About your motorcycle?"

"Nah, he pissed me off. I just told him I needed some air."

"That wasn't very smart."

"I know that now. He could have verified my story if I'd said anything, but at the time, I didn't figure it was any of his business."

"You didn't say anything to your coworker either?"

"Nope."

This guy is either really dumb, thought Jane, or really clever. She wasn't sure which. "So what did your boss say when you told him you needed some air?"

Emery snorted. "He fired me."

"And of course, he can testify that you weren't at work right around the time Charlotte was murdered. So, essentially, you have no alibi."

"Yeah, I guess so."

She paused. "This call, did the person give a name?"

He shook his head.

"Could you tell if it was a man or a woman?"

"Your father asked me the same question. I've thought about it, but I'm not certain. Could have been a man *or* a woman. It was that kind of voice, you know? And they spoke softly. I asked them to speak up, but instead they hung up."

Jane wondered if her father couldn't subpoena the record of phone calls to the answering service that night. Something might turn up. Then again, if Emery did get this anonymous call, the individual in question could have phoned from anywhere. It was probably useless. "I was told that fibers from one of your jackets were found on Charlotte's raincoat. And some of her hair was found on the same jacket. How do you explain that?"

He rubbed the back of his neck. "I can't. That's what bothers me the most. The only conclusion I can come to is that I was set up. I mean, I had to be! I didn't do it, Jane. I despised that woman, I made no secret of it. But I didn't kill her. I couldn't. I couldn't kill anyone. You may not believe this, but I'm totally against violence. Politically, I'm a pacifist. I would have been marching with you in the sixties, don't ever doubt it."

Jane blinked. She wondered just how old she must look to this young man. "Is that right? Well, whatever the case, I'd say you're in a lot of trouble."

He set his jaw grimly. "That pipe bomb sent to your

father really got to me. Who would do something like that?" He waited. When she didn't respond, he continued. "I'll tell you. It's someone who doesn't want to see me helped by the best defense attorney in town. See, the less experienced my attorney, the worse my defense, the more chance there is that I'll be convicted. Now ask yourself, who would benefit if I'm convicted?" He paused for effect. "The real killer, that's who! Simple."

Jane didn't find his scenario all that self-evident. "You think that's why it was sent?"

"Of course! It's part of the setup. Plain as the nose on your face. And I've been thinking about something else, too. Maybe Rose's death is related. Someone could have pushed her down those steps. The newspaper said she fell, but it also said she was alone. Now, how on earth can they know for sure she was alone?"

Good question, thought Jane. They had finally moved to the subject in which she was most interested. Rose Gower. "You knew her pretty well. Did she have any enemies that you know of?"

"Rose? She was as decent as they come. Encouraging. Helpful. She did have one kind of odd quirk. She was what I'd call a mystic. She always wanted to read my tea leaves. Rose really believed in that spirit world stuff. But then everyone's entitled to a few eccentricities, right? I can't believe she had an enemy in the world. Then again." He thought for a moment. "I did hear her arguing recently with Miriam Cipriani. She's one of the other board members over there. They were really going at it. I didn't think the old gal had it in her."

"Do you know what it was about?"

"Something about AIDS research. I didn't get it all. They stopped when they realized I'd come into the room."

Interesting, thought Jane. A coincidence? "Who do you think murdered her then—if it wasn't an accident? You aren't suggesting Miriam—"

He shrugged. "Who knows? Maybe the same person

114

who stuck it to Charlotte got Rose too."

"Did she ever mention anything about being frightened?"

"Nah. Never."

"Do you ever recall her talking about The Chamber?"

"The what?" He looked totally lost.

Jane couldn't help but feel his confusion was genuine. "Ok, but what about the motive for her death?"

"How should I know? Maybe it had something to do with that club. She and Charlotte were both board members. Just because those other two were supposed to be her best friends, doesn't mean they actually were."

Jane still resisted this conclusion. "Well, all I can say is that I've talked to lots of people there. Most everyone agrees with the police. It was accidental."

"What do they know?" His fingers curled into tight fists. "Anyway, like who?"

She had to think fast. Both Mae and Miriam agreed with *him*. What other people might there be that he would remember? "Well, Julia Fortnum for one. And her sister, Evie."

Emery's fair skin colored. "I could care less what either of them think."

He said the words with such unmistakable venom, Jane wondered what was behind it. She knew he'd dated Evie. Perhaps they'd ended their relationship on a sour note. Still, her father might want to use Evie as a character witness. Since Emery had been in town less than a year, he was badly in need of people to testify that he was a decent guy. If he and Evie could settle their differences, it might be to his advantage. "Do you plan on seeing Evie now that you're out?"

Emery narrowed one eye. "What do you mean by that?"

"Well, I know you two've dated some."

"What have you heard?"

He seemed more touchy about this subject than any

115

they'd discussed so far. "Nothing, really. Just that Rose introduced you."

"Yeah. Well, you can tell Evie from me that maybe I'll try to catch her act over at Wizards sometime soon. I'm sure she'll be overjoyed. If she knows I'm coming, she'll be able to bring along her stooge to protect her."

"Her stooge?"

"Sure. Freddy Lindhurst. You met him yet? Mr. Mighty Mind. Just the kind of guy I'd like to wipe the floor up with."

"Not particularly pacifistic, Emery."

"Hey." He scowled. "I think your time's up. I believe I've had enough of this conversation. You can tell your daddy I'm doing fine. No problems. And tell that assistant of his—Norman—that if he comes by and I'm out, he can leave a message." His easy smile returned. "I'll have my secretary return the call as soon as possible."

Casually, Emery rose and walked to the door, holding it open. "It was nice meeting you, Jane. I suppose you like working with your father."

"Pardon me?"

"You know. You work for him, right? As a paralegal or something."

"No. Sorry."

For the first time, his eyes really took her in. "Lawless didn't send you?"

She shook her head.

"You're not a reporter, are you?"

"I own a restaurant."

"Then why are you here?"

Jane could see the muscles in his neck tense. It was time to leave. "Because I wanted to meet you. Ask you some questions."

"I don't get it? Are you some kind of crime junky or something?"

"No."

He moved menacingly towards her. "Listen lady, I

116

don't know what you're up to, but stay out of my business. You got that?"

She walked past him into the hallway.

He followed, shouting, "I don't like games, missy, but if you suck me into one, I warn you, I play to win. You're a weirdo, you know that? Either that or—" For some reason, the end of the sentence was abandoned.

Jane found the stairs and started down. Emery Gower was a man with a short fuse. She thought it best not to stand around waiting for the elevator to arrive. By that time, Emery might be hurling more than verbal abuse.

19

JANE took her after dinner coffee and strolled into the club's first floor library. It was a sunless, highly formal room, with floor to ceiling bookcases on three walls, and a series of oil portraits of the Gower family on the fourth. She'd left Cordelia sitting in the dining room, finishing a conversation she'd begun with several other diners on the art of the silent film. Silent films were one of Cordelia's passions. She maintained firmly that women's roles took a nose dive after the advent of sound. Since Jane had heard the argument many times before, she decided to check out the rest of the first floor instead of remaining at the table and trying to stifle a yawn. It wasn't that she had no interest in silent films. It just seemed that every conversation about them dead-ended with a discussion of whether or not Rudolph Valentino was gay. To Jane, it felt much like having a conversation about rock-n-roll disintegrate into a heartfelt testimonial on *what Elvis meant to me*. Somehow, the point got lost.

"Ah, there you are," said Mae Williams, bustling into the room. Slung over one shoulder was her ever present book sack. "Someone said you were here. I was hoping we might talk for a moment."

Jane waited as she dumped the sack on one of the

small reading tables and then walked back and closed the library door. She seemed like a different person tonight. Gone was the quiet, earnest confidence of the other evening. It had been replaced by a kind of fidgety restlessness.

"That's better," said Mae, smiling. "We need some privacy. So." She turned her full attention on Jane. "Anything to report?"

"I'm sorry. Nothing yet."

"Well, we can't expect miracles."

"No. I did speak with Miriam Cipriani yesterday."

"Yes, she told me."

Jane moved over to one of the paintings and studied it for a moment. "Not a profitable conversation."

"Oh?"

"I got the feeling she didn't like me very much. I find that a bit strange since we've never met."

"Well, sometimes when she's hanging a new exhibit, she becomes distracted. I wouldn't worry about it."

Jane turned around. "I'm not worried. I'm curious."

Mae seemed flustered by Jane's direct gaze. She straightened her sweater and tried another less than confident smile. "I was wondering. Have you had a chance to examine the attic room yet?"

So that was it. Mae wanted to know if they'd sanitized the place well enough. "Yes. Last night."

"Did you find anything?"

It was Jane's turn to smile. "You mean, did you miss anything?"

Mae raised an eyebrow. "I—"

"How could I? The interior had been gutted. I can't imagine it looks much like its former self. Did you think vacuuming away everything but the light fixtures was a good way to help me find Rose's murderer?"

"We felt . . . that is to say, certain things had to be removed. However, you must understand, it will not impede your investigation. The room itself is not important. Miriam and I went over it with a fine tooth comb after

Rose's death. We found nothing. Consequently, what we did to . . . clean it, should not be an issue."

"Not an issue!" Jane couldn't believe her ears. "Look, I'm beginning to wonder if you even want me to find out what happened the night Rose died."

"Of course we do!"

"Then prove it! Give me something to go on."

Mae began to pace. "It's complicated. More complicated than you realize."

"What do you mean by that?"

She wrung her hands. "I want to tell you, but I can't."

"Why? Miriam won't allow it?"

"It's not that simple."

"No?" These half answers were beginning to rankle. "Tell me what The Chamber is, Mae. You can give me that much."

Mae refused to meet her eyes. "I can't."

"Why not?"

"Because . . . I've taken an oath."

Jane didn't know what to say. She hadn't expected that.

Mae moved over to her book bag and began to straighten the straps. Without looking at Jane, she said, "You must believe me when I tell you we do want you to find out what happened to Rose. We *must* find that stolen property. It's absolutely imperative." She hesitated. "And . . . I'll speak with Miriam. Perhaps there's more we could tell you about . . . certain matters. I'm not promising anything, but we'll talk again. Now." She hoisted the book bag over her shoulder. "I'm late for an important appointment." She started for the door.

"When?"

Mae stopped. "When what?"

"When will we talk again?"

As she turned around, a certain annoyance was clearly visible in her eyes. "Soon."

"Soon?" Jane let the word hang in the air. "I suppose

that will have to do. Maybe when we next meet you can explain to me all about your interest in AIDS research. Might even be illegal AIDS research, Mae. Experimental drugs." It was a guess, but she hoped it would pay off.

Mae's entire body froze.

"Hum. Seems I've hit a nerve."

"Who . . . told you that?"

"Why don't you call me sometime *soon*. We'll talk."

Mae stared at the floor for a long minute before looking up.

For the first time, Jane could see the toll this was taking on her. Mae's face looked haggard, deeply shaken.

"I'm not cut out for this kind of cloak and dagger crap, Jane. I'm a poet, not a spy. Besides, unlike Miriam, I happen to trust you. Believe me when I say that I'd like to explain everything to you right now—but I can't." Her jaw tightened. "I simply can't."

As Jane watched her, she came to one important conclusion. She may not understand what was going on, but she felt truly sorry for this woman and the stress she was under. "Look, I think I better give that check back to you. I'm obviously not getting anywhere you haven't already been."

"No." Vehemently, Mae shook her head. "You keep trying. Who knows, you might come up with something." She opened the door. Again, she hesitated. "One more thing. Don't say anything to Miriam about that AIDS business. I don't know how you found out about it, but you won't get any further with her than you have with me. And . . . I *will* call you soon. I promise." With that, she rushed down the hall and disappeared out the front door.

At that same moment, Cordelia ambled out of the dining room, patting her stomach. She gave Jane a small wave.

"Well," said Jane, waiting for her to approach. "Did you convince the hordes to go see *Birth of a Nation*?"

"Are you kidding?" With great solemnity, she closed

her eyes and shuddered.

"Rudolph Valentino, right?"

"Who else?"

"What did you tell them this time?"

Cordelia put her arm around Jane's shoulder and whispered, "That he was really Elvis Presley's grandfather."

Jane nodded. "Good thinking."

20

JANE handed Cordelia a flashlight and then put a finger to her lips. "Now, when we get on the other side of the bookcase, we have to be quiet. I don't know where this leads, but there are lots of people around here tonight. We don't want to be discovered."

Cordelia gave her a knowing nod.

The attic looked just as it had the other night. Jane felt like she was in a hospital room after the patient had died. Everything swept and tidy, empty of the life it had once contained. "And remember," she added, "we stay together." She lit the oil lamp and crossed to the entrance. "Ready?"

Cordelia took a deep breath. "As I'll ever be."

They stepped together into the darkness. Silently, they scurried down a narrow corridor, the flickering flame throwing long shadows against the exposed brick walls. Thankfully, the passage had been swept and obviously cared for. No huge spider webs hung from the ceiling.

As Jane moved along, steadying herself on a small railing, she came to a steep wooden stairway. "I wonder where it leads?"

"Down," whispered Cordelia, shining her flashlight on a three-inch centipede about a foot from her nose. "The torture chamber is on the second floor."

Jane turned and gave her a sickly smile. "Follow me."

As they came to the bottom of the steps, Jane saw that there was a door blocking their path. It appeared to be a recent installation. The wood still looked new. She tried the knob. "It's locked."

"Figures."

"I wonder." She dug deep in her pocket for her keys. "Maybe the key to the attic door fits this one."

Cordelia watched as Jane slipped it into the lock.

The door creaked open.

"Stout woman."

"Do you suppose many people know about these passageways?" asked Jane, raising the lamp. In front of them stretched another long, narrow corridor.

"Only the monks who make the wine."

"Look at this." Jane stopped in front of what looked like another bookcase entrance. "This probably leads into one of the apartments."

Cordelia moved closer. "What's this thing?" She pointed to a small piece of wood attached to the wall by a hinge. Shining her flashlight down the hall, she counted at least six more.

"Beats me." Jane lifted it as far away from the wall as it would go. "Look. It's a peephole." She leaned down and looked through it. "We can see into one of the guest apartments. But it's empty. There's nothing in the closet."

"Must have been Charlotte's. Her daughter just moved out. And say, don't be such a hog." Cordelia nudged her out of the way. "Give someone else a chance to look. Sure. I was in there once. I remember that painting over the bed. *Pretentious Drivel* I believe the title was. This is definitely attached to another bookcase. I remember one in the room." She felt along the wall for an opening.

"Come on," said Jane. "Let's see if we can get to the first floor from here."

They continued on.

"Why do you suppose the house was built like this?" asked Cordelia. "There must have been some reason."

"You know, before dinner tonight, I was talking with that woman who owns the flower shop. The one with all the beautiful Native American jewelry."

"Emma Little Horn."

"Right. She said the house was built in 1903 by a man who'd made his fortune in flour milling. But get this. His real passion was magic. Emma said it was very popular back then. He was also known for being kind of eccentric. Apparently, there were times when he'd have a houseful of guests and he'd just disappear. Sometimes for hours. He'd be in a room one minute, and the next he'd be gone. I guess he really had everyone spooked. According to Emma, he didn't live long after the house was built."

"Shouldn't wonder," said Cordelia, ducking her head under a low hanging beam. "One of his guests probably got sick of being ignored."

"Here we go," whispered Jane, coming to another stairs. It appeared to lead down to the first floor. This time, there was no door blocking their access.

"Did you see any more of those wall entrances as we went along?" asked Cordelia.

Jane shook her head. "There seems to be only one entrance and exit from the second floor."

"Through Charlotte's apartment."

"You got it."

Once downstairs, Jane looked first to the right and then to the left. The right side seemed to dead end a few yards from the stairs. "Which way?"

"I lean a little left, myself."

They proceeded slowly down the darkened hall. "There's another entrance."

"And a peephole," whispered Cordelia. "Let *me* look first this time." She flipped back the piece of wood. "The Library. Wouldn't you know it. There's three of the women we had dinner with looking at an Encyclopedia

Britannica. I'll bet I can guess the subject."

"Valentino."

Cordelia nodded.

Jane walked a few paces further to another hidden door. "Look at this, Cordelia." She squinted through the peephole. "This leads to a small conference room. Just one long table."

"Yeah, I had a private meeting in there once with Rose. It was right before I joined. They had some questions they wanted to ask me."

"And for privacy they pick a room where everything can easily be overheard." This was too much. But what did it mean? Unless Jane could tie the discovery of these passageways to something specific, the mere fact of their existence meant nothing. It was just a useless curiosity. An old house with a secret. The attic chamber was an entrance or exit—however you wanted to look at it. So was Charlotte's apartment. But so what? As her mood turned sour, she gave the wall a kick.

"Temper, temper."

"I want to get out of here," said Jane. "This is a waste of time." She bent down to rub her big toe. "Cordelia?"

"What?"

"Move your foot."

"Why?"

"Just move for a minute." As Cordelia retreated, Jane picked up a small, gold pin. "Look at this. *Sigma Delta.* It's a fraternity pin."

Cordelia cocked her head. "Funny place to pin your sweetheart."

"I wonder who it belongs to?"

"Oh, I'd say he's about five-foot-ten. Cocky. Drives a Jeep Cherokee, or if his parents are particularly cheap, a Suzuki. Probably a few pimples. A good, suburban tan. Majoring in communications, or if he's really smart, business administration."

"Cordelia, that's a stereotype."

"So?"

"It's like someone assuming *you* love to play softball."

"Heavens!"

"See? It's annoying."

"I should say."

Jane held the pin closer to the lamp. "This means something, I'll bet on it."

"You do that, Janey." Cordelia's voice held little interest. "You now have a small conundrum on which to dwell for the rest of the evening. Me, I've had enough of this Daphne Du Maurier novel for one night. I'm heading back up to the attic."

"All right," conceded Jane. "You're probably right. We've found all we're going to find."

Together, they climbed slowly to the third floor.

"Well," said Cordelia, catching her breath as she flopped into one of the attic chairs, "that was definitely an experience."

Jane allowed herself a small degree of hope. "It was."

"Now, even though I know you'll want to talk—ad nauseam—about the ramifications of this discovery upon Rose and Charlotte's untimely demise—assuming there are ramifications—and even though I hate to rush off, I must. I have a date."

Jane carefully replaced the filing cabinets in front of the bookcase. "Anyone I know?"

"Andromeda and I are taking in a late movie. Do you want to come along?"

"No thanks. Actually, I have a date of my own."

"Dorrie."

"Who else?" Jane switched off the light and started down the stairs. Before she got to the bottom step, she heard someone running away from the attic door. "What the—?" She hurried into the hall. Rose's door stood wide open.

"Who do you suppose that was?" Cordelia puffed to a stop directly behind her.

"You got me." Jane looked around. Everything was quiet. "We can't leave that door unlocked. Maybe we should check out the apartment. See if anything was stolen." Carefully, she entered the front hall. She immediately spied a book resting precariously on top of a small oak table. "I don't remember seeing this in here before." A gold "C" was stamped into the leather cover. Jane's eyes opened wide. "Cordelia! Look at this." She picked it up and flipped through the first few pages. "It's the ledger! I'm positive. It's even in code."

"Let me look at it." Cordelia whipped it out of her hands. "Yup. Code." She handed it back.

"I have to call Mae right away."

Cordelia hesitated, putting her hand over Jane's arm. "Wait just a minute there sweetie."

"Why?"

She clasped her hands behind her back and began to pace. Back and forth. Back and forth.

"You look like General Patton about to brief the troops."

"Very funny." She pointed a finger at Jane. "You want to solve this, don't you?"

"Of course."

"Then consider this. That book may be the only leverage you've got in dealing with Mae and Miriam. You want some straight answers. They want the ledger. Tit for tat."

"What are you saying?"

"I'm saying, dearheart, don't give it back to them *unless* they agree to give you something in return."

"You mean information."

"Ah, all those synapses are standing at attention now."

Jane thought it over. "You could be right."

"Of course I'm right."

"But I'll have to decide just how to do it."

"Good. *You* decide." Cordelia ducked her head briefly into the front room and looked around. "All quiet on the western front. Now, this has been truly swell, Janey, but I'm late for my date." She waited for Jane to walk in front of her and then switched off the lights in the apartment and shut the door. "Give my regards to Dorrie."

"I will."

"Oh, and one more thing. Tomorrow is Saturday. Remember? Say it with me now. *Sa-tur-day*. Therefore . . . even if you discover a cure for the common cold or win the lottery, *don't* call me before noon. Got it?" She scuttled to the elevator. "Well?"

"Why Cordelia, I wouldn't dream of interrupting your slumber."

Cordelia raised an eyebrow. "Why don't I believe you?"

21

AFTER Cordelia had left the club, Jane stood in the front doorway a few moments before going back inside to pick up her backpack. Ominous thunder clouds had erupted in the western sky and a stiff wind had begun to blow. Unfortunately, Jane had ignored today's unseasonably high temperatures and growing humidity and was going to be caught without a rain coat or an umbrella to protect her from the downpour. Oh well. Maybe she'd get lucky and make it to Dorrie's before the storm hit.

Seeing Freddy Lindhurst coming up the walk, she held the door open for him. Again this evening, he was weighed down by two heavy sacks filled with canned goods and packaged food. He nodded his thanks as he passed in front of her.

"We meet again," he smiled, starting down the hall.

"Where do you get all this stuff?" asked Jane, taking one of the sacks from his arms.

"My wife is an art therapist. She teaches several classes through the Pinewood Institute in Golden Valley. She's organized a food shelf drop-off point there and I'm generally elected to see that it gets delivered to the club."

"That's nice of you," said Jane, following him into the storage room.

"Julia even promised to do the inventory until they can find someone to permanently take over Rose's duties. She wanted to come tonight but she was too tired. It's the pregnancy. I left her sleeping on the couch." He set his sack down.

Jane did the same. She was struck again by his wholesome, choir boy appearance. "Has anyone ever told you that you look like a Renaissance angel?"

He gave a self-conscious laugh. "No, that's a new one. But I know what you mean. I do my best to look macho, but somehow, it never works."

As they returned to the hallway, Freddy stopped and turned around. "I suppose I should apologize to you for my wife's behavior the other day. Generally, she's very friendly. In this case, however, I think you can understand why she wasn't delighted to see you. She thinks your father is defending the man who murdered her mother. Intellectually, she knows Emery has a right to a defense, but it's hard being reminded of him."

Jane did understand. "It's no problem. I'd probably feel the same way."

Freddy went on. "She thinks you're snooping around here to find something to help Emery's case. Is that true?"

Jane could tell he was watching her carefully. She was glad she didn't have to lie. "No, not really. Although, my father does think there's a reasonable doubt about his guilt."

Freddy gave an indignant grunt. "Oh, he's guilty, all right. You don't know him, but he's . . . he's utterly unfeeling. *Scum*, that's what I'd call him."

Freddy and Emery's feelings about each other appeared to be mutual. "But didn't Evie date him for a while?"

Freddy straightened his tie. "She did. I'll never understand what she saw in that brainless buffoon—other than a certain animal charm."

Jane had to agree. She distrusted charm about as much

131

as she did angelic faces.

"Anyway," he said, glancing over her shoulder into the dining room, "let's not talk about Emery. He's not worth the effort." He put his hands casually in his pockets. "What brings you here this evening?"

Well, thought Jane, he seems to want to talk. That was fine with her. "I had dinner with a friend. If you're staying, the leg of lamb is particularly good."

He smiled. "I don't have time tonight. By the way, you haven't seen Doyle Benedict, have you?"

"You mean the steward?"

"Yeah." He leaned over and peaked into the great hall. "I'm supposed to . . . uh . . . give him something." At Jane's questioning look he added, "I teach a class in first year German over at the University. He's one of my students."

"Ah. Then can I assume you and Charlotte Fortnum were colleagues?"

Again, he straightened his tie. It seemed to be a nervous gesture. "We were."

"I understand she was quite a well-loved professor."

"I suppose."

"You don't agree?"

He shrugged. "I think, like everything else, it depends on your point of view. She didn't much care for my presence in her life. She didn't formally disapprove of Julia's and my marriage, but let's just say I wasn't her first choice. Julia's had to live with that niggardly approval for the past several years. It was beginning to get on both our nerves. It's always been my plan to make Minneapolis my permanent home. After getting my doctorate, I was hoping to be offered an assistant professorship at the U of M."

"And Charlotte might have prevented that?"

"No, I'm not saying she had any particular interest in ruining my career plans, but sometimes she just didn't realize her own power. People took what she said very seriously. Even small comments. The fact that we had visible disagreements wasn't a plus for my side. But, we would have worked things out. If nothing else, for Julia's sake."

Interesting, thought Jane. "Did most of your problems center on work disagreements?" As soon as she'd asked the question, she could tell she'd stepped over the line. This was beginning to sound too much like an interrogation.

Freddy took a moment before answering. "You know, Ms. Lawless, for someone who isn't gathering information for her father, you have quite an energetic interest in other people's affairs."

Jane held up her hand in protest.

"No, that's all right. I'll answer your question. But be sure, when the time comes, to quote me correctly. Charlotte Fortnum and I did not get along. Period. I found her to be opinionated and . . . moralistic."

"Moralistic?"

"Her beliefs came before everything. Perhaps I'm in the minority today, but I think that's a brutal way to live your life. Have you ever read much George Bernard Shaw?"

"Some."

"Well, he said once that true humanitarianism lay in never sacrificing people to principle."

"That's quite a statement. You think it applies to Charlotte?"

His lips curled into a faint smile. "I think . . . I've said more than I intended. But let me just add one final thought. Even though my relationship with Charlotte wasn't great, I didn't wish her any ill. I truly didn't. You may not believe this, Ms. Lawless, but the county already has Charlotte's murderer. He may get off on some stupid technicality, but if he does, your father will have to live with that for the rest of his life. All I can say is, I'm glad Emery's behind bars. Someone should throw away the key while there's still time."

Obviously, Freddy didn't know Emery had been released. "Actually, he's out on bail. He left the county jail this afternoon."

Freddy's mouth dropped open. "You're joking?"

"I'm afraid not."

Without thinking, he pulled his keys out of his pocket and began to play with them. Another nervous tic? "Did he go back to his apartment?"

"I don't know." Jane decided to play dumb.

"This is awful. You don't understand." He shook his head again and again. "Do you know what your father's done? That man is a menace!"

Just then, Doyle sauntered out of the dining room. He was whistling a rather silly, cheerful song. It happened to be one Jane hated. "Hey, Mr. Lindhurst. I thought I might see you tonight."

Freddy barely registered his presence.

"Mr. Lindhurst?" Doyle waved a hand in front of Freddy's face.

"Oh. Hi."

"Right. Well, now that you're here, maybe we should go someplace more . . . private." He wiggled his eyebrows at Jane in greeting.

"Sure. But I've got to make a phone call first."

Doyle seemed frustrated by the potential interruption. "I don't have much time. I'm on duty so we have to do this . . ." He glanced at Jane. ". . . quickly."

"Ok. Sorry. I understand."

She wondered what all *this* was about. Were they planning to speed through some verb conjugations?

"Well," said Freddy, pulling thoughtfully on his chin as he turned back to Jane, "I've got to run. Tell your father from me he's made a huge mistake. If he wanted proof Emery was Charlotte's murderer, he may get it sooner than he realizes. That guy is a loose cannon. God, how anyone could let such an animal out!" His jaw set angrily.

Jane stared as the two men retreated into the food shelf room. The heavy door clanged shut behind them. What was going on? Why the need for such privacy? It might not have anything to do with Charlotte Fortnum's murder, but then again Jane doubted the point of the meeting was to sample packaged cookies.

134

22

"WHY are you singing that idiotic song?" asked Dorrie. She carried an empty tray into the kitchen and set it on the counter next to where Jane was working.

Immediately, Jane stopped and looked up. "I don't know. It just popped into my head."

"In case you didn't know this, hon, *Zippity Doo Da* is not good mood music."

Jane raised an eyebrow. "I don't know what came over me. I suppose to redeem myself I should hum a few bars of Mahler's first."

"You do that." Dorrie sat down behind the kitchen table. "You're in a pretty good mood tonight."

"Yes. I guess I am."

"Care to share the reason why?"

"Well, for one thing, I got the quarterly report for the restaurant back today. The figures look really solid. I couldn't be more pleased."

"That's great." She paused. "Anything else?"

Jane wondered what she was fishing for. *Stop*, she ordered herself. She'd been distrusting people's reactions for so many days now it was starting to become a habit. Dorrie was merely asking a simple question. "Well, actually there is one more thing. My father and Marilyn left today for a few days in Italy. He's going to ask her to marry him. That is, unless Marilyn pops the question first."

Dorrie's smile broadened. "That's wonderful, Jane. I really like Marilyn."

"I do too." Jane placed the Cornish pasties on the tray with a small salad. "Here you go. Dinner is served." She wiped her chef's knife with a soft cloth. "Not everyone has her own personal restaurateur catering meals, you know."

"Don't think I don't appreciate it," said Dorrie coming up behind Jane and giving her a hug.

She held on so long Jane wondered what was going on. "You better lead the way or this meal is never going to get eaten." She turned and, for a moment, held Dorrie's face in her hands. "I kind of like you, you know that?"

"I know," said Dorrie.

Jane handed her the tray. Once in the living room, she made herself comfortable on one end of the couch. The weather was too threatening to sit out on the deck. "Ok, so what's the good news you were going to tell me? That business you mentioned on the phone this morning."

Looking like the proverbial cat that ate the proverbial canary, Dorrie spread a napkin in her lap. She tasted the pastie before speaking. "Superb, as usual."

"You're stalling."

"Oh, Jane, just wait till you hear this. It's such a great opportunity." She patted her mouth with the napkin and leaned back against the cushions. "You know my Uncle Morris is a publisher in New York."

"I think you mentioned it once."

"Well, his publishing house wants to bring out a new line of cookbooks based on famous restaurants around the country. I talked to him this morning and Jane...he wants to include The Lyme House!"

Jane was stunned. She'd always had it in mind to do a cookbook, but to have a publisher come to her with an offer, well, Dorrie was right. This was simply incredible. "I don't know what to say?"

"Say yes, dummy! Do you know what a nationally promoted cookbook could do for your restaurant—for your *career*?"

Jane had a pretty good idea.

"The only problem is, they want to publish your book first. That would mean you'd have to drop everything you're doing right now so you could work on it. I told him I knew you'd be thrilled."

Jane's mind was swimming. She couldn't pass up something like this. On the other hand, how could she stop her investigation over at the club? It no longer seemed like just a matter of doing a job. Jane was deeply invested in finding the truth.

"So?" said Dorrie. "Earth to Jane. Are you still with me?"

Jane took a deep breath. "Are you sure they want The Lyme House Cookbook first? They couldn't change the schedule around?"

Dorrie shook her head. "Uncle Morris was adamant about that. Don't go screwing this up, Jane. It's the chance of a lifetime. Besides, you aren't all *that* busy right now. I know for a fact your new fall menu is almost done. Your heavy catering won't start until December. You could handle the extra load."

Normally, that would be the case. But Jane could tell something else was at work here. Dorrie's demeanor just didn't ring true. She turned and for a moment, looked Dorrie straight in the eye. "Did your uncle call you or did you call him?"

Dorrie glanced down, playing with her salad. "What's the difference?"

"There's a big difference." The light was beginning to dawn.

"Well, if you mean did I suggest your restaurant to him, the answer is yes. I don't see anything wrong with that."

Of course, that was true. She'd used a connection to

help a friend. Nothing wrong with that. Nevertheless, Jane couldn't help but wonder if this had something to do with her own recent refusal to stop *snooping around*, as Dorrie put it, over at the club. This was one very seductive way to get her to stop. If Jane had no free time, she'd have to give up the investigation. "I appreciate the fact that you mentioned my restaurant to him. Don't get me wrong."

"Well, he's eaten there, Jane. Many times. It wasn't like I had to twist his arm. He simply hadn't considered The Lyme House before I talked to him. He's making a special space on the schedule just to include you. You'd be a complete fool to turn it down."

"Do you have his phone number? I think we should talk."

"Oh, he's going to call you. I think he said something about Monday morning. If you're out, he'll leave a message. Actually, the reason I thought of calling him was because he'd just sent me a packet of cookbooks in the mail. His publishing house does them so beautifully. Now, where did I put them?" She got up and walked over to her bookshelf. "Oh, I know. I left them in the car." She picked up her keys and crossed to the door. "Don't eat any of that food while I'm gone or your name is *mud*. I'll be back in a minute."

Jane got up and stood in front of the doors which opened onto the deck. A soft rain had begun to fall. She knew she had to make a decision about all this, and quickly, but her mind felt about as agile as a block of cement. She was tired. It'd been a long day. Leaning against the cool glass, she looked out on the walk which surrounded Lake Harriet. Street lamps lighted the deserted paths. According to the radio in the car on the way over, the predicted thunderstorm was still an hour or so away.

Jane turned at the sound of the phone. It rang three times before Dorrie's answering machine clicked on. Sluggishly, Jane's mind focused on the voice.

"*Dorrie? It's Miriam.*" There was a pause. "*I can't leave it the way we did last night. My work is beginning to suffer. We have to talk."* Another pause. *"You have to give me another chance. I'm not the same person I used to be. We've both grown up."* An even longer silence this time. *"I'll never believe you don't feel the same. Never. Not after last night."* Her voice broke with emotion. *"This is ludicrous. I hate these machines. Just call me."* The line clicked.

For an instant, Jane was thrown. Then, the meaning of the words began to penetrate. Stiffly, she sat down. She was still sitting like that when Dorrie returned.

"Here they are," said Dorrie, re-entering the living room. She paged through the top book. "This one is my favorite. I was hoping your restaurant would get the same kind of treatment." She stopped when she saw Jane's face. "What's wrong?"

Jane looked up. She wanted to say something but no words formed.

Dorrie knelt down. "Are you all right?" She smoothed back the fine hairs around Jane's forehead.

Jane glanced at the blinking light on the answering machine. "No. I'm not all right."

Dorrie followed her eyes. "Who called? Cordelia? Is it your father?"

Jane shook her head. She knew she had to get a grip. She had to say something. "No. It was...Miriam Cipriani."

Dorrie closed her mouth. After a long moment she said, "Really? I wonder what she wanted."

"You, Dorrie. It seems she wants you."

Dorrie removed her hand from Jane's arm. Slowly, she rose from her crouching position and moved to a chair. She perched uncomfortably on the edge. Remaining very still, she said, "I never wanted you to find out like that."

"Find out *what?*" Jane could feel the anger welling up inside her. Then again, any emotion was better than the horrible numbness which had possessed her for the past few minutes.

"Will you listen to me for a moment?"

Jane kept her eyes averted but she didn't move. She waited.

"The truth is, I've known Miriam since I was nineteen. We lived together for almost a year during our junior year at Northwestern. It didn't work out. I wasn't ready to settle down and Miriam was...well, she was pretty intense back then. Angry at the world. She couldn't understand my attraction to men. She thought I should just make a decision to be straight or gay and stick with it." She sighed wistfully. "You know, I'm not sure our understanding of bisexuality has progressed very far from that point even today. We had so many arguments. It was a terrible time. When I left Illinois to come here, I thought I was leaving her forever. I didn't realize she'd taken a job in St. Paul about a year later. Anyway, as luck would have it, I finally ran into her. For some idiotic reason, we began to date again. We even moved in together for a short time, but just like before, it didn't work. I think our attraction was so strong, we ignored our basic incompatibility. You didn't know Miriam back then, but she was very volatile. I guess I found her exciting. What can I say? We were both young and headstrong, unwilling to give an inch because we thought it meant being controlled by the other person. You get into that mind game Jane, and you never get out. I finally left her.

"Several years later I met the man who later became my husband. But there again, things don't always end happily ever after. I knew when I married him that he wasn't well. He lived for six years before he died. They were the six best years of my life. I've dated here and there since, but I've never been serious about anyone." She paused. "Not until you."

"I don't understand," said Jane. "What's going on with you and Miriam?"

Dorrie rubbed her hands together nervously. "When I was elected to the city council last year, Miriam sent congratulations. It was just a small card with her name signed at the bottom. I knew she was heavily involved with The Gower Foundation. That's one reason I never wanted to join the club. But as time went on, I realized so many of the women I needed to network with met there for lunch. It seemed silly to boycott the place just because I might bump into an old flame. Besides, I'd heard she was personally involved with someone else. So . . . I joined.

"For the first few months, every time we ran into each other we were polite, but it went no further. I'd already begun to date you. I had absolutely no interest in her. Then, about a month ago, we were on a panel together. You remember. It was about future arts funding for Hennepin County. Afterwards, she invited me out for coffee. She told me that Charlotte Fortnum, the woman she'd lived with for many years, had recently left her. It was a mutual decision. She felt the break up was final. Later, she brought the conversation around to me. She asked if I was dating anyone. I told her about you. I think she could tell by the way I spoke that we'd become quite serious, so she just let the subject drop.

"Then, about two weeks ago, she dropped by one evening. Needless to say, I wasn't thrilled to see her, but she said she wanted to speak with me about The Gower Foundation. That night she asked me a lot of questions. I wasn't sure where it was all leading until five days ago. That's when she dropped a broad hint that I might be asked to join the board. The thing is, as we were talking, the conversation came around again and again to things of a more personal nature. She wanted to talk about the past. She told me a lot about her relationship with Charlotte. I won't lie to you, that old attraction was still there. We both felt it. And if we were going to be working together, we couldn't ignore it. In some manner, it had to be addressed and resolved."

This was not what Jane wanted to hear. "So? Where does that leave *us*?"

Dorrie seemed to grow pale. "I was officially asked to

join the board of directors last night. Miriam came here with the offer. Another directorship is also going to be offered to someone else very soon. They've given me two weeks to decide. But during the conversation, Miriam made it quite clear she still cares about me. She wants to try it again. She maintains she's not the same person she once was. I know she still has that volatile nature, but she's mellowed considerably. We...last night we...I don't know how to tell you this, Jane. I didn't plan it. I didn't even want it."

Jane felt her heart pounding. "God, Dorrie, what were you thinking?" She looked away. "I don't need pictures."

The silence in the room seemed to engulf them. "Can you believe that I love both of you?"

For an instant, Jane flashed on the conversation she'd had with her father just that morning. How glad he was he didn't have to choose between Jane's mother and Marilyn. "I'm not sure," she said.

"Oh Jane, don't give up on me. I just need some time. It's a lot to sort out."

Jane could see Dorrie's eyes imploring her. Her own eyes were burning. "All right." She knew her voice sounded wooden, but the effort to alter it was too much. "I think I'd better go."

"Aren't you going to say *anything?* Please!"

Jane got up and walked slowly into the front hall. "I can't stay." She turned around for a moment.

Looking hopeful, Dorrie stood.

"Goodnight." Jane opened the door and left.

23

As the thunderstorm broke, Jane found herself sitting on a bench in her backyard garden. Going indoors right now felt too confining. She needed space, both physical and mental, in which to think.

As the heavy rain soaked into her light cotton clothing, she realized that Dorrie's revelation explained a great deal more than she'd intended. So *this* was why Miriam had been so hostile to her when she'd gone to the art museum two days ago. It seemed surprising, given such a set of circumstances, that Miriam had agreed to work with her at all. But, at least for now, Miriam wasn't her concern. It was Dorrie and the decision they must both make that filled her mind with dread.

On the way home in the car it had occurred to her that, when it came to relationships, she'd already lived through her worst nightmare. Christine's illness and subsequent death had been the single most devastating thing she'd ever experienced. It'd taken her years to recover, but the bottom line was, she *had*. She'd survived. And she would survive this as well. The problem was, no matter what their final decision was, the relationship would never be the same. The one thing Jane and Christine had always agreed on was that a good relationship was too complex and simply too precious to play around with—especially in a world where love and commitment were hard to find. Trust was central. And Jane's trust had been severely shaken. Right now, Dorrie had some hard deciding to do. Then again, so did Jane. Things would simply take some time. Unfortunately, *patience*, as Cordelia liked to point out, was a quality Jane entirely lacked.

A crack of thunder broke her concentration. The trees had begun to strain against the force of the wind. From her standpoint, it was a perfect night. The weather exactly mirrored her mood. In the rain, her tears were invisible—they blended right into the scenery. For that, she was grateful. She knew nothing was going to be settled sitting outside and getting soaked to the skin, yet one thought kept gnawing at her. It was the fact that Miriam had offered Dorrie a seat on The Gower Foundation board of directors.

Jane had meant what she'd said the other night. The attrition rate in that particular job seemed frighteningly high. Dorrie had two weeks before she needed to give them an answer. She simply mustn't accept the offer until someone, Jane or the police, knew the whole story behind the deaths of Charlotte and Rose. It was too perilous. However, convincing Dorrie of that was going to be a problem. Jane knew there was a strong chance she would see any negative comments or any attempt to get her to hold off on a decision as simple jealousy. And since this whole investigation had to remain a secret, there was nothing Jane could do to remedy the situation, except of course, heartfelt denial. Fat lot of good that would do her. No, her hands were tied. That is, unless she could do something to untie them. She thought of the ledger.

A powerful bolt of lightening lit up the night sky. The crack of thunder which followed sent her ducking for cover. Realizing the storm was getting dangerous, she headed quickly for the back porch.

The house was dark and quiet as she entered through

144

the kitchen. Beryl was undoubtedly asleep upstairs. Sometimes when it appeared that Jane was going to be late, Beryl took the dogs with her into her bedroom and shut the door. That way, her sleep was uninterrupted by barking animals intent on waking the entire neighborhood.

As she crossed into the front hall, she noticed a reading lamp on in the living room. Normally, except for a small light in the kitchen, Beryl turned everything out before going to bed. She must have forgotten tonight. Realizing she was dripping water all over the rug, Jane tip-toed into the room and switched it off. She checked the front door to make sure it was locked and then headed upstairs.

After a hot shower, she put on some fresh pajamas and crawled under the covers. She knew sleep wasn't going to come easily tonight. She contemplated calling Dorrie, but thought better of it. Just as she closed her eyes and got comfortable, the doorbell rang.

God in heaven! She glanced at the clock. It was nearly 2 A.M. Who on earth would have the nerve to ring a doorbell at this time of night? The answer was obvious.

Cordelia.

Putting on her robe, Jane bolted down the stairs before the bell could ring again. Without even looking through the peephole, she whipped the door open. "All right. You better have a pretty good ex—" She stopped. "Cordelia?" She took a step outside. No one was there. In the distance she could hear the faint sound of thunder. The storm had finally passed over the house.

Scratching her head, she shut the door and stood staring absently at the water on the floor. At that same moment she became aware of a tinkling sound coming from the living room. She turned and noticed that the light she'd switched off earlier had been turned back on. Had Beryl come down while she was taking a shower? She hadn't heard anything, but then again, she wouldn't. Taking a few steps further into the room, the tinkling became more distinct. There, sitting on the mantle, almost hidden in the shadows, was a small, wooden music box. Something about it instantly struck her as grotesque. In the silence of the house, the cheery melody seemed sinister. Off kilter.

Zippity Doo Da, Zippity-A. My oh my what a wonderful day.

Jane stood mesmerized. She couldn't seem to move.

Upstairs, she heard a door open. An instant later, Bean and Gulliver came scrambling down the stairs, barking past her into the living room. They had obviously caught the intruder's scent. Beryl followed close behind them, rubbing the sleep out of her eyes. "Who was at the door, Janey?"

Stiffly, Jane turned. She watched her aunt as she too became aware of the song.

"Where did that come from?"

Jane glanced at it out of the corner of her eye. "I don't know."

"Is Cordelia here?"

She shook her head. She didn't want to frighten her aunt unnecessarily, but she couldn't exactly hide what was happening. "Listen, Beryl, I'm afraid someone must have gotten into the house. I don't know how they did it, but they left that . . . thing."

Their eyes returned to the mantle as the song wound down and then stopped.

"But who was at the door?"

"No one," said Jane. "I think it was just a way to get me downstairs. Someone wanted me to find that while it was still playing." Was this intruder already in the house when she'd come in from the garden? She thought of the light in the living room.

"Who would be calling us this time of night?" asked Beryl, hearing the phone ring in the kitchen.

Jane could see her hesitate. Her aunt was clearly frightened. "I'll get it," said Jane. She hurried to pick it up. "Hello?"

Silence.

"Who is this?" she demanded.

"Did you get my present?" The voice whispered.

Jane could barely make out the words. "Who are you? What do you want?"

Again silence.

"I'm going to call the police!" she insisted. "How did you get into my house?"

"I'm watching you, Jane. Watching and waiting. Stay out of my business and...stay away from the club." The line clicked.

For a moment, she held on to the phone, too stunned to hang it back on its hook. Had the caller been a man or a woman? She couldn't tell. She closed her eyes and took several deep breaths before turning around.

Beryl must have followed her. She was standing next to the refrigerator. "What did they say?"

"Nothing that made any sense."

"I don't believe you." Beryl reached for Jane's hand. "This has something to do with that man your father is defending, doesn't it? Something to do with that women's club."

Jane slipped her arm around her aunt's waist. "We'll talk about it in the morning. I promise. Right now, I want you to go upstairs and pack a small suitcase. I don't want to worry you, but I want to leave here as quickly as possible."

"But shouldn't we call the police?"

"I...I'll handle it."

"But Jane!"

"We're going to spend the rest of the night at Dad's house. He's out of town right now, so it won't be any problem."

"Where did he go? He never said anything to me."

Whoops. Another area to stay away from. "He and Marilyn decided, kind of spur of the moment, to take a few days vacation."

"Humph. He might let a person know."

Jane began to walk her towards the stairs. "Tomorrow I'm going to have someone come over and check out the house. I want to know how this person got in. I don't mean to upset you, but we're not safe here until I find out."

Beryl glanced into the living room. "All right. I won't be but a minute."

Jane smiled. "And don't worry. We'll be fine."

After her aunt was gone, she crossed to the music box and lifted it down from the mantle. It was cheaply made. A magician dressed all in black, pulling a rabbit out of a hat. She turned it upside down and gave it several cranks. The music started again.

Zippity Doo Da. Zippity-A. My oh my what a wonderful day.

In total aggravation, she put her hand over it to make it stop. Not even taking into account the fact that there was a lunatic out there trying to scare the shit out of her, the song, in and of itself, was bad enough. It was as if some giggling idiot was pointing a finger at her and laughing.

A wonderful day. Right. Tell me another.

24

SATURDAY mornings had always been Mae's favorites. She would get up early to play with the kids while Bill made a big breakfast. Bill was a much better cook. Even after the kids had grown and begun lives of their own, she still found him every Saturday morning, brewing fresh coffee, chopping vegetables for omelets. She loved to watch him. His elegant doctor's hands moved so competently. Sometimes, she even allowed herself the luxury of feeling safe. She wouldn't let it last for long. She recognized a middle-class American fiction when she saw one. But, once in a while, it couldn't hurt.

That's what she'd told herself. Before. Before the *accident*. Before Bill's right eye was damaged beyond repair. He might never perform surgery again. That's what his own doctors were telling him. And he would have some trouble with his equilibrium until he got used to living with only one eye. It was a prognosis she could see him resisting with each new day. She could see him now. In the kitchen. Steadying himself on the counter as he buttered their breakfast toast. Moving carefully to the refrigerator to get out the juice. The will inside him was still strong. He insisted he was going back to the clinic. No *terrorist for God* was going to dictate to him what he could believe or where he could work. If nothing else, he would simply *counsel* all the women who came seeking an abortion. Mae knew he felt very strongly about counseling. Abortion opponents always suggested clinics like the one he gave his free time to were nothing but mills. Baby killing mills. Bill knew that wasn't true. He had personally talked to hundreds of women, both rich and poor, about every current option available. But he believed firmly that in the end, the final decision was the woman's. Even after the accident. . . .

Why did she still call it an accident? Bill had been sitting in his reading chair one evening, paging through the newspaper. Unfortunately, the chair happened to be right next to a window. Voices outside the house began chanting moments before the brick came crashing though the glass. She'd rushed him to the emergency room, but the damage was already done. Even as they were pulling out of the drive, stones and bricks were hurled at the car. One woman ran up to her as she was helping him into the front seat. She urged them both to accept Jesus as their personal savior. To understand that God had a plan for their lives. She said God loved them. Mae remembered turning to look this person straight in the eye. *These* were God's messengers? This rabble filled with hate and intolerance and arrogance? The windshield was partially smashed as they made their way slowly down the street. The car looked like it had been through a war. It had. But none of that mattered. Only Bill. And he was alive. One of the terrorists shouted that maybe, next time, he wouldn't be.

"We're ready to eat," called her husband from the kitchen.

"And it better be good, darlin', cause I'm hungry!"

She thought of the day she'd been offered the seat on The Gower Foundation board of directors. The night before, Rose and Charlotte and Miriam had patiently explained to her the ramifications of the position. There was an element of danger. They couldn't deny that. The Chamber had been active since 1922. It would be active long after they were all dead. Could she take the oath of loyalty and secrecy? Did she have that kind of commitment? After all, she was essentially a writer. A poet.

At that point, Mae remembered laughing out loud. Commitment? Why honey, they were talking to a grand master. Her entire life had been committed to fighting for freedom and personal dignity. Did they want credentials? She'd fought in Alabama for civil rights in the sixties. For women's rights, and gay rights in the seventies. She'd struggled for economic rights for the poor and disadvantaged in the eighties. And now, in the nineties, she found herself fighting... Miriam. Yet, when she thought of Bill, she knew it had to be done. And she would win. She would win because it was *necessary* to win.

"It's getting cold," he hollered.

"I'm coming." She stood, wiping a tear off her cheek. No time for that. Rearranging her face into a smile, she strolled calmly into the kitchen.

25

CORDELIA fluffed a bed pillow and stuffed it resentfully behind her head. She was not going to get up. Through clenched teeth she said, "I thought we'd already discussed my...*schedule* today. It's not even 9 A.M., Janey. Look out there. It's still dark."

"That's because it's cloudy and you have all your shades pulled. The sun rises at six twenty-one, Cordelia."

She humphed, grabbing her favorite teddy bear and closing her eyes. "You are *such* a store of useless information."

Jane continued to pace. "I called my brother before I came over here. He knows an ex-policeman. I think his name is Mugs Lonetto."

"With a name like that, he'd hardly be a ballet dancer."

"They're dropping by my house in an hour. Mugs is going to check the place over. See how the intruder got in."

"Splendid."

"I said we'd met them there."

Cordelia opened one eye. "*We?*"

"It's that song, Cordelia. The song that music box played. *Zippity Doo Da.* I was humming it earlier in the evening. Over at Dorrie's."

Cordelia let out a muffled shriek. "Not exactly your style, dearheart. I would have pictured you more in an *Unchained Melody* mood last night."

"I was—when I first got there."

"Uh oh. Trouble in paradise?"

"You could say that."

"Care to talk about it?"

Jane kicked a stuffed dragon out of her way. "It's Miriam. It seems she and Dorrie were once an item. Years ago. She wants her back, Cordelia."

"So? Dorrie gave her the heave ho, right?"

"Not exactly."

"What do you mean?"

Jane swallowed hard. "They slept together. Two nights ago."

Cordelia's eyes opened wide.

"Dorrie's not sure what she wants."

"And what do you want, dearheart?" Cordelia's voice was gentle.

"I don't know." Jane dumped herself into a chair.

"I see."

"Right now, I'm just not sure where I'm at. I can't tell Dorrie about my investigation over at the club. And to make matters worse, Miriam has just offered her a seat on The Gower Foundation board of directors."

Cordelia whistled. "To quote the King James version, The plot doth thicken." She tapped a finger against her chin.

"Those board members seem to be dying at a rather high rate. I feel like I should warn Dorrie about all of it, but I can't."

Cordelia lifted a cat off her knees and dropped him on the floor. "All right. What can I do?"

"Help me think this through! Who could have broken into my house last night and left that...that sniggering obscenity."

Cordelia smoothed a wrinkle in her comforter. "You

think Miriam was responsible?"

"That's just it. I don't know."

"What about Emery?"

"What about him?"

"Well, he certainly didn't wish you a wonderful life when you left his hotel suite yesterday. At dinner last night, you mentioned that he thought you were snooping. Messing in his business."

"True."

"If he *is* guilty of Charlotte's murder, then I'd say you may have poked your head into a hornet's nest. I'd stay away from him if I were you."

Jane leaned forward and rested her chin on her hands. "You know, when I told Freddy Lindhurst last night that Emery had been released on bail, he got all hot and bothered. I think he really believes the guy is guilty. I know his wife sure does."

"It's what that entire family wants to believe. And frankly, contrary to what your father may feel, I think they're right. All the evidence points to Emery."

"I wonder," said Jane.

"You wonder what?"

"Well, whoever left that music box last night is obviously trying to get me to back off. That could mean someone is concerned about what I might discover."

"You mean about Rose."

"Or Charlotte. If the deaths are connected, then one person is probably behind it. If not, then we have to look at each case individually. The problem is, Rose and Charlotte were friends. Their lives were deeply intertwined. Rose was like a grandmother to Charlotte's children. Mae was a longtime friend of both. My guess is that the motive for their deaths is also connected. And that leads me to wonder about Charlotte's family. As far as I know, as soon as the police picked Emery up, that was the end of any far-ranging investigation."

"You mean you think Evie or Julia might have had

154

something to do with their mother's death?"

"I don't know. Family problems can often be intense. And by the way, Cordelia, aren't you forgetting an important member of that family?"

"Who?"

"Charlotte's son-in-law. Freddy Lindhurst. He and Charlotte didn't get along. I found that out last night."

"Hardly a motive for murder."

Jane nearly exploded out of the chair. "I simply don't have enough information! And unlike the police, I can't go around demanding that people talk to me."

Cordelia clasped her hands over her imposing bosom and stared patiently at the underside of her canopied bed. "Does that exhaust your list of suspects?"

"Cordelia, what if I'm getting close to something important and I don't even know it? If I'm not, then why would someone be trying to scare me off?"

"Good point." She managed a look of great patience. "Jane, will you please stop pacing. You're wearing a groove in my rug."

Jane looked down at her feet. "When are you going to get rid of this brown shag? They don't even make it anymore."

"If I wait long enough, dearheart, it will come back into style. Sort of like your wardrobe." She pulled herself up into a sitting position. "And now that I am fully awake, I have remembered something important. I have news, dear one."

"About what?"

"Sit down, first. I feel like I'm watching a tennis match."

Dragging herself back to the chair, Jane sat.

"All right. Now. You know that list of drugs we found in the attic? The ones that seemed to have something to do with AIDS?"

"How can I forget?"

"Well, I was curious. I called The Gower Foundation

155

general offices yesterday and I asked if any of my donations went to AIDS research."

"Your donations?"

"Don't interrupt." She removed her long, black and green striped night cap and casually fluffed her thick auburn curls. "The woman said the only thing she could find was a large grant recently given to some center in St. Louis. I asked if she could be more specific, and that's when she got out this year's financial report. There was nothing about drugs. It appears this center is involved only in educational outreach. You know, AIDS prevention. Sending people around to schools. Things like that."

"Then I wonder what that list of drugs meant? Maybe I jumped to a wrong conclusion."

Cordelia held up her hand for quiet. "To continue," she said, exaggerating her patient expression, "I then called a friend of mine. Cissy Bergman. She's an RN who works with AIDS hospices around town. She also organizes and teaches workshops. Does a lot of writing on the subject. Anyway, I read the list to her. She recognized five or six of the names as drugs being used in Europe. One in Asia. You were right. Most are still experimental. The FDA is being pressured to allow two of them into the country, but so far, they haven't."

"Interesting. But what would Charlotte be doing with that list? And why would it be in a file upstairs in the attic room?"

"I suppose it could be just a coincidence."

Jane shook her head. "I don't think so." She noticed Melville, one of Cordelia's cats, peek his head out from under the bed. His nose was almost entirely encased in dust. "You know, as I see it, I've got one chance here. The ledger. It's the only means I have of forcing some cooperation out of those two women."

"I wonder why they want it so badly?"

"Beats me. I was looking through it last night. Maybe I'm wrong, but it appeared to contain a lot of names and addresses."

"A list of contributors?"

"Possibly. But those names should be a matter of public record."

Cordelia kicked off her satin quilt and swung her feet over the side of the bed. She felt around on the floor until she found her Daffy Duck slippers.

"Are those new?" asked Jane, trying not to stare. She couldn't believe even Cordelia could wear something so . . . so ridiculous.

"I got them in Chicago last spring. And no, you may not borrow them." She lifted Miss Blanche, her oldest feline, to her lips and gave her a small peck. "So, give! What are you going to ask for in return for that ledger?"

Again, Jane stood. Her nervous energy was too strong to allow her to remain seated. "I couldn't sleep when we finally got to my father's house last night, so I just sat up on his couch with a brandy . . . and I thought. I came up with two things. First, before I promise to give the ledger back, I want both Mae and Miriam's word that they won't add any more members to the board of directors until all this is settled. Until we've reached some conclusion about Rose's death."

"And the second demand?"

"I want to know what The Chamber is. I have a gut feeling that *that* particular piece of information is central to any solution."

"Well," said Cordelia, rising and slipping into her fake zebra skin robe, "I wish you luck. Now. Would you care to join me for a cup of Darjeeling and a Ding Dong? If I'm going to be made to get up at this hour of the night, I have to have some sustenance."

Jane checked her watch. "Ok. We have a good fifteen minutes before we need to be at my house."

Cordelia stopped, squared her shoulders and then proceeded out the door. "On second thought," she muttered, "this just may turn out to be a two Ding Dong day."

26

"WAS that Peter's jeep in front of your house?" asked Cordelia, sweeping into the front hall and shaking the rain out of her umbrella.

"He must already be here." Jane stepped to the stairs and called up. "Anybody home?"

"Be right down," came a deep voice. The wood floors creaked under the weight of a tall, bearded man as he came bounding down the stairs. He gave them both a hug before stuffing a screwdriver into the back pocket of his cords.

"Where's your ex-policeman friend?" asked Jane, glancing around.

"In the basement. So far, everything checks out tight as a drum. No pry marks on the windows. No evidence anywhere of breaking and entering."

"You know," said Cordelia, standing back to look at them, "I forget sometimes how much you two look alike."

"Especially when I put on my fake beard," said Jane, slipping an arm around her brother's shoulder. She gave his curly brown hair a playful yank. "But I'm older. And wiser."

"And crazier," said Peter, nodding at the music box still sitting on the mantle in the living room. "What have you gotten yourself into this time?" Together, they walked away, leaving Cordelia standing alone in the hall.

Catching the unmistakable scent of fresh brewed coffee, she began to edge her way into the kitchen. After a quick perusal of the refrigerator, she selected a loaf of English muffin bread and popped two slices into the toaster. Then, getting down a mug, she sidled over to the coffee maker.

"Who are you?" asked a husky voice from the doorway to the basement stairs.

Cordelia turned, holding the coffee pot in mid air. "I . . . I might ask you the same question." She blinked several times as she beheld a robust, highly attractive bleached-blond, wearing a pair of white bib overalls, a red bandana tied around her hair.

"Mugs Lonetto." She held out a meaty hand.

Cordelia shook it limply. "Cordelia Thorn. I thought you were supposed to be . . . a man."

Mugs looked down at her rather prominent chest. "Not likely." She gave Cordelia a devastating smile.

Cordelia nearly dropped the coffee pot.

"Ah, there you are," said Peter, walking briskly into the room. "I see you two have already met. Mugs, this is my sister, Jane."

"Glad to meet you," said Mugs, once again extending her hand.

"So," continued Peter, "what did you find downstairs?"

Mugs shoved her hands into her pockets. "No problems. The security in this house is pretty good. Not that you couldn't use a burglar alarm system. But I'd say your visitor last night had to have a key. There's no other way he could have broken in without us seeing some signs."

"A key," repeated Jane. "How could someone get a key to this house?"

"Oh, you'd be surprised how easy it is. I don't suppose you've lost yours recently?"

"Well . . . I mean, I left them in the ignition of my car a

few days ago. But I don't think anyone touched them. Otherwise, why didn't they steal the car?"

Peter brushed a hand over his mouth to hide a smile.

"I saw that," said Jane.

"Nothing," said Peter, grinning. "I said nothing. Why, I wouldn't trade your car for two BMWs."

"It's a real wreck, is it?" asked Mugs.

Jane shook her head. She noticed that Cordelia had said nothing. Generally, she never missed a chance to defame the prehistoric Saab. This morning she merely stood in the corner with an inane smile plastered on her face. What was *her* problem?

"Anyway, I suggest you get a locksmith out here today," continued Mugs. "I'll give you the name of a woman who'll do it right. And cheap." She walked over to Cordelia, took the coffee pot out of her hand and poured herself a cup.

"Great," said Peter.

"It wasn't a professional job," said Mugs, leaning her elbow on the counter and flashing Cordelia another gorgeous grin. "At least you're lucky there. If a professional wanted to make a point, they'd grab you, drag you into a dark ally and kick the shit out of you. That tends to scare a person real good. If you know what I mean." She sniffed. "Then again, sometimes the nonprofessionals are the most dangerous. They're unpredictable. Unfortunately, the police won't be much help. Not unless you can prove a threat was made."

"Well," sighed Jane, sitting down at the kitchen table, "I guess I'll just have to wait and see what develops."

"All you can do," agreed Mugs. She turned to Cordelia. "You a friend of the family?"

Cordelia managed to flutter her eyes.

"Where did you get the name Mugs?" asked Jane. "It's kind of unusual."

"Yeah. I know. My real name is Mary. Mary Katherine Lonetto. I come from a big Catholic family over near

Crocus Hill. Ever since I was a kid, I insisted people call me Mugs. I guess it was my way of telling the folks I wasn't headed for the convent." She gave Cordelia a small wink.

"This has been fun," said Peter, picking up his umbrella, "but I'm afraid I've got to run. I'm already late for a shoot. Thanks Mugs. I owe you one." He turned to his sister. "Janey, I'll talk to you later. In the meantime, be careful. If you need anything, you call, ok? And make sure you change those locks today." He gave Cordelia a peck on the cheek as he left through the kitchen door.

"Well," said Jane, leaning back and putting her feet up on another chair, "at least I know more than I did last night. I better call my aunt. I promised I'd come get her as soon as I got the verdict." She rubbed her tired eyes. "Thanks for coming over, Mugs. You've really been a big help."

"No problem."

Jane glanced at Cordelia. "I suppose you'll want to get home so you can catch a nap before bed."

"Really?" said Mugs, taking a sip of coffee. "You been up a long time?"

Cordelia shot Jane a withering look. "No. Actually, I was planning to head over to...the gym. Yes! For my morning workout."

Jane stood, her eyes opening wide. She silently mouthed the word *gym*, making a question mark out of her face.

Mugs nodded her approval. "I've got some stuff to do too. I wanted to get in some target practice today. Keep up the skills." She set her cup down. "I thought maybe we might go get some breakfast first. What do you say, Cordelia? You up for a little ham and eggs?"

Cordelia elbowed her way past Jane as she followed Mugs out into the dining room. "I know just the place. If you like grease."

Jane rolled her eyes to an empty room.

"Here's that name and number," said Mugs, writing it

down on a slip of paper. She left it on the dining room table. "Well, better shove off." She glanced at Cordelia. "Ready?"

"Yes. I mean, *yeah*."

Jane dragged herself into the front hall in time to see two backs retreat out the door. Oh well, she thought. At least she didn't have to drive Cordelia home.

And buy her a quart of chocolate milk to placate her world-weary soul.

Mugs could be in charge of that. Poor woman.

27

BERYL read the next name in the column. *Peglow Novelties*. She'd been calling around all afternoon, trying to find out where someone might buy a cheap music box. If Jane didn't have time to pursue it, she might as well make herself useful. Even after the locksmith had come and gone, she still felt nervous about being in the house alone. Of course, she'd told Jane she was just fine. Her niece didn't need any more stress in her life right now. She looked so tired. Beryl had suggested some rest, but Jane insisted she had to get to work. And Beryl knew when Jane was in one of her stubborn moods, there was no reasoning with her.

She picked up the phone and dialed the number.

A man's voice answered. "Peglow's."

"Hello. Yes. I wonder if you could help me?"

"That's what I'm here for."

She cleared her throat. "Do you sell music boxes?"

"Biggest selection in town."

Wonderful, thought Beryl. Except, this was the third man who'd said exactly the same thing. "I'm looking for something in particular. It's painted wood. Small. I believe it plays a song called, *Zippity Doo Da*."

"Sure. The magician pulling the rabbit out of a hat. We sell those. But, hold your horses. I think we may be all out." He dropped the phone.

Beryl waited, elated by her good luck.

"Yup. We got a shipment in last Monday. Haven't had any of those in months. To tell you the truth, they aren't usually that popular. But last Tuesday, this guy strolls in and buys the whole lot. All twelve. I doubt we'll be getting in another shipment for at least a couple months. I could take your number. Give you a call."

"You wouldn't by any chance remember the name of the man who purchased them? Or his address?"

"Sure. It's no skin off my nose." He paged through some papers. "I got the invoice right in front of me. His name was D. Benedict. He put his address down as 1603 University Avenue."

Beryl wrote it down on a note pad. "You've been very helpful."

"Stop by any time. We're open seven days a week."

"I'll do that." She tore off the page as she hung up.

What incredible luck! This might just be the break Jane needed. Beryl grabbed her purse and car keys and headed out the door. No need for an umbrella. The sun had finally reappeared.

1603 University Avenue. Beryl knew Jane kept a map in the boot of her car. It shouldn't be hard to find. She even had a vague idea where University Avenue was. This sleuthing business wasn't so hard. Why did everyone make such a fuss?

Half an hour later, Beryl pulled up in front of a disheveled, three story building. The untidy front yard contained two cement elephants painted a brilliant shade of orange. Several tall, Greek letters were affixed to the face of the house. As she looked down the street, she noticed that all the houses had similar letters attached to the front.

She quickly got out of the car and approached the front door, stepping over an empty bottle of Jack Daniels and a particularly filthy pair of sneakers on her way.

As she was about to ring the doorbell, a young man leaned out of a second story window. "Can I help you?" he asked.

She moved back a few paces and looked up. "Indeed you may. I'm looking for a D. Benedict. I was told he lived here."

The young man started to laugh. "Are you English? Pip pip and all that?"

Beryl didn't see what her place of birth had to do with anything. Besides, she didn't like his tone. "I am."

"Well, shiver me-timbers. No that isn't right. Oh hell." He held up a beer can in salute.

She tried again. "Is Mr. Benedict at home?"

The man took a swallow before turning to face some of his buddies inside the building. "Hey, Jason. Lance. Is Master D. Benedict at home?"

She could tell he was mocking her accent. Behind him came a roar of laughter.

He returned to the window. "Sorry, old bean. No such luck."

"He does live here, doesn't he?"

The young man took another sip. "Sometimes. This is a frat house, lady. The guy you're looking for . . . his name's Doyle. Not D."

"I see. Thank you for that clarification. Perhaps, since you're being so helpful, you could assist me with one other thing. Do you know about a series of music boxes Mr. Benedict purchased from *Peglow Novelties?*"

"Music boxes?" He burped. "Sure. We gave them away as door prizes last night. It was our big homecoming bash."

She glanced at the yard. Scrutinizing it a bit more carefully, she could see it was positively thick with beer cans. "Is that right?"

"Yup. Sorry about the mess. The butler hasn't had a chance to clean it up yet." He tipped the can back and emptied it. "You want to leave him a message?"

"Thank you, no." Carefully avoiding the debris, she began to back away. After moving only a few paces, she noticed the front door open. Out walked one of the most lovely men she had ever seen. His clear, china-blue eyes glanced up at the young man leaning out of the window.

"May I help you?" he asked, brushing an errant blond curl away from his eyes.

"Why, no. I was just leaving." She hesitated. "Are you . . . one of the members?"

The man smiled. "No. Actually, I work just across the street. I'm a teaching assistant in the German department." He pointed to a brick building. "I stopped by to see a friend."

"Ah. I see."

He offered her his arm and together they started down the walk. "You're English. Or am I wrong?"

"I seem to be a curiosity."

Again, he laughed. "Not really. Where's your car?"

"It's right over there. That old green Saab." Was it her imagination or did the sight of it seem to startle him?

"There you go," he said, opening the door. "You're sure you're going to make it home in this thing?"

"I usually do. It belongs to my niece. She doesn't feel she can afford a new one right now." As she climbed in, she noticed him tilt his head to one side. Oh, he *was* handsome. Just about the right age for her friend, Evelyn Bratrude's oldest granddaughter. Then, she noticed the wedding ring.

"What brings you over to the University?" he asked, a shadow falling across his face.

"Oh, well I wanted to speak to a man by the name of Doyle Benedict. Do you know him?"

"I do. Did you find him?"

"Alas, no. He wasn't at home."

"I see. You know, I could give him a message next time I see him. He's in one of my classes."

166

Beryl got comfortable in the front seat. "That won't be necessary. But thank you anyway."

He shut the door. "Of course. Well...have a nice day."

"I shall," said Beryl. She gave him a small wave as she started the motor and pulled away from the curb. At the end of the block, she glanced in her rear view mirror. Odd that he should still be standing there, watching her.

28

MAE pushed away from her desk and reached in back of her for the phone. "Black Writers Minnesota," she said absently into the receiver. It was Saturday afternoon. The secretary was gone.

"This is Jane Lawless."

"Oh...hi. What can I do for you?" Damn. She should have let the answering machine take it. She hadn't had a chance to speak with Miriam yet.

"I need to talk to you."

"Yes...of course. But I haven't—"

"Listen to me for a moment. I have something. Something you want. I'm willing to give it to you, but only if we talk first."

"Can you be more specific?"

There was a long silence. "All right. I have the ledger."

"I don't believe it! That's wonderful. When do you want to meet?"

"I want Miriam there too."

"Why? She'd have no problem with you giving it to me."

"You're not listening, Mae. I said I wanted to talk first."

"About what?"

"I'll tell you that when I see you. I want to do it to-night."

"Tonight? Well—" She knew it wasn't smart to stall. Every minute that ledger was out of their hands was a minute too long. "Where?"

"How about at my restaurant?"

"I'm not sure I can get Miriam there on such short no-tice."

"Then you won't get the ledger."

Mae felt her breath catch in her throat.

"I want some answers. I mean it. I'm not playing games. Either we work together or I keep the thing until we can come to some sort of agreement."

"I . . . you can't do that. It doesn't belong to you."

"You're right. But my life does, and right now I'm pretty sure it's in danger."

"What do you mean?"

"Those are my terms. Take it or leave it."

Mae had to think fast. Miriam was supposed to host an art opening tonight at eight. She might be at the mu-seum right now attending to last minute details. "I'll do what I can. But Jane?"

"What?"

"I don't think we should meet at your restaurant. It's too . . . public. How about the attic room at the club?" She could sense Jane's hesitation. "Is something wrong?" She waited.

"All right. Nine o'clock."

"That should be fine. See you then." She dropped the receiver back on the hook.

Damn it all. Her eyes fell to her keys. She'd better move fast. Miriam was not going to be happy with this turn of events. From the very first, Miriam had insisted that hiring Jane was a stupid, unnecessary indulgence. If that was true, if she had made a mistake, they would all end up paying for it—in spades.

* * *

At nine that evening, Jane walked resolutely up the steps to the attic room. Since a soft light glowed from under the door, she assumed Mae and Miriam were already there. It was a case of now or never.

"Good evening," said Mae, as Jane entered. Miriam's face was partially hidden by shadow. The oil lamp burned in one corner of the room. Three chairs had been placed around the round, oak table. Mae was seated to Jane's left, Miriam to her right. Neither looked particularly happy. Well, that was to be expected. Jane had backed them into a corner.

"Did you bring the ledger?" asked Mae.

Jane sat down. "Before we discuss that, I want to talk for a few minutes."

"You do have it?" said Miriam. Once again, she was the picture of understated elegance in her silks and pearls.

"Yes. I do. But before I give it to you, there are two specific things I want." She looked from face to face. Both seemed set in stone. Patiently, she folded her hands on the table. "As far as I'm concerned, this meeting doesn't have to be adversarial. Correct me if I'm wrong, but I think we all want the same thing. We want to establish how Rose died. We also want to know if the stolen ledger and the stolen jewels had anything to do with her death. Rose was in a meeting late that night. A Chamber meeting, I believe it's called. Now, unless I'm very much mistaken, both of you know what that is. You might even have been there. So, before I give you the ledger, I want to know what happened that night. What this Chamber is all about. Who the members are. I need the information so that I can begin to examine Rose's last hours."

Mae took a deep breath. "Can't you take our word that the meeting had nothing to do with her death?"

"No."

"What's the second thing you want?" asked Miriam,

her voice distant and slightly imperial. "Let's put everything on the table."

"Fair enough. I want your word that you won't install any new board members until we reach some sort of conclusion about Rose's death."

"Not possible," said Miriam, dismissing her immediately. "Gower Foundation affairs are none of your business. Now, you have a piece of property that belongs to us and we want it back."

"Sorry," said Jane, realizing Miriam had merely come to issue an ultimatum. "No deals." She crossed her arms and waited. As far as she was concerned, it was their move.

Miriam stood. "This is a waste of time. I, for one, have better things to do with my evening. For your own good I suggest you rethink your position, Jane." She let the threat hang in the air. Without further comment she swept around the table and out the door.

Jane remained seated. Mae had not yet spoken. Had she misjudged the relative importance of the ledger to these two women? If so, Miriam was right. This was indeed a waste of time.

Mae shifted in her seat. She seemed to be listening to Miriam's footsteps as they retreated down the hall. Once the room was quiet, she got up and stepped over to the door. She closed it softly and then returned to her seat, pausing a few moments before saying, "You have us over a barrel. I assume you know that."

Jane gave a small nod.

"Miriam told me a few minutes ago about... well, about Dorrie. It came as a revelation. I didn't know of your... mutual relationship. She never mentioned anything about it when I suggested hiring you. That was a mistake." Mae sighed and looked down. "I will admit you have me stymied. I don't know how to proceed. If I tell you about The Chamber, I'm breaking an oath. If I don't—" She let her voice trail off. After a moment she said, "So tell me Jane, which is more important? My own integrity or other people's lives?"

Even though the question was serious, Jane relaxed a bit. At least Mae was being honest. "Only you can answer that."

Mae gave a rueful smile. "Such talent for stating the obvious."

"Look, you said the other day that you trusted me. I hope that's still true. I would never do anything to hurt any legitimate aspect of this club or the Foundation."

"That's just the problem," said Mae, drumming her nails on the table. "How do you feel about *non*-legitimate aspects?"

Jane cocked her head. She wasn't sure what she meant.

Mae glanced at the bookcase before getting up and walking over to it. She leaned an arm against the edge. "You know what's behind here, don't you?" It was more of a statement than a question.

Jane nodded.

"You're very clever, you know that? And tough. You're not as flawed by what I call *Minnesota Nice* as I thought. Unfortunately, that wasn't in your dossier. Had it been, I might never have come to you. But don't get me wrong. I respect those qualities, Jane. I don't want you for an enemy. Somehow, I feel that even if I don't give you the information you want, you're going to get it. God knows how, but you will."

She returned to her seat. "All right. You want to know about The Chamber. And so . . . I'll tell you." She rested her elbows on the table, dropping her chin on her hands. "A little more than seventy years ago, Amelia Gower came up with an idea. She wanted to start a philanthropic foundation primarily aimed at the needs of women. She was a suffragist, as well as an early pioneer for all of women's rights. Several years after starting The Gower Foundation—and endowing it with her own fortune, as well as that of her deceased husband—she realized some of the things she wanted to accomplish couldn't be done, shall we say, *legally*. That's when she came up with the idea for The Chamber. It was begun in the spring of 1922 with five women. Amelia and the other four Gower Foundation board of directors. These were women she'd hand picked. She knew them intimately. Trusted them implicitly. The Chamber itself was to be kept entirely secret. The meetings took place in this room. Ideas were kicked around. Plans were made. Some of the early proposals involved such issues as prostitution, contraception—many of the things we're still dealing with today.

"Five years after its inception, Amelia became gravely ill. One evening, she called The Chamber members together around her bed and spoke of her hope that, even after her death, The Chamber would remain alive. She explained her ideas for codifying The Chamber rules. Number one—absolute secrecy. Number two—how projects would be financed. Three—how, after the death of a member, new members would be initiated. At her insistence, the number of members would now remain at four. Issues would still be debated. Once every two years, a new project would be selected. If there was a deadlock in the voting—in other words, if two women favored one proposal and the other two favored a different proposal— Amelia left her two most beloved jewels, those her husband had given to her on their wedding day, as a means of breaking the tie. One jewel would represent each side. Each jewel had been cut exactly alike. To break the deadlock, one of the members would put on a blindfold and select a jewel from a small enamel box. In a sense, Amelia would still have a say in some of the decisions. Even after her death, those jewels were her voice. The fifth voice. That's what we called them. That's how we looked upon them. That is, until they were stolen."

Jane was fascinated. Still, she knew she had even more questions now than when they'd started. "You said you thought Miriam might have had something to do with stealing the jewels? Why?"

Mae picked up a pencil and began to play with it. "Last June, we began debate on a new project. As usual, two proposals were offered for consideration. The first had to do with AIDS research. Miriam suggested we look into the acquisition of certain drugs, legal in other parts of the world, but illegal here in the states. These drugs, even though they are experimental, present the best hope right now for desperate people who already have the virus, but whose immune systems haven't totally broken down. A nationwide distribution system was suggested. All covert. Rose and Charlotte seemed interested, though they wanted more information. For the last three months, Miriam has been working hard to provide it."

"What was the other proposal?

"There was a suggestion that we develop fifteen to twenty teams of trained—"commandos," for want of a better word—to monitor the activities of certain anti-abortion terrorists. These teams would discourage—forcefully if necessary—the terrorists' participation in the harassment of certain clinics and doctors. As it happens, this was my proposal. I felt it was more in keeping with the original guidelines of The Chamber and I argued that point very strongly. Again, both Charlotte and Rose seemed interested. Two days before we were to take a vote, Charlotte . . . was murdered. Emery took her life and at the same time put all of ours in limbo."

"Both seem like worthy proposals."

"They were."

"Do you have any idea how Charlotte was going to vote?"

"I don't. Though I know she'd finally made a decision. She'd been having some problems with it. In the past, because of her relationship with Miriam, they'd generally voted as a block. They tended to talk things over together and most often reached the same conclusion. But recently, they'd let on that they were having some personal problems. I know Miriam felt Charlotte might vote against her proposal merely out of spite. Knowing Charlotte as I did, I was positive that would never happen. But, even before Charlotte's death, Miriam was crying foul."

"What about Rose?"

"Privately, she told me she was committed to my proposal."

"Did Miriam know that?"

"I think she had a pretty good idea."

"So, if Charlotte voted with you and Rose..."

"Exactly. All Miriam's work was for nothing."

"And if she voted against you?"

"We were deadlocked. The jewels would need to be used to break the tie. But then, Charlotte died. Several weeks later, Rose was gone. I can't say for sure Rose was murdered, but the death was certainly suspicious. The ledger was taken, as were the jewels. Even if I wanted to force a vote now, I couldn't. There'd be no point. Without the jewels, we have no means to make a decision. With them we could have proceeded. Each of us had a fifty-fifty chance our proposal would win."

"And you think those odds weren't good enough for Miriam?"

"I don't know."

It was all becoming clear. "But if she packs the board with people she can sway—" She thought of Dorrie. "Does Dorrie know the full extent of your current problems?"

"No. As a potential board member, she's been told about the history of The Chamber. The rules. And she's been appraised of the potential dangers. But the specifics would come later."

"I see."

"Do you understand now why we couldn't call the police?"

Silently, Jane nodded.

"The thing is, the two most recent proposals were powerfully argued. Emotions were running very high. A lot was at stake. Under normal circumstances, we would have made a decision within a month. But Charlotte kept insisting we gather more information. It was obvious to anyone with eyes to see that she was stalling. She didn't want to make a decision because she knew if she voted against Miriam's proposal, it would be the end of their relationship. At least, that's what I thought. Rose was certain Charlotte was in a genuine quandary. It had nothing to do with Miriam. Whatever the case, we'll never know how she was going to vote because she died before she could tell anyone."

"What about Dorrie? Are you going to allow that offer to go through?"

"Knowing what I know now, no. Miriam and Charlotte's personal ups and downs were enough. Rest assured, I'm not going to deal with a situation like that again. I realize all marriages have their moments, but it doesn't belong in this room."

Jane felt immensely relieved. "Thank you."

"So," said Mae, leaning back in her chair and tossing the pencil on top of the table. "Does that answer all of your questions?"

"What about the ledger? What does it mean? Why is it in code?"

Mae studied her for a moment. "Well, I suppose since you already know this much, I might as well trust you with the rest. You understand, of course, that everything I've told you tonight has to remain a secret. Your silence must be absolute. The work of generations and the reputations of many fine women would be destroyed if you make it public."

"I realize that. You have my word."

"Good. All right. About the ledger. Five years ago The Chamber began to develop a series of safe-houses all over the country. Women could take their children and finally get some help in running away from abusive spouses. As you might well imagine, no one would use this kind of network unless they feared for their lives, or the lives of their sons and daughters. Nobody would willingly leave their homes and jobs unless they were absolutely desperate. We can now keep these folks safe in an underground network for years. We've even developed the means to give them new identities. A new start somewhere else. The ledger is a coded record of all these activities. We decided not to put it on a computer because that was too easy to access. As you might guess, there are many individuals, as well as groups, who'd like to get their hands on this information. The ledger contains everything. And you have it. I hope you put it in a safe place."

Jane smiled. "It's safe."

"When do we get it back?"

Jane got up and walked over to the bookcase. She bent down and pulled it from one of the lower shelves. "I came up here earlier this afternoon. Just to check things out. I thought this was a great hiding spot. It would be the last place you'd look."

Mae took it and hugged it to her chest, tears forming in her eyes. "Thank you, Jane." She started to laugh. "A woman with a sense of humor. You're ok. But how did you find it?"

"To tell you the truth, I just got lucky. Someone left it in Rose's apartment. It was Thursday afternoon. Cordelia and I had been up here in the attic room looking around. When we got downstairs, we heard footsteps running away from us down the hall. Rose's door was open. We decided we'd better check it out so we went inside. I noticed it right away. It was sitting on that small oak table."

"I know the one," said Mae, still smiling.

"Now, if I could only find the jewels as easily. And figure out what happened to Rose."

Mae's smile faded.

"That last Chamber meeting—"

"You mean the night Rose died?"

Jane nodded. "Did anything unusual happen?"

"No. Not really. We discussed taking a vote by using

the jewels, but since we were one member shy, Miriam wouldn't hear of it."

"I see. But technically, at that point you weren't deadlocked. You and Rose could out-vote Miriam."

"True. But Miriam convinced us not to look at it that way. According to the bylaws, she had a point. So, the majority of the evening was spent discussing potential replacements for the position Charlotte's death had left vacant."

"And then Rose died."

"What are you saying? That Miriam might have had something to do with Rose's death?" Mae shook her head. "I'll never believe that. The jewels are one thing, but Miriam is a decent woman. Sure, she's got a temper, but she'd never do something like that. I'd stake my life on it."

Jane hoped that wouldn't be necessary. "All right. But you were the one who said there was a lot at stake here. Could she have some personal reason for wanting these drugs to be available?"

"Everything," said Mae, her voice taking on a hard edge, "is personal." She seemed startled by her own vehemence. "Just like everything is political." She said the last sentence quickly, pushing away from the table.

Jane found the answer too pat. It was the first time tonight she'd felt Mae was holding back. Her demeanor almost shouted that Jane was about to cross some invisible line. "I guess our meeting is over."

Mae's expression softened. "I'm sorry. But you're right. I have to get home. My . . . husband is recovering from a recent surgery."

"I didn't know."

"He's going to be fine. I just don't like to leave him alone in the evenings. It's kind of a hard time for him."

"I understand."

"I'll let you lock up." She opened the door and stepped out onto the landing. "And Jane." She turned. "Remember, you just pledged your word. I'm holding you to it." She gave a rueful smile. "That from a woman who has just broken hers. I hope I made the right decision. I guess only time will tell."

29

JANE wasted no time in leaving the club. After last night's bizarre turn of events, all she wanted was a hot shower and a quiet cup of tea before bed. She'd been toying all afternoon with the idea of calling Dorrie, but perhaps it was too soon. They both needed time and space in which to think things out. Maybe she should give it a couple more days. That seemed sensible. Not that she felt like being sensible.

As she crossed to the parking lot, she noticed someone leaning against the hood of her car. In the darkness, she couldn't immediately make out who it was. She slowed her pace until she could get a better look. Her heart sank when she saw that it was Miriam.

"Was there an ultimatum you forgot to issue?" she asked, opening the trunk and dumping her backpack inside.

Miriam remained still.

"Look, I've had kind of a hard day. Why don't you go glower at someone else for a while."

At that, Miriam looked up. "You were right."

"About what?"

"We do need to talk."

"Fine. Call my secretary. Make an appointment." Jane knew that would be hard to do, since she didn't have one.

Miriam put out a hand, blocking Jane's access to the front seat. "Will you follow me? My home isn't far."

"Give me one reason why I should?"

Softly, Miriam said, "Dorrie."

Bingo. Right answer. "All right. I guess I could do that. You lead the way." As she started her engine, waiting to see if it would die, she noticed Miriam get into a new Lincoln Continental. That figured. Jane backed out of her space and followed her out of the lot.

Ten minutes later, the Lincoln pulled into the drive of a lovely, wood and stucco mock Tudor just west of Nicollet and Fiftieth. So this was where she and Charlotte had lived lo these many years. It must have been difficult to move into a small room at the club after such spaciousness.

Entering the front door, Jane was struck by the amount of artwork filling the rooms. All of the walls were painted white. The natural wood floor was bare except for one dramatically large Native American rug in the center of the living room. The furnishings were sparse but expensive. It wasn't a house in which to kick off your shoes and have a beer. It was more of a house in which to keep your shoes on and sip from a glass of Barsac. Since Jane enjoyed both, she wasn't sure what to make of it. One thing she did know, the artwork was amazing. She stood in front of a many-faceted glass sculpture, watching the track lighting play tricks with her eyes.

"Have a seat," said Miriam, walking to a table against the far wall and pouring herself a scotch. "Can I get you anything?"

"Some Barsac would be nice."

Miriam turned. "Barsac? I'm not sure we have any right now. Would you settle for a Piesporter?"

"Fine." Jane made herself comfortable on the sofa. At least when it came to food, she wasn't out of her depth.

Miriam poured the wine. "Did you give Mae the ledger, or do we still have to convince you we're not the enemy?"

"I never thought you were."

She handed Jane the glass and then sat down. "That's not an answer."

"The answer is yes. I gave Mae the ledger."

"Good. When it comes to negotiations, I bow to her greater diplomatic skills."

They each sat silently for a few moments, sipping their drinks.

"Does all this artwork belong to you?" asked Jane.

Miriam nodded. "Charlotte enjoyed it, but I'm afraid, over the years, we'd reached a parting of the ways when it came to...new acquisitions. All Charlotte wanted were her books and her nightly glass of Cognac. Beyond that, she couldn't have cared less if she was sitting in a palace or, like Thoreau, on a pumpkin. I'm afraid she thought my priorities were...misplaced. My surroundings have always been important to me. I'm very proud of this house. To be honest, I think it embarrassed Charlotte."

Since they were obviously talking personally, Jane decided to ask a personal question. "Is that why you and Charlotte broke up?" She knew this was simplistic, but hoped it might lead somewhere interesting.

Miriam stretched her arm over the back of one of the sofa cushions. "No, though I think the argument became an outward manifestation of our inward drift. When we first met, we knew we were different, but at the time, that difference seemed like flint and steel. It generated an incredible spark. We forged a great deal of our ideas and our own maturity in the fire it produced. I'll never regret our relationship, but...things had begun to sour. It happened long before Dorrie joined the club. Seeing her again only reminded me of what I'd lost—of what had been missing in my life for some years. Then again, the more we talked, the more I felt Dorrie and I still had a chance. That old attraction was still there. I don't know what there is about a first love, but it never really seems to die."

Just dandy, thought Jane. Miriam had brought her all the way over here just to tell her it was impossible to do battle with nostalgia. "I'm not going to roll over and play dead. Dorrie means a lot to me too."

"I know that. I suppose that's why I felt we should clear the air." She took a sip of her scotch. "I want you to understand that I didn't plan for this to happen. It just happened. I still love Dorrie, and if she decides to take the position on the board of directors, we will be working together closely. I think that would make your relationship with her completely untenable."

Jane could feel the anger rising in her chest. She would've loved to jump up and tell *Ms. Understated Elegance* that Mae wasn't going to allow that offer to go through. But if she did, she'd only open up another can of worms. It wasn't worth it. Miriam would find out soon enough. "We'll see."

"Yes. We will."

As much as Jane wanted to like some part of this woman, she simply couldn't. Miriam was an ass. Why didn't Dorrie see it?

Both women turned at the sound of the back door opening.

"Evie? Is that you?" called Miriam.

Evie Fortnum, her hair now a florescent shade of pink, entered through the rounded dining room arch. "I'm beat," she said, throwing herself into a chair. She glanced at Miriam's drink.

Jane nodded a greeting.

"I told the guys to use Brenda for the last set. I have to get some serious rest. We're playing that pool party tomorrow over at Cuthburts. That should go until one or two in the morning. And then both Julia and I want to be to the lawyer's bright and early Monday morning for the reading of Rose's will."

"I sent your red dress to the cleaners," said Miriam. "Oh, and the black one too."

"Great. Thanks." She fished in her purse and brought out a package of gum. "Is Ben here?"

Miriam shook her head.

"Oh well. I'm too tired for a late night talk, anyway. I gotta get to bed." She remained seated, kicking off one shoe. "You know, it was that dumb frat party on Friday night. That's what really wiped me out."

"What fraternity?" asked Jane.

"Sigma Delta."

Immediately, she thought of the fraternity pin she and Cordelia had found. That was Sigma Delta too. Since Jane didn't believe in coincidences, she asked, "Are you a friend of someone who's a member there?"

"Sort of," said Evie, unwrapping a stick and folding it into her mouth. "He works at the club. Doyle Benedict. He asked me if my group would like to play a couple of sets at their homecoming bash on Friday night. It turned into five hours of non-stop revelry. I didn't get to bed until after four. *Big mistake.*" She bugged out her eyes.

Curious, thought Jane. Finally, here was a connection. Then again, how did Doyle's pin, if it was Doyle's pin—and she'd bet money that it was—get behind that conference room door? "Are you two dating?"

"Nah," said Evie, snapping her gum. "Only in his mind. We're really just friends. He's ROTC. Not exactly my type."

Jane wondered if Emery was still her type.

"Well, I better mosey on upstairs. Hit the sheets." She got up and gave Miriam a peck on the cheek. Before she left the room, she paused in front of the beverage table eyeing a bottle of vodka. Realizing everyone was staring at her, she turned and smiled. "What did you say your name was again?" she asked Jane.

"Jane Lawless."

"We've met, right?"

"Once."

She nodded, quickly stuffing the bottle into her large purse and hurrying out.

"Excuse me for a moment," said Miriam. She rose and

followed Evie into the kitchen.

As the grandfather clock by the patio doors struck eleven, Jane took this lull in the evening's merriment to study the rest of the room. On a glass end table next to her, she noticed a framed picture of three teenagers sitting on a park bench. She recognized Evie and Julia at once. The third was a boy. He looked about the same age. Cuddled in his arms was a small puppy.

Miriam returned, briskly striding back to the sofa. She set the bottle of vodka on the floor next to her and then attempted a confident smile. "Sometimes Evie gets a bit carried away. She's taken her mother's death pretty hard. And, of course, she was close to Rose too." She paused, straightening her strand of pearls. "It's been a rough couple months for us all, I'm afraid." She noticed the photo Jane was holding.

"You helped raise Julia and Evie, didn't you?" asked Jane.

"I did."

"Who's the other one in this picture? The boy?"

Miriam took it from her hand and stared at it for a moment. "That's Ben. My nephew. I couldn't love him any more if he were my own son. His mother left when he was only five. Nobody knows why. One day, she just took off. My brother never heard from her again. Unfortunately, Ben had some...problems when he was in high school. My brother kicked him out. He came to live with us during his junior and senior year."

Remembering Evie's comment, she asked, "Is he still living with you?"

Miriam's mouth drew into a thin, grim line. "No. He has a lovely home, but he does spend the night here once in a while. He's general manager of Barton Toys in Eagen. And he was going to be married this fall, but his fiancé... died. It was rather sudden."

"I'm sorry to hear that."

"Yes." She put her hand over the picture as if to caress

his face. "She died of complications arising from . . ." Her voice caught in her throat. Slowly, she set the picture down. "She had AIDS. We don't know exactly how she got it, but it must have been sexually transmitted. That was before she and Ben met. She didn't know she had it until just before they got engaged."

"Is Ben all right?" asked Jane.

Miriam took a long time before answering. "No. He misses her terribly. They were so much in love." She looked up. "Oh. You mean . . . does he have the virus? Yes, he's HIV positive, though he's still healthy. The doctors check his immune system all the time. It's a vicious waiting game. If you ask me, it saps all a person's strength to just remain positive. You don't know him, but he's a great kid. So decent. So loving." She stood and walked to the patio doors, keeping her face averted. "This wretched disease is killing us all. One way or another, it's going to destroy our bodies and our hearts. I simply can't lose him. Not Ben . . . it's not fair. This damnable FDA. Who do they think they are? I lost two of my dearest friends last year to the disease. One was an assistant curator at The Stroud. The other an artist. Both were so talented and bright. Sometimes I feel like there's a fire inside me. If I don't do something to put it out, I'm going to turn to ash. Of all people, you would think Charlotte would have understood. She loved Ben too. But she argued. She nitpicked. She wanted more information about this. More clarification of that. Every night was like a wrestling match. I couldn't stand it anymore."

Jane felt the back of her neck prickle with a cold dread. Was it possible? Could it be that Miriam was admitting to a murder? If she had any sense that Mae had told her the truth about The Chamber, Miriam would never be talking like this. But she felt safe in the presence of Jane's perceived ignorance. Either that or she was totally innocent and was just venting emotions to an empty room. Jane felt certain her presence in the house carried about as much weight as a buzzing fly. She looked up when she saw Miriam watching her. "I'm sorry things didn't work out for you and Charlotte." There. That was suitably mealy-mouthed.

Miriam narrowed one eye. "Thank you." She seemed to have regained her composure. Moving around a welded metal sculpture that looked for all the world like a buffalo charging an ice cream cone, Miriam stood rigidly next to the sofa. "It's getting late. I don't want to keep you any longer. It's good, don't you agree, that we had this talk?"

Jane set her unfinished glass of wine on the table. "I do. I've learned a lot." She stood, coming eye to eye with her host.

"Have you?"

"Indeed I have. And before I leave, I have one more thing to say. I want you to know that if Dorrie gets a kick out of her current *retro-mood*, I guess that's her business. Living in the past can be seductive. But it's also a waste of time. And you're her past, Miriam. I hope to god you stay there."

Miriam accompanied her to the front door. "Don't count on it."

Jane nodded. "I don't count on anything these days. Thanks for the wine. It was a bad year, Miriam. I suggest you use the rest for a marinade."

30

EVIE and Julia stepped onto the elevator and glanced simultaneously at their reflection in the tinted mirrors. Had they still been children, they would have said or done something ridiculous to annoy the other passengers crammed into the small space. Since that was no longer an option, they waited until they reached ground level to continue their conversation.

Once out on the street, Evie noticed that the traffic on Marquette Avenue wasn't as heavy as when they'd arrived. Kloster, Morescki & Bitz, Rose Gower's attorneys, opened for business at 9 A.M. They had been ushered into a private office for the reading of the will at exactly nine-fifteen. It was the first time Evie had seen Emery since the night she'd escaped from his apartment, her body bruised and bloodied, her clothing torn. Even now, it was hard to sit in the same room with him, but she couldn't let on to Julia what had really happened. Something inside her told her the entire evening had been her fault. During the reading, she'd managed to sit behind Emery so that his face wasn't visible. When he spoke up to ask a question, she could feel her body tense, but thankfully, Julia hadn't noticed. After it was over, Emery had merely nodded to her as if she were a stranger and then left. She could still feel her body trembling. She never wanted to get this close to him again.

"That bastard," said Julia, marching down the street toward the parking ramp. "The nerve of that guy to show up this morning. I think I could kill him with my bare hands."

"Rose left part of her estate at the disposal of his defense. He had a right to be there."

"Sure. Defend the ex-boyfriend. He killed our mother, Evie. Or have you forgotten?"

That stung. The last thing she wanted to do was defend Emery. "I didn't mean it that way."

Julia grumbled something unintelligible. As they reached the corner, both women stopped, waiting for the light to turn green. Julia glanced at her sister. "You look awful."

"Thanks."

"Are you getting enough sleep?"

Sleep, thought Evie. That was a laugh. Even when she tried, it didn't happen. "Sure. I'm fine. But Julia, I was wondering. I'd like to talk to you sometime soon. You know. Like old times. I sort of feel, now that Mom's gone...like...well, like there were things we never resolved. Important things. And I can't seem to let it go. I feel so alone. Confused."

"Join the club."

"You feel the same way?"

"Of course."

Yet Evie knew it wasn't the same. How could it be? Julia was the good child. Charlotte was proud of her eldest daughter's accomplishments. And especially of her good judgment. That was always the issue. Judgment. Dating Emery had been clear evidence of Evie's lack of good judgment. She could still hear her mother's voice on the phone. Emery was a mistake. Why didn't she see it? And then, after that awful night in his apartment, how could she admit her mother had been right? After all, she had *some* pride left. But then, something else happened—something which took her mother's mind off Emery forever. Evie had posed nude for a men's magazine. She'd been desperate for money. So what if her values didn't exactly mirror her mother's? It was her body, wasn't it? Her life. She could live it any way she pleased. Except Charlotte hadn't seen it that way. Somehow, she'd found out about the shoot. The pictures hadn't even been published yet, but she knew. The argument which followed was too horrible to think about. Even now, Evie shuddered when she recalled the look on her mother's face that last afternoon. Before—.

"I agree," said Julia, her voice breaking roughly into Evie's thoughts. "You and I should spend more time together. It's just . . . right now, I'm so busy with work. And I've taken on extra responsibilities at the club. I almost feel like my life is out of control."

By the shrill quality of her sister's voice, Evie could tell she wasn't kidding. "I understand."

"And this pregnancy has really exhausted me. Maybe we could get together for lunch . . . early next week? Would that be soon enough?"

"Fine."

The light changed. Julia strode briskly across the street. She was so much like their mother. She rarely complained. Everything was taken with a stiff upper lip. For her to say she felt stressed, well, it really had to be bad. Once again, Evie felt guilty for needing something. She had to get it together on her own. Be an adult. As she hopped up on the curb, she began to cry. Julia was already halfway up the block.

A drink. That's what she needed. She wiped the tears away from her face as she ran to catch up. "How's everything with you and Freddy these days?"

"What do you mean by that?" snapped Julia.

"Nothing! Jesus, cut me some slack."

"We're fine, Evie. Everything's fine."

Evie could tell Julia was covering. Something was wrong. From Evie's perspective, all this romance and happily-ever-after stuff was a crock of you know what. Julia might be older, but she had a lot to learn about life.

As they reached the lot, Julia searched through her purse for her car keys.

Evie tried again. Maybe a joke would lighten the mood. "God, Julia, you could be a night watchman at the Mall of America with that set of keys. How many do you have?"

"As many as I need," came the terse reply.

"Look, I'm not your punching bag. I'm merely trying to make conversation. You're as tight as a drum."

"I'm sorry." Julia put her hand on the hood of the car and leaned over, trying to catch her breath.

"And for god's sake, don't make everything into a marathon. You're pregnant, remember? You have to take it easy."

She nodded, looking up into Evie's face. "I really am sorry. I guess I got up on the wrong side of the bed."

Evie giggled. "Remember when we used to try to figure out which side that was? Mom caught us under Rose's bed that one time. We were poking the frame. Pulling on the springs. I couldn't have been more than five or six."

"I remember," sighed Julia. "And Rose got all hot and bothered. She thought the thing might fall on us."

"From the looks of the frame, we should have realized she was right."

Both sisters laughed.

"We will have that lunch, Evie. I promise." Julia slid behind the wheel.

Evie stood by the door.

"Aren't you coming?"

"Nah. I thought I might take a walk."

"Do a little shopping you mean. Now that we've both inherited a sizable amount of money from Rose's estate, you want to celebrate."

"Right." Evie smiled. If only that windfall could have come sooner.

"Her personal things mean the most to me," said

Julia, putting the key in the ignition. "The cloisonné. That antique comb and brush set we used to play with when we were kids."

"Yup. The personal stuff's the best."

"You made out all right too," said Julia, patting Evie's hand.

"Sure did."

"Well . . . I've got to run. I'll call you."

"Great."

"Maybe Freddy and I can make it to one of your performances next week."

"That would be nice."

"Evie?" Julia leaned her head a little way out of the car window. "Are you ok? Did I say something to upset you?"

"Nope. We'll . . . ah, talk soon then."

"Right."

Still looking hesitant, Julia backed the car up and headed for the exit. She gave a wave as she pulled out into traffic.

Evie collapsed against a pillar, checking her watch for the exact time. Almost eleven. Surely there had to be a bar open somewhere. She felt in her pocket to see how much cash she'd brought with her. A twenty. That was enough. At least for starters.

31

JANE picked up the phone and dialed her father's office. It was time for a break. She'd spent most of the day at her restaurant, catching up on paperwork.

"Law offices," said a voice Jane recognized. It belonged to Norman Tascalia, her father's clerk.

"Norm. Hi. This is Jane. Do you know when my father's expected back from Europe?"

"Last I heard, he and Marilyn were flying in late Wednesday night. I can give you the flight number if you'd like."

"That won't be necessary. Do you expect him in the office on Thursday?"

"Sure do. We've had kind of a breakthrough on the Fortnum murder case."

"Really?" That was interesting. "Care to share the information?"

"I don't see why not. The news services will have it by the end of the day. We petitioned the phone company for a record of calls made to the answering service where Emery Gower was working the night of Charlotte's death."

"Right. He said he'd gotten a call about eight telling him someone was messing with his motorcycle."

"You sound like you know the story. Well, it was a

long shot, but we came up with something important. We checked the origin of all the calls received by the answering service around eight. And guess what? The call was placed from the phone in Emery's own apartment. Someone was in there, Jane. God knows who. The thing is, we know Emery himself was at work. There was a witness. He insists no one else has keys to his place. The landlord didn't see anyone."

"Does my father know about this yet?"

"I talked to him a few minutes ago. He was the one who said to release it to the press."

Fascinating, thought Jane. She picked up a pencil and began drawing a telephone sitting on top of a question mark. "I assume you have investigators working on it."

"We do. Something may turn up at any time."

"Thanks Norm. Talk to you later."

No sooner had she hung up the phone than it began to ring. She grabbed it, placing the receiver between her shoulder and her ear. "Jane Lawless. May I help you?"

"I hope so," came a deep, rumbling voice. "This is Morris Nesbit. I believe you know my niece, Dorrie."

"Oh, hi! Sure. It's good to hear from you, Mr. Nesbit. Dorrie said you might call."

"I take it she gave you the news about our latest cookbook series."

"She did."

"Good. Good. Then I assume you're getting ready for a busy couple of months, Ms. Lawless. We don't want to skimp on any of this. Let's see. It's Monday. I would think we'd be sending a team of photographers out to your place sometime towards the end of the week. I'll see to it they make an attempt to accommodate your schedule as much as possible."

"Thanks. Ah . . . Mr. Nesbit?"

"Call me Morris."

"Right. Morris?"

"I'll put the legal department to work on the contract

ASAP. We can talk more specifics later. I think you'll be pleased with the deal."

"I'm sure I will. But I have a couple of—."

"All in good time. I can't tell you how delighted I am to have your restaurant included in our growing list. You'll be surprised at how this kind of publicity can boost your sales."

"I'm sure that's true."

"Well, nice talking to you Joan. I'll be calling you again early next week. In the meantime, start thinking about how you want to arrange the recipes. Look through some of the books I sent Dorrie. That should help. You'll want to alert your executive chef to what's happening. We want only the most current offerings. And of course, your classics. The Yorkshire Puddings. The Beef Wellingtons. Those wonderful scones I had for breakfast early one cold January morning. Ah, I remember your restaurant well. We'll talk soon. Bye for now." The line clicked.

Morris Nesbit was obviously a man used to *directing*. Jane dropped the receiver back on the hook and leaned back wearily in her chair. What was she going to do about all this? He'd taken her acceptance as a matter of course.

Outside her door, Jane heard the unmistakable sound of Cordelia's voice. She braced herself for the usual dramatic entrance.

Instead, Cordelia limped into the room with some difficulty, carrying a large bed pillow under one arm. With a pathetic look on her face, she hobbled over to Jane's desk.

"Planning on spending the night?" asked Jane, raising an eyebrow.

Cordelia grunted, placing the pillow in a chair and then easing herself down. "I've just come from the Allen Grimby. You can imagine how delightful it was trying to stuff this thing into one of those narrow theatre seats. Absolutely everyone was enjoying my discomfort immensely. That idiot lighting engineer kept shining a spot on me every time I got up to offer my words of wisdom to this actor, or that. My efforts to sit down were particularly appreciated. Consequently, I spent the day directing a vaudeville. True, the play *is* a comedy, but today even the straight lines were a cause for unprecedented hilarity. As I was leaving the theatre, I was treated to an especially ribald rendition of *She's an Old Cow Hand From the Rio Grande.*" She closed her eyes. "It was a ghastly day."

"I can see that." Jane leaned forward to examine the pillow more closely. "If I might be so . . . indelicate. Why are you sitting on that thing?"

Cordelia raised her eyes to the ceiling, her expression one of supplication. "Six hours on a horse."

"Excuse me?"

"Mugs and I went horseback riding yesterday."

"Ah."

"It was nothing but an ordeal from start to finish. I am not a pioneer, Janey."

"I never said you were."

"Be it ever so humble, there's no place like the front seat of my Buick Le Sabre for getting a person around."

"Indeed."

Her head sank down on her chest. "My horse didn't like me."

"Oh, I'm sure you're wrong."

"No. It tried to bite me. Twice."

"That's terrible."

"And it stepped on my foot when I was trying to give it a friendly pat."

"I'm sure it was an accident."

"Why do I always fail at these . . . these naturalistic experiences, Janey?"

"You're being too hard on yourself."

"*Because*," she shrieked, "I do not belong in the woods! That's why." She yanked her blouse into place. "Furry things belong in the woods. Slithery, odd-smelling . . . creeping things." She hunched her shoulders and made a creeping movement with her fingers.

196

"And you would never creep."

"Exactly!" She glanced at the doodles on Jane's desk. "Now, not to change the subject too abruptly, but I see *you've* certainly been hard at work today."

Jane grinned. "I suppose, given your present damaged state, that I can't coerce you into accompanying me to Wizards tonight."

"What could you possibly need to do at such a . . . tacky establishment?"

"I want to talk to Evie Fortnum. That's where she's singing."

"Figures. Last time I saw her, her hair looked like a badly arranged mound of cotton candy." She shifted uncomfortably in her chair. "Anything in particular you want to talk to her about?"

"Two things, actually. I found out she's a friend of Doyle Benedict's."

"The steward at the club."

"Right. Interestingly, he belongs to Sigma Delta Fraternity over at the U."

"Sigma Delta? Wasn't that the name on that pin we found behind the wall?"

"It was. Beryl also discovered something equally interesting. It seems Doyle was in charge of the door prizes given out at the Sigma Delta homecoming bash last Friday night. Guess what they were?"

"Gilded jock straps? Personalized condoms?"

"Music boxes, Cordelia. A magician pulling a rabbit out of a hat."

"No kidding." She whistled.

"Evie sang at that party. I want to ask her a couple of questions."

"I don't doubt it. But be careful now, dearheart. That business at your house on Friday night should give you great pause. Somebody out there's playing pretty nasty. By the way, not to change the subject again, but how's Beryl taking all this?"

"She's not saying much, but I know it's bothering her. I suggested she stay with Peter and Sigrid until this is all over. I think she's going to do it."

"I don't know if that's good or bad."

"What do you mean?"

"Leaving you alone in that house."

"I'll be fine."

"Right. Famous last words."

Jane smiled. "Your concern is touching. So? Are you game? Do you want to come with me tonight?"

Cordelia's expression again grew pathetic. "Oh Janey, I can barely walk, let alone sit. I'm afraid I'll have to pass. You understand."

Jane nodded. "Go home and take a hot bath."

"Come to think of it, you shouldn't be going to a place like that alone. Why don't you wait a day. I should be right as rain by tomorrow night. I promise. We'll storm the citadel together. Tie Evie up by her thumbs and demand she tell us everything she knows. That should take about a minute and a half."

Again, Jane smiled. "I'll think about it."

"Good. Say, by the way . . ." Cordelia hesitated.

"What?"

"Well, have you . . . you know. Talked to Dorrie recently?"

Jane tossed her pencil on the desk. "I thought I'd give myself the weekend to cool off. Try to gain some perspective."

"She'll call."

Jane's expression was bleak. "I don't have the time to dwell on it right now anyway. I suppose that's good."

Cordelia unclogged herself from the chair and stood, rubbing the small of her back. "It is. Now. I'm going to let you get back to your doodling."

"Thanks a lot."

"And call me tomorrow."

"I will."

Cordelia held up one hand. "Don't get up, Janey. I have every confidence I can make it to the parking lot before I collapse. I *will* say, I think the person who invented the horse was undoubtedly a sadist. Something's obviously wrong with the basic design." She passed into the hallway.

Jane could hear her spouting inanities all the way to the front door. She couldn't help but shake her head and wonder what the world be like without Cordelia Thorn. It was too dreadful to even contemplate.

32

JANE knocked on Evie's dressing room door. Even this far back of Wizards' main stage, the air was thick with smoke and the acrid smell of sweat. Since no response was forthcoming, she knocked harder, calling, "Anybody here?"

"It's open," came a thick, slurred voice.

Cautiously, Jane stepped inside.

The room was tiny. Musty and windowless. An ancient folding chair stood in one corner, a bunch of coats tossed haphazardly over the seat. Ripped rock posters dangled from the scuffed walls. A single mirror had been hung low over what remained of a card table. There was only one comfortable resting place in the entire room. A dark green, mohair couch, circa 1950. Evie's thin body was slumped against one of the arms, her head in her hands.

"What do you want?" She didn't look up.

"It's Jane Lawless. Remember me?"

Evie lifted her head. She'd been crying. Her eyes also seemed something less than focused. "Oh. Yeah. Hi." She closed her eyes again and leaned her head back slowly.

"Are you all right?" Jane could smell the alcohol on her breath.

Evie began to laugh. "Oh, I'm just dandy. Never better." She tried to wave her arm but it fell limply to her lap.

"Would you like me to get you anything?"

"Someone already is. That is, unless you're offering a new life." She attempted to open one eye.

"No. Sorry."

She grew very still. Jane began to wonder if she'd fallen asleep. Then, stirring, Evie asked, "How's that rich daddy of yours?"

It was a stab at conversation. Jane was grateful. "He's fine."

"Oh, good. I wouldn't want him to be anything less than fine."

"Look," said Jane, perching on the other end of the couch, "I was wondering if you could help me with a couple of things." She knew this wasn't a very good time, but since she was already here, she felt compelled to give it a shot.

"Like what?"

"Well, first. I was curious about your friend, Doyle Benedict. Did you ever see him with a Sigma Delta fraternity pin?"

Evie coughed a couple of times, passing a hand through her pink hair. "He had one a couple weeks ago. Bogus piece of shit. He won't get a pin of his own until sometime around Christmas. I think he won it in a poker game."

"Did he ever offer it to you?"

"Sure. He tried. But I'm not that hard up." She rubbed her temples and sat up a bit.

"So you never took it?"

"Do I look that stupid?"

"You said the other night that you'd sung at the Sigma Delta Homecoming party."

"Lucky me."

"Do you remember the door prizes that were given out?"

She scrunched her face together and tried to focus her eyes. "You mean those music boxes?"

"I don't suppose you noticed who received them?"

She shrugged, glancing at Jane out of the corner of her eye. "Nope."

Jane paused for a moment. "Who are Doyle's friends?"

"His...friends? Well, I suppose guys from the frat house mainly."

"Anybody from the club?"

Her eyes narrowed. "Yeah. Well, before Emery was arrested, they hung around some. No accounting for taste."

"But you dated Emery. You must have thought he was ok once."

"Maybe."

"Forgive my curiosity, but what did you see in him? I met him a couple of days ago. I wasn't terribly impressed."

Evie gave her head a tiny shake. "You'd probably think I'm seriously shallow if I tell you the truth."

"Try me."

She stifled a small hiccup. "Well...see, he has a great body. That's it. I was attracted, ok? His mind was another thing." Her head tilted back. "I couldn't believe he'd treat me that way this morning. That royal fucking bastard."

"This morning?"

"At the lawyers' office. Julia and I went there 'cause they were reading Rose's will."

"Emery was there too?"

"He looked right through me! Like I was invisible. Like nothing had ever happened. God, he makes my skin crawl." She scraped at her arms with the palms of her hands.

"Were you and Julia mentioned in Rose's will?"

Evie suddenly tensed. She sat up very straight. "Fifty thousand dollars each. But the personal possessions mean the most." Her voice had become flat, mechanical.

"What personal possessions?"

"Julia got the cloisonné flower pots, a carved ivory let-

202

ter opener, and Rose's comb and brush set."

"And you?"

"Oh, I was the luckiest of all. I got Rose's collection of children's books. The ones she used to read to us when we were small. And of course, her favorite shawl."

"Does that make you happy?"

"Happy? Why in my book Peter Rabbit is right up there with Jackie Collins. All that sex and scandal in the cabbage patch. My kind of stuff. Oh, and I really want to wear something someone died in. That would definitely make my day."

Jane heard a soft knock on the door. A second later Freddy backed into the room, carrying a tray spread with coffee and donuts. When he saw her, his worried expression turned to one of anger. "What are you doing here?" he demanded.

Jane stood. "Freddy. Hi. I just wanted to speak with Evie for a few moments."

He set the metal tray on the card table and then turned. "Well, as you may have already seen, she's in no shape for a social call." He seemed terribly agitated.

Evie lifted her head when she smelled the coffee. "Yuk. I told you to bring me a vodka."

Freddy's frown deepened as he handed Evie a mug. "I'm afraid I'm going to have to ask you to leave, Jane."

"Of course. If there's anything I can do—."

"Nothing."

Since she already felt like an intruder, she quickly crossed to the door, closing it softly behind her.

She hurried to the rear exit. Suddenly, a metal tray crashed violently to the floor. She could hear Evie begin to sob, calling out something about her sister, Julia. Then another crash. Probably the mug of coffee hitting the wall. Jane could hear Freddy's voice trying to calm her down.

Gratefully, Jane stepped into the cool night air. Freddy had his hands full. At least Evie had somebody with her who cared. She was obviously a very troubled young woman. Jane felt guilty for having to pump her for information—especially in the state she was in tonight. But she'd learned something important. That fraternity pin had belonged to Doyle. And Doyle had also purchased the music boxes for Sigma Delta. It was all connected. All she had to do was follow the trail and see where it led.

Jane inhaled deeply, trying to rid her lungs of the smell of Wizards. Then, taking a moment to get her bearings, she made her way out of the dark alley. As she walked along, an idea was forming in her mind. On her way home, why not make a run over to the club? See if Doyle was working tonight. If he was, she had a few questions she wanted to ask him as well.

At the edge of the building a figure stepped out of the shadows, blocking her exit. "Ms. Lawless. How nice to see you again."

Jane stopped dead. "Emery."

"I'm flattered that you'd remember me." His smile was more of a sneer. "I understand your father will be back in town Wednesday night. What do you think of a lawyer who goes off and leaves his client high and dry in the middle of a murder investigation?"

"He's hardly left you high and dry."

"No?" His mouth twitched.

What did he want? She tried to move around him, but he continued to block her path.

"I've been sitting across the street over there"—he pointed—"on my motorcycle. I saw Freddy bring Evie in. She didn't look too good, if you ask me. Poor girl. She has a lot of problems."

"And you feel sorry for her."

"Why certainly I do. What kind of man do you think I am?"

Best not to answer that one, thought Jane. "Well, if you'll excuse me." Once again, she tried to move around him.

He put out his hand. "I was hoping you'd stay and

have a drink with me. I know what you're thinking, you know. How could this young stud be attracted to an older woman. But, actually, you're quite . . . quite lovely. I suppose guys tell you that all the time."

"Not really."

"No?" He moved closer. "I've thought about you a lot since you came to visit me. I understand now. You probably saw my picture in the paper. It's all right. I'm not mad." He stroked her arm. "I was mad for a while, but I got over it. Most of the time I'm a nice guy. Real nice."

She backed up several steps. "Look, I'm already late for an appointment."

"No you're not," he said, his voice dropping to its most seductive register. This time he grabbed her roughly, pinning her against the brick wall.

"Get . . . get away from me!" She struggled to free her wrists.

"Why? You like this. I can tell. You wanted it the other day but you were too shy to ask."

"I'll scream!"

"Great. I like feisty women." He put one hand on her breast and spread his legs, pressing his mouth hard against hers.

Realizing it was now or never, Jane brought her free hand around behind his neck and grabbed his hair, yanking it back with all her might. Startled, Emery released her other hand. In an instant, she smashed a finger into his right eye. She knew her aim had been bad, yet it was enough to send him howling to the ground.

It was no longer time for conversation. She took off around the corner, running as fast as she could. When she got to her car, she saw that every tire was flat. "Great!" she shouted to no one in particular. She looked behind her, noticing a taxi pull around the corner. She waved furiously but it drove past without stopping. Damn! This wasn't rational, but she felt as if Emery was everywhere. She even glanced at the tree tops. Then, another taxi pulled around the corner. This time, she was prepared. She dashed into the street and held up her arms. The driver either had to hit her or stop. He honked his horn.

"This is an emergency!" she shouted, pounding on the hood. She reached into her pocket and drew out two twenty dollar bills, waving them over her head. The driver hesitated for a moment and then waved to the rear door. Jane hopped in. "Do you know where The Amelia Gower Women's Club is?"

"I'm on my way to another fare, lady."

She threw the money at him.

He turned to stare at her. One look must have convinced him she wasn't kidding about the emergency. "Ok. Over by the Walker, right?"

"Right." As they sped past Wizards, she caught sight of Emery coming out of the alley. He was looking in the direction of her car. "Step on it, will you?"

"You got it." He clicked on the meter.

Shivering, Jane leaned back into the seat, folding her arms tightly over her chest. It was just beginning to dawn on her what kind of danger she'd actually been in. Breathe, she ordered herself. Just calm down. As she rested her head against the glass, looking out at the city speeding past, her thoughts turned to Evie. That poor kid had terminally bad judgment to get mixed up with someone like Emery Gower. Had she been treated to this same kind of violent behavior? Jane closed her eyes. In the end, that might turn out to be the sixty-four thousand dollar question.

33

JANE thanked the taxi driver and then climbed the steps to the front door of the club. Since it was just after nine, with no special activities scheduled for the evening, the main floor rooms contained very few members. Jane walked slowly and a bit shakily down the hall, peeking into this door and that. Only in the food storage room did she find any activity. Julia and Mae were calling out the names of food items as they unpacked the donated bags and boxes. Two women sat in the back with clipboards, checking items off a prepared list.

Retracing her steps to the dining room, Jane entered and sat at one of the tables in the back. She glanced briefly at the painting of Amelia Gower, realizing the woman's quiet bearing and composed face were in sharp contrast to her own. At some point, she knew the trembling would stop, but for now, all she could do was take deep breaths and try to relax. Here, at least, she was safe. She waited, biding her time by looking out the window, until a waiter arrived.

"Good evening," he said pleasantly. "The soup this evening is a cream of potato and leek."

Jane smiled at him, taking the menu from his hand. "I don't suppose Doyle Benedict is working tonight?"

"Doyle? Sure. Would you like me to get him? I think he's taking a break in the kitchen."

"That would be great. Thanks."

"Can I bring you anything from the bar?"

Jane glanced up at the doorway. Julia was standing alone near the receptionist's desk, staring at her. Her scowl was intense, almost threatening. Hearing someone call her name, Julia turned her face to the side and nodded. Her eyes found Jane's for one last second before she strode away.

The young man cleared his throat. "Ma'am?"

"What?"

"Anything from the bar?"

"Ah...sure. I'd like a Manhattan. On second thought, tell the bartender to make it a double." Thanks to Emery, all four of the tires on her car were flat. She wasn't going to be doing any driving tonight. Once again, her mind flashed to the scene in that dark alley. She shuddered as she thought of his mouth on hers. Her father was going to hit the ceiling when he found out. Emery Gower would no doubt be looking for a new lawyer. Picking up the menu, she noticed her waiter enter the kitchen. A few moments later, Doyle came out into the dining room, giving her a wave before ducking into the bar. After what seemed like an eternity, he reappeared carrying her drink.

"Might as well make myself useful," he smiled, setting it down in front of her. "All my tables have already left for the night."

She motioned him to a chair.

"I understand you wanted to talk to me."

"I did." She felt inside the pocket of her jeans for the fraternity pin. "Have you ever seen this before?"

He took it from her hand, saying nothing as he rolled it between his fingers.

"Well?"

"Where did you get it?"

"Is it yours?"

"Maybe." He placed it on the table. "Technically, it belongs to a guy named Jason Price. But he had two measly pair to my three of a kind. What can I say? I'm lucky."

Jane took several sips of her drink.

"You didn't answer my question, Ms. Lawless. Where did you find it?"

Jane suspected he already knew. "In the passageway behind the conference room bookcase. You know the spot."

He spent a moment realigning the silverware. "And what if I do?"

"Let's quit beating around the bush, ok? How did you find out about those passageways?" She took another sip and held the glass in front of her, waiting.

"Well," he smiled, "it's kind of a long story."

"I've got plenty of time."

He ran a hand over his crew cut. "All right. But on one condition."

"What's that?"

"You have to promise not to tell anyone I was behind there. I could lose my job."

"We'll see."

"No promise, no deal."

Jane thought for a moment. What did she have to lose? "Ok, it's a deal."

He gave her a smug smile. Leaning back in his chair, he said, "After Charlotte Fortnum moved into that apartment up on second floor, Evie used to come into the club late at night, when she was all done at Wizards. Sometimes she was pretty far gone—you know what I mean. Since we sort of liked each other for a while, she'd wait for me either in the library or that conference room. I'd come in here, work for a while, and then take a break. Then I'd sneak back to where she was supposedly waiting. One night I caught her going through the bookcase. That's it. She couldn't exactly hide what she was up to. So she took me back there and showed me around. This may sound strange, but I found it . . . romantic. That's where I tried to give her the pin."

"Did she take it?"

He shook his head. "It wasn't my night. And then I lost it. The next day I went back . . . I felt kind of strange about it. But it was such a hoot. I even started eating lunch in there, when I knew no one was around. It was sort of peaceful."

"Peaceful?"

He shrugged.

"How did you usually enter?"

"Always through the conference room bookcase. Most of the time, that room is empty."

Jane continued to sip her drink. "Did anyone ever come into the conference room while you were back there?"

"Nope. Never."

She didn't believe him, but what could she do? She couldn't beat the truth out of him. "I understand you're a pretty good friend of Emery Gower's."

"Who told you that?"

"From what I can tell, it's common knowledge."

He stuck a finger between his tight collar and his very thick neck, tugging the fabric away from his skin. "Sure. We played some handball together a few times. Had a few beers."

"Have you ever been in his apartment?"

"His apartment? No, not that I recall." He fidgeted with his tie for a moment and then made a move to get up.

She didn't want to spook him. She still had one more question. "Just one other thing. It's about those music boxes you bought for Sigma Delta."

"What about them?"

"Do you remember anybody who might have received one the night of the homecoming party?"

"I bought them, but I didn't have anything to do with that. I was busy . . . elsewhere." His grin was pregnant with meaning.

Jane got the point. "You don't remember *anybody* who walked out with one?"

He shook his head.

"Was anyone from the women's club there that night?"

"Just Evie. And I suppose she's not really even a member here."

"How many music boxes did you buy—originally."

"Twelve. It was all the place had."

"Were all twelve still available for prizes the night of the party?"

"How should I know? Besides, why all the questions about a stupid music box? Do you want to buy one or something?"

This time, he didn't appear to be lying. Then again, he could also be a good actor. He pushed away from the table. "You're weird, you know that? And anyway, my break is about over. I think I'd better get back to the kitchen."

"All right."

"Since I'm headed that direction, can I get you anything else?" His eyes fell to her drink.

"Sure. Some of that potato leek soup would be nice."

"Ok. I'll tell your waiter." He got up quickly and dashed back to the kitchen.

Jane was starting to feel a slight buzz. It felt good to finally relax. And anyway, the idea of going home depressed her. She'd come to rely on the companionship and love of her aunt. Without her there, the house seemed uninviting. As she was toying with the idea of spending the night at Cordelia's, her waiter walked up carrying a small silver plate.

"For you," he said, bowing slightly as he left it on the table. In the center was a small piece of paper, the name *Jane* written on the outside.

She finished her drink and then picked it up, unfolding it and reading silently.

211

Meet me outside by the back gate.
I need to talk to you.

Julia

Jane looked up, lost in thought. After a few minutes, the waiter returned, this time carrying the steaming soup and a basket of bread. Before he reached the table, Jane had slipped out of her chair. She was about to tell him to just leave it—she'd be right back—when her legs suddenly buckled and she stumbled against a wooden pillar.

"Whoa," he said, catching her by the arm.

She steadied herself, a surprised look on her face. "I must be a little high." She felt momentarily dizzy.

"Are you all right?"

"Alcohol doesn't usually affect me this way." She smiled apologetically.

"Maybe you should sit for a minute. Have something to eat."

"No. I'm fine." She passed a hand over her eyes. I have to . . . I'll be right back."

"Of course."

Feeling a bit embarrassed, she headed directly for the rear delivery entrance. A good dose of fresh air would clear her head. The back gate was about thirty yards from the main house. Unfortunately, the parking lot lights didn't reach quite that far. By the time she got to the appointed spot, the dizziness was becoming worse. She put out a hand and leaned against a rock wall, shaking her head again and again. Julia was nowhere in sight. Since Jane didn't have a jacket—and since the night wind had turned bitter—she hoped she wouldn't have long to wait.

She sat down on a bench. Glancing up at the sky, she noticed the clouds part, revealing a full, harvest moon. But . . . something was wrong. She rubbed her eyes and looked again. The moon was a bloody shade of red! And it seemed to be throbbing. She got up immediately and started for the back door of the club. She had to get some help. She could feel her body shutting down. As she moved along, the ground seemed to draw her toward it like a magnet. Worst of all, her mind was descending deeper and deeper into a strange place. When her legs finally gave out and she felt her body hit the concrete, the reverie was so intense and so pleasant, she almost didn't care.

34

THE tranquil sound of water lapping against wood woke Jane from a deep sleep. As her grasp on consciousness became more firm, she found herself lying flat on her stomach on the sandy floor of what appeared to be a shed. Her hands were tied securely behind her back, a piece of heavy tape stretched across her mouth. Her feet were also bound. She made a valiant attempt to roll over, but found her body bruised and stiff. Any movement caused pain. Realizing the futility of her situation—at least for now—she lay very still. She moved her head slightly to the side and saw through an open door that she was mere yards from a rather weedy lake shore. A sailboat was moored about twenty feet from the end of a metal dock. Another boat, this one a rowboat, was tied to the center of the dock. In the distance a lawn mower buzzed. She listened for a moment, realizing it was coming nearer.

What had happened? Her mind struggled to recover the details of—had it been last night? How long had she been out of it? She remembered the note from Julia. She also recalled walking out by the stone gate in back of the club. Then?

Her most vivid recollection was the feeling of weakness and disorientation which had gripped her so suddenly. Someone must have put something in the Manhattan she'd been drinking. But who? And where was she now? Somewhere during all of this, she remembered opening her eyes. She was inside a car. It was pitch dark and she was being driven down a bumpy, country road. She knew she was out of the city because the smell of sweet grass was so strong. And then . . . nothing. She couldn't remember a single thing until a few minutes ago. As she closed her eyes in an attempt to concentrate all her effort, she realized the lawn mower was almost on top of her. Suddenly, the motor died. She could hear someone muttering. Then, the sound of wooden steps creaking under the weight of heavy boots. She stretched her neck and saw a shadow fall across the open doorway.

"Goddamn piece of shit," said a male voice. A second later, Freddy walked into the shed, kicking an empty paint can out of his way.

Jane felt herself freeze. Her breathing became rapid and shallow.

He stopped next to a work bench. Jane watched as he rummaged through a drawer. She didn't know whether to lie still and hope he went away, or thrash around to get his attention. Most of her body was hidden behind a stack of boxes. If she didn't move, he might not see her. Then again, he might be her only hope. She decided to wait.

Still muttering about the lawn mower, she saw him bend down and search through a bunch of small cans near the door. "Success!" he whispered, apparently finding the one he wanted. "Now." He turned, his eyes taking in the entire room. "If I were a funnel, where would I hide?" He walked a few paces toward the back. "What the—?"

Jane saw his feet as they moved in front of her face.

Quickly, he knelt down, grabbing her by the shoulders. "Are you all right?" He attempted to turn her over. "Jane!"

She felt him lean over her, yanking the ropes away from her hands.

"You take that tape off your mouth. I'll get your feet."

She rubbed her wrists for a few moments to get the feeling back in her fingers. Slowly, she pulled off the tape.

"How did you get here?" he asked, tossing the ropes in a corner. His face was full of concern.

"I don't know." Her voice was hoarse, her reactions thick and slow. She decided she was probably still affected by whatever had knocked her out. "Where am I?"

"Do you want some water? There's a sink upstairs."

She shook her head.

He watched her for a moment and then leaned down and helped her to a sitting position. "This is The Gower Foundation summer lodge." When she continued to look confused, he added, "Brown Deer is the closest town. Do you know where that is?"

She nodded. "My family has a cabin on Blackberry Lake."

"Sure. That's less than five miles from here."

"What lake is this?" She glanced again at the sailboat, rubbing the back of her neck.

"Old Sawmill."

"What day is it?"

"What day? Why, it's Tuesday." He checked his watch. "It's nearly five in the afternoon."

Five P.M. She'd been asleep for . . . her mind resisted the arithmetic. "I'm cold."

"Of course. What am I thinking." He took off his jacket and wrapped it around her shoulders.

"How . . . why are you here?"

"Well. . . ." He sat down next to her. "I drive up on the weekends to mow the grass. I like the exercise and the extra money comes in handy. I didn't get a chance to do it last weekend, so that's why I came today. Nobody was scheduled. I didn't think it was a big deal."

"What do you mean scheduled?" She ran a hand through her hair, brushing out the sand. None of this was making any sense. She felt an overpowering urge to giggle.

216

When Freddy spoke, his nose twitched like some cherubic cartoon rabbit. She knew her reactions were...inappropriate—a good nineties word—since every minute she sat here chatting with him, her life was probably in danger. Nevertheless, she couldn't seem to move.

"Is something funny?" He looked down at his chambray shirt.

She shook her head, rearranging her face into something more suitably grim. "Go on."

"Well, Miriam Cipriani insisted on buying this place several years ago. It was a good tax write-off for the foundation, and it allowed the top brass and their families access to some summer boating and fishing. The main house is about half a mile up the road which runs just back of the boat house here. Anyway, there's a sign-up sheet kept by the secretary at the main offices, downtown. I checked to see if anyone was going to use the lodge this past weekend. With all the problems right now, no one had signed up. So, I figured if the grass didn't get cut right on schedule no one would be the wiser."

"I heard the lawn mower." There. That was a sensible thing to say.

"Yeah." He glanced at the can of oil. "It's an old one. I keep it in the machine shed in back of the main house. I filled the thing with gas, as usual, but it cut out on me just as I came up over the rise. I think it needs oil. I knew the boat shed probably had some, so that's why I came in. Good thing I did."

Jane smiled amiably. Then she frowned. She didn't know what to do. If he was here, maybe he was the one who'd brought her in the first place. Perhaps this was all some kind of elaborate charade.

"Do you remember how you got here?" asked Freddy.

She eased herself back against the wall, summoning all her strength to clear her mind. "I don't remember much of anything. I was at the club one minute. The next, I woke up with sand in my face."

"The club?"

She could see a look of surprise grow in his eyes. It was probably best to say as little as possible. Until she knew more, she couldn't trust anyone.

"Look, I think I should call the police. I don't mean to alarm you, but you don't look so hot."

From outside came the sound of a car. Freddy got up and moved to a small window. "Hum. Looks like Miriam's Lincoln. God, she's going to have my ass." He rubbed his hands against the sides of his jeans.

At the sound of her name, a jolt of adrenaline shot through Jane's body, sobering her up like nothing else could. What was *she* doing here? "Don't tell her about me."

He turned around. "What?"

"Is the car stopping? Does she look like she's coming in?"

He returned his gaze to the window. "Yeah. She's pulled up next to the big willow. She probably saw my car up by the main house and then noticed the lawn was half cut."

Jane began to search for a way of escape. There was only one door. The one he'd come in. "Freddy, you've got to do me a huge favor. Don't tell her you found me in here. Play dumb."

"What? Why? You're going to call the police, aren't you? This has to be reported."

"There's no time to explain. Just get rid of her."

"But . . ."

"Please!" Her vehemence said it all.

"Ok." He hesitated. "I'll take care of it. Just sit tight." He grabbed the oil can and strode confidently outside to her car.

Jane eased herself into a standing position and peeked out through a crack in the wall. Freddy seemed to be doing a lot of smiling and gesturing. Miriam glanced several times at the boathouse, but didn't make a move toward it.

After issuing her normal commands, she got back in her car and backed up, returning down the road toward the lodge. Shielding his eyes from the bright sun, Freddy waited until the car was out of sight and then returned to the shed.

"All clear."

"Thanks." Her legs felt like rubber.

Seeing she was about to fall, Freddy rushed over and put his arm around her waist. "Are you all right? Maybe we should get you to a doctor first? I can call the police from the hospital."

"What did Miriam say?"

"She wants to take the sailboat out."

"That's all?"

"She asked me what I was doing in the boat shed. I told her I needed some oil."

"And?"

"I told her I'd found it. Then she said to cut the damn grass and leave *ASAP*. I got the impression she's expecting someone. She wants to be alone."

Jane's first thought was of Dorrie. Then again, maybe there was another reason she wanted to be alone.

"So." Freddy helped her over to an ancient lawn chair. "What do you want me to do?"

All she wanted was to lie back down in the sand and go to sleep. Not a good sign. "I . . . I don't know. I'm not sure." Her brain felt completely scrambled. She had to concentrate.

"Look, I've got an idea. About thirty yards down the shore there's another dock. The Gower houseboat is moored there. Why don't I help you out to it. You can rest on one of the beds until I'm done with the grass. Then, I'll take you to the sheriff in Brown Deer. Or back to Minneapolis. Whatever you want."

Yes. Fine idea. She nodded her assent. Still, something inside her continued to resist the notion of trusting him. Unfortunately, in this weakened state, she had little choice.

She couldn't run. Her brain was too thick to think her way out. As far as she could see, it was Freddy or Miriam. Take your pick.

Freddy helped her to her feet. "Everything's going to be fine. You'll see."

Right, thought Jane. Famous last words. She leaned her weight on his shoulder and together they started for the houseboat.

35

"Just pull into the drive," said Jane, feeling like she could kiss the ground under which Cordelia's car was parked. True to his word, Freddy had finished mowing the grass and then brought her in his Oldsmobile all the way back to Cordelia's doorstep. She hadn't spoken much during the drive, dozing off and on. She did remember Freddy trying to make conversation. He said something about proposing marriage to Julia while standing under the big willow, just in back of the boathouse. He loved the area. The lake especially. Jane realized she was picturing all of this in her mind's eye, Freddy taking Julia's hand in his, slipping on the engagement ring. The two of them kissing under the delicate willow branches. As he talked, she continued to see pictures inside her mind. Freddy said he and Julia took the houseboat out at least once a month. He'd even done some of the work for his doctoral thesis while sitting at the small table in the aft cabin. He'd done his best thinking there, calling those times the happiest and most peaceful he'd ever known.

"Do you want me to help you to the door?" he asked, ready to jump out of the front seat.

Jane shook her head. "I think I can make it that far under my own steam." She smiled, taking in his handsome face. She had to admit, she was curious about Freddy

Lindhurst, and about his marriage to Julia. Had she been in better mental shape, she would have taken this as an opportunity to find out more about the family. About Charlotte and Evie. But, as it was, she was doing well just to stay awake.

"I'd like to ask you one question before I go," said Freddy, putting his hands on the wheel and looking straight ahead. "Correct me if I'm wrong, but you seemed kind of...scared of Miriam when I first found you. Why?"

The question took her by surprise. All she could manage to say was, "I don't trust her."

"Do you think she was responsible for dumping you in that shed?"

"Right now, I don't know anything for sure."

He revved the motor, giving himself a moment to think. "Well. I guess I'd better shove off. I told Julia I'd be home by seven. If I'm late, she worries." He smiled. "I hope you feel better soon. Let me know if there's anything I can do."

"Thanks for everything, Freddy. You may have saved my life. I won't forget it." Slowly, she got out and closed the door behind her. After he'd driven away, she dragged herself up the steps to Cordelia's front door. When Freddy had asked what she wanted to do, all she could think about was getting back to Minneapolis. Yet, she realized she couldn't stand the idea of going home to an empty house. She was frightened of spending the night all alone. Beryl had contacted Evelyn Bratrude, their next door neighbor, about taking care of the dogs while she was staying with Peter. So, nothing to worry about there. The house was locked securely. Another night away shouldn't be a problem. Besides, she was still weak. And Cordelia had a nice, soft couch.

She rang the doorbell.

No answer.

She waited for a reasonable period of time and then

knocked. This time, the door swung open almost instantly.

Cordelia, dressed like a matador and holding a cat under each arm, gave a whoop of surprise. "Get in here," she ordered, turning her back and charging into the living room. She dropped the cats on a chair and then whirled around. "Where were you? I just got off the phone with your brother. Your restaurant has been calling him all day looking for you." She stopped when she saw Jane begin to collapse against the archway. "Janey!" She rushed to her side and helped her to the couch. "What's wrong?"

"It's a long story. Let's just say I had quite a night. Oh, and I guess a day too. I've kind of lost track of time."

"Look at you! Your face is bruised and scratched. And your clothes. They're all dirty and torn." She grabbed Jane's hands. "And your wrists!" She grimaced.

"I'll tell you everything if you make me a cup of tea."

Cordelia pressed her hand against Jane's forehead. "*Tea* my Aunt Clarice. You have a fever. You need to see a doctor."

"No doctors."

"No? We'll see about that." She straightened her cape and marched out into the hall, throwing open the front door and disappearing down the steps.

Jane took the opportunity to kick off her shoes and drink in the safety and comfort of Cordelia's theatrically embellished living room. The softness of the sofa felt like heaven. A few minutes later she heard Cordelia return. This time, there was another voice.

"Arnold, this is Jane Lawless. Don't get up, Jane. Arnold is my neighbor. He's also a GP. And a damn good one, as he so often likes to point out. He's going to check you over."

Jane groaned.

"No carping. Just shut up and let him do his job. Now, I shall retire to the kitchen and put on the kettle. Give a holler when the examination is done. I shall want a complete report."

Arnold pulled up the coffee table and sat down. He set his medical bag on the floor. "So, what seems to be the trouble?"

Fifteen minutes later, Arnold entered the kitchen. Cordelia was just putting the finishing touches on a linen-covered tray spread with snacks and her favorite china tea service. She'd taken off her cape and matador's hat and tossed them on the counter near the sink.

"Food is a good idea," said Arnold, making himself comfortable at the kitchen table. "She's had a rough time of it."

"Did she tell you the whole story?"

"I doubt it." He reached for a slice of apple. "Just what she wanted me to know for medical reasons. Someone slipped something into a Manhattan she'd been drinking last night. It knocked her out cold. When she came to, she was in an unheated shed about fifty miles north of the city. She wouldn't be any more specific than that. It gets pretty cold during the early morning hours this time of year. Especially out in the country. She's suffering from exposure. The cuts and bruises will heal in time. I think she's pretty sore. She must have been dragged for some distance. As far as the drug that's in her system, I can't be sure what it is unless I do some blood work. She insists she feels much better and doesn't want to go to that kind of trouble. I can't force her, so I let it drop. Just make sure she drinks a lot of liquids." He popped the apple into his mouth. "Suffice it to say, she's going to live."

"You're such a poet, Arnold."

"Thank you." As he was about to grab another slice, Cordelia slapped his hand.

"Now. You toodle on home. I wouldn't want you to miss another moment of CNN."

"We can't let the world pass us by."

"Certainly not." She lifted the tray and walked behind

him into the front hall. "Give my love to Grace."

"Will do. And one more thing." He lowered his voice. "My advice to your friend in there was to report this to the police as soon as possible. This is a clear case of kidnapping—possibly even attempted murder."

"What did she say when you told her that?"

"She said she'd think about it. I don't know what there is to think about," he grumbled. "At any rate, be sure to keep her warm and quiet. At least for the next twenty-four hours."

Cordelia lowered her chin and raised one eyebrow. "I'm afraid for that, dear Arnold, I shall need a pair of handcuffs and a gun."

Cordelia entered the living room and immediately brushed away a cat who had just taken up residence on the coffee table. She set the tray down and then eased onto the couch next to Jane. "The doctor says you'll live."

"But will I find true happiness?" she asked, eyeing the plate of food. Apples, cheese and crackers, and two Twinkies. How utterly Cordelia.

"You have your sense of humor back, I see. Such as it is. I suppose that's a good sign." She poured the tea. "Now drink up. Doctor's orders."

Jane welcomed the cup, taking it from Cordelia's hand. Beryl had said once that Jane must certainly be half English. At times like this, she knew her aunt was right. A cup of Earl Grey didn't solve everything, but it certainly helped.

"Now," said Cordelia, "I want the details. What happened to you last night?"

Jane savored the tea a moment before answering. It felt so good to be warm and looked after. For more years than she dared count, Cordelia had been her lifeline. Through all the agony of Christine's illness and then the aftermath of her death, she'd been there, a staunch support and source of comfort.

"Come on, dearheart. I'm sitting on pins and needles!"

"Speaking of pins and needles," said Jane, "how's your back? Have you made another date to go horseback riding with Mugs?"

"I'm happy to say that several hot baths did the trick. This morning I was right as rain. And indeed, Mugs is coming to the Allen Grimby on Friday night. It surprised me, but she absolutely adores the theatre."

"Wonderful," said Jane. "At last. Someone who can appreciate you for your mind."

"I beg your pardon?"

Jane finished her cup and held it out for a refill. As Cordelia poured, she couldn't help but notice how badly her own hand was shaking.

"This good cheer is just a cover, isn't it? Come on. Exactly what happened to you?"

Jane held the cup as firmly as she could in both hands and took another sip. "I guess nobody's as strong as they think."

"Meaning?"

She looked away. "I'm . . . scared, Cordelia. Really frightened. And I don't know what to do with that feeling. Do I stop this investigation? Simply bury my head in the sand and hope everything goes away? Something tells me it's too late for that, even if it's what I wanted." With all her might, she resisted the urge to cry.

"So, what did happen last night? Did you go to Wizards?"

"Unfortunately, yes. That's where the nightmare began. First, I talked to Evie. She'd been drinking pretty heavily. I asked her all the questions I could think of—about Doyle Benedict, about the fraternity party she'd sung at on Friday night." She reached absently for a piece of cheese. "Apparently, she and Julia had gone to a lawyer's office earlier in the day for the reading of Rose's will."

"Is that why she got drunk? She didn't like the terms?"

Jane shook her head. "Not that I could tell. Both she and her sister received fifty thousand dollars."

Cordelia whistled.

"As well as some of Rose's personal possessions."

"Like what?"

"Well, I think Julia got a comb and brush set. And some cloisonné vases. I remember seeing them in Rose's living room. And Rose willed Evie some children's books. Peter Rabbit. That sort of thing. Rose left Evie her shawl."

"Nothing to get all worked up about there."

Jane nodded her agreement. "Except Evie did say she wasn't delighted at the prospect of owning a piece of clothing someone had died in."

"That might get to me too. Depending on my mood."

Jane nibbled on the cheese. "She did seem awfully depressed. To be honest, every time I've ever talked to her she's been drunk or depressed. Freddy seems very protective of her. I'm sure she's still upset about her mother's death."

"Jane?"

"Mmm?"

Cordelia picked up one of the Twinkies and held it inches from her lips. "How did Evie know Rose died in that shawl? I thought the details of her death were supposed to be hush hush."

Jane stopped nibbling. "What?"

"Well, didn't you tell me to keep my mouth zipped about the whole thing?"

"You're right. I did."

"Then?"

Jane could feel a faint crackle in the back of her mind, like a radio that wasn't quite tuned to the right station. But almost. "Cordelia? Do you realize what you just said?"

"Well—"

Jane thought for a moment. "That's it! Evie was there that night. She had to be. Do you realize what this could mean?"

"Evie murdered Rose?"

Jane swung her feet off the couch and started to get up.

"Wait a minute, buster. What do you think you're doing?"

"We've got to find her, Cordelia. I've got to talk to her right away."

"Oh no you don't. I promised Arnold—and myself—that I was going to keep you quiet and safe for at least twenty-four hours."

"But don't you see—?"

"I see nothing that can't wait until you're stronger." Half of the Twinkie disappeared into her mouth as a way of putting a period on the end of the sentence.

Jane searched the room for a compromise. "Ok, how about this. You call Wizards. See if she's there."

"To what end, Jane dear?" Cordelia's rounded tones spoke louder than anger.

"If she *is*...maybe I can get her to come over. Sure, that's it. I'll tell her I want to talk to her about...about Emery."

"Why would she care?"

Jane set her cup down. "I met him coming out of the bar last night, Cordelia. He...assaulted me." She looked down at her hands. "As I was coming out of the alley next to Wizards he grabbed me and pinned me against the wall. He...thought I was coming on to him when I went to visit him at the Maxfield Plaza." As she closed her eyes and lowered her head, the fear she'd felt last night all came rushing back. "I got away. I hurt him—at least I hope I did. But he scared me pretty badly. Evie must have seen that side of him too. If I tell her what happened, she might be willing to talk to me."

Gently, Cordelia touched Jane's arm. "God...why didn't you say something right away?"

Jane covered her face with her hands. "It's too much, Cordelia." Again, she resisted the urge to cry. "Right now, I've just got to get through this. I've got to talk to Evie. The

228

only way out of this nightmare is to find the truth. I'm so close. I know it."

Gravely, Cordelia nodded. "All right. I'll call." She got up and walked over to her favorite easy chair. The phone was sitting on a huge plastic gargoyle, a discarded prop from one of her earlier plays. After a quick search of the yellow pages, she found the number.

Jane poured herself another cup of tea.

"Good evening," said Cordelia into the receiver. "I'd like to speak to Evie Fortnum." She paused for several seconds, listening. "I see. Do you know *why* she isn't coming in?" Another pause. "No. No message. Thanks."

"Not there?"

Cordelia shook her head.

"All right. This time, let's try Miriam's home. That's where Evie lives. If she's sick or something, she'd probably be in bed."

"Good idea." Cordelia searched the white pages. "Here it is." She dialed the number.

Jane waited. "No one home?" she asked after almost a minute.

"So it would seem." Cordelia put down the receiver, slumping against the arm of the chair. "I wonder where she could be?"

"Well, I know Miriam's up at the Gower summer lodge."

"How did you find out about that place?"

Jane cocked her head. "How did *you?*"

"Mae spent a good hour telling me about it at dinner one night. She drives up quite often. She loves it. It's so remote. So cut off from the hustle of the city."

"An apt description. That's where I was last night, Cordelia. Someone put something into my drink. After I passed out, they tied me up and brought me to this shed under a boathouse on Old Sawmill lake. Freddy mows the lawn there every weekend. He found me."

"This gets worse by the minute!"

"It's a long story, but while I was there, Miriam showed up. She was anxious for Freddy to leave so she could have some privacy. She wanted to take out the sailboat."

"And?"

"Well, my first thought was that maybe she'd made a date with Dorrie. Then again, it occurred to me she might want to be alone to . . ."

"Finish you off? What a horrible thought!" Cordelia sat forward, rubbing her palms together nervously. "Janey, I know you may resist this idea, but I think my next call should be to the police."

Without hesitation Jane said, "No."

"Why not?"

"I can't talk to them about any of this. You must know why, Cordelia. I promised Mae my silence. I won't go back on my word. The Chamber is too important to put in jeopardy."

"So is your life!"

Jane pinched the bridge of her nose. "I agree with you. But how are the police going to protect me? Put an armed guard around my house?"

"By finding the truth!"

"At what expense? And how long do you think that will take? No, I want to handle this my way."

"You realize what killed Cock Robin, don't you?"

"I'm sure you're going to tell me."

"Stubbornness, my dear. Pure and simple."

Jane took a deep breath. "Look, I've already told you I'm frightened. I'm not going to take any chances. But I've got to pursue this on my own. At least until I have some hard evidence. Do you understand?"

Cordelia gave one, very grudging, nod.

"Good. Now, back to Evie. As I think about it, maybe she was the one who was going to meet Miriam at the lodge. That's why she canceled her performance tonight."

"Well," said Cordelia, slapping her thighs, "only one way to find out. I've got the number here somewhere." She paged through her personal directory. "Yes. Here it is. The Gower Foundation Summer Lodge. Now then, if Evie answers, do you want to talk to her?"

Jane thought for a moment. "Not with Miriam standing by, listening. See if you can find out what her plans are. Where she'll be tomorrow."

"All right. Hum. Now what kind of excuse. . . . I've got it. This should work." Rummaging through a wicker basket on the floor next to her chair, Cordelia found a stick of gum and folded it quickly into her mouth. She picked up the phone and dialed the number. "It's ringing," she said in a heavily nasal voice. Then, chewing loudly, she continued into the receiver, "To whom am I speaking? Who? Ah yes, Ms. Cipriani." She paused. "My name is Flora Seitz. I'm the personal assistant to Winona Elderberry, Senior Editor of WHAM magazine. What? You've never heard of us? Well, my dear, welcome to the twentieth century. We're one of the fastest growing rock monthlies in the nation. It just so happens that Ms. Elderberry was in your town two weeks ago. She had the pleasure of hearing a young woman by the name of Evangeline Fortnum. I was told I might talk to her if I called this number." She snapped her gum. "It's about a possible interview, Ms. Cipriani. Is she there?" Cordelia waited, giving Jane a knowing nod. "Oh yes. Hello. Ms. Fortnum? Isabel Seitz here."

"Flora," Jane corrected her.

Cordelia shot her a nasty look. "Sometimes I go by the name of Flora Seitz. Take your pick. It's all the same to me. Anyway, the reason I'm calling. . . I'm the personal assistant to . . ."

"Winona Elderberry," Jane prompted.

"Yes . . . Ms. Winona Elderberry, Senior Editor of WHAM magazine. What? You've never heard of WHAM either? Well darlin', you've heard of *Rolling Stone* haven't you? You have? Well, there you go. Now. Ms. Elderberry was in town two weeks ago and heard you sing. She wanted me to call and see if you'd be available to do a preliminary interview. If all goes well, we'd like to feature you in the December issue of our magazine." She chewed on her thumbnail. "Of course. I could explain all the details to you tomorrow. If you could give me an address and a time?"

"Ask if Miriam will be there," whispered Jane.

Cordelia held up a hand. "I see. Brown Deer. Yes, I'm sure I can find it. County Road Five. Three miles. Then right at Hoeburg Road. Good, good. Yes, I can remember that. About what time? No, I'm not an early riser either. I entirely understand. Four P.M. would be fine. Oh, and Ms. Fortnum? Will we be alone?" She spit out a piece of nail. "Splendid. I do so like to have some privacy—especially during the preliminary interview. See you then." She dropped the phone back on the hook.

"Bravo." Jane would have stood to clap, but her sore muscles protested.

"Tut tut. Now. You can spend the rest of the night, and most of tomorrow *resting*. Do I have your word of honor that you'll cooperate? No more guff?"

For the first time since she'd walked in the door, Jane felt some hope. "Absolutely no more guff. I am in your hands."

"Splendid. First thing on the agenda is some Rachmaninoff. I'd say the second piano concerto is in order. Then, a soothing, hot bath."

"That sounds like heaven," said Jane. "Oh, and Cordelia?"

"Yes?"

"Thanks." She could feel her eyes begin to tear.

Cordelia was clearly touched. "You would do the same for me, dear one. Now. I'm off to the bathroom to draw you a tubby. What you need are lots of bubbles and rubber duckies. You just relax until I come back. Then, after your bath we'll . . ."

Jane closed her eyes, letting Cordelia's voice wash over her like waves lapping against a grateful shore.

36

At ten minutes to four the following afternoon, Jane and Cordelia found themselves bumping down the winding back road to the Gower summer lodge. Tall white pines obscured the sun, making an otherwise beautiful drive feel strangely gloomy and remote.

Before leaving Minneapolis, Jane had stopped briefly at her house to get her phone messages. As she suspected, Dorrie had called, suggesting that they meet tomorrow afternoon at Loring Park. Neutral turf. Jane left a message on Dorrie's answering machine accepting the invitation. Perhaps, by then, she would feel she had a better grip on her own life. Only time would tell.

"You're sure Mugs said my car would be taken care of by the time we get back," said Jane, tapping her fingers impatiently on the arm rest.

"Absolutely. She promised that a friend of hers would fill all the tires with air and then drive it to my house. That is, unless the engine falls out first."

"Very funny." Jane was anxious to talk to Evie. She was having trouble concentrating on anything else. "Where's your gun?" she asked, fidgeting with the loop of her seat belt.

"In the glove compartment, dearheart. Just calm

down. I have everything under control. As I said this morning, I'm not letting you go into that cabin alone, unprotected. If Evie was with Rose the night she died, she *could* be responsible for Rose's death—and god knows what else. You might be in danger. Lucky for you I did a bit of target practice with Mugs the other day. My skills were a bit rusty."

Jane felt the conversation with Evie could end up going in many different directions. The best case scenario was that Evie would simply break down and tell her the entire story. In an effort to think positively, Jane restrained herself from a detailed examination of the worst case.

The country air was doing wonders to clear her head, yet her body, if it was possible, felt even worse today than yesterday. Cordelia's suggestion of renting a walker did little to lift her spirits.

"There it is," said Cordelia. She nodded to a sprawling, one story log cabin sitting on a rolling hill overlooking the lake. Across the entire front was a screened-in porch. "Looks kind of homey."

Jane gave her a sickly smile.

Cordelia drove the car to the side of the building and stopped. "Remember, dearheart, leave the door open after you get inside. I'll be right behind you. Quiet as a church mouse."

"Be sure you stay out of sight. I don't want to spook her. And I think Evie might be more inclined to talk if she doesn't feel outnumbered." Jane paused for a moment before getting out. "You know something, Cordelia? While we were driving up here, I got to thinking. Of all the people who might've been responsible for abducting me last night, the only one who couldn't have done it was Evie."

"Because?"

"She was much too drunk. Freddy was doing his best to sober her up in that dressing room at the back of Wizards, but it couldn't have happened fast enough."

"So that leaves Doyle. Julia. Emery. And of course, Freddy himself. Don't make the mistake of counting him out, Janey. After all, he found you. I'd say that puts him at the top of the list."

"I haven't counted *anyone* out."

Cordelia narrowed one eye. "Is that a veiled reference to Miriam?"

"I suppose it is." Jane eased out of the car. Leaning her head inside the open window she continued, "Whoever drugged and kidnapped me was undoubtedly the same person who left that music box at my house. The latter was simply meant to frighten. While the former—." She glanced away. "By all rights, I should be dead, Cordelia. I can't figure out why I'm not."

Cordelia took hold of her hand, giving it a reassuring squeeze. "Do you think your abductor was the same person who mailed the pipe bomb to your father?"

"I do. When you think about it, it all fits. It's all part of the same fabric. And that means whoever is responsible, also had something to do with Charlotte Fortnum's death. If we find my kidnapper, I'll bet you anything we find her murderer."

Cordelia shivered.

"The thing is, if Emery is responsible, then the motivation for Charlotte's death seems obvious. On the other hand, if it was someone else, I'm not so sure where that leaves us. If it was Miriam, it might have had something to do with The Chamber and the vote they were about to take. At this point, I think that's a strong possibility. But if it was Freddy or Julia—someone in Charlotte's family—what was the reason? And believe me, Cordelia, there was a very specific reason for Charlotte Fortnum's murder. It was no random act."

"Do you think Rose's death is connected to Charlotte's?"

"That's what we're here to find out." She glanced over her shoulder at the cabin. "Look, give me a few moments to get Evie away from the front door. Then you can follow."

Cordelia opened the glove compartment and removed a small pistol. "Remember, Janey, I'll just be in the next room."

"Thanks. I hope *that*—" she nodded to the gun "—won't be necessary." Limping slightly, Jane walked off toward the front porch.

"What are you doing here?" asked Evie. She held a nearly empty brandy snifter in one hand, a copy of *City Pages* tucked under one arm.

"I need to talk to you," said Jane.

"I've got an appointment. You'll have to come back another time." Today, her pink hair looked clean and combed. The bright yellow sun dress she wore flattered her thin figure. Yet the puffiness around her eyes told Jane something was very wrong.

"I'm afraid I have a confession to make."

"Like what?" Evie took a sip of the caramel colored liquid, leaning against the door frame.

"I'm sorry to do this to you, but . . . I'm your appointment."

Evie appeared confused. A look of anger slowly crept across her face. "What the hell?"

"It was Cordelia who called you last night. I really am sorry I had to handle it this way. But I had to talk to you . . . alone."

Evie wiped a hand across her mouth, taking in Jane's appearance. "You're a mess, you know that? You look like you've gone ten rounds with a rabid mongoose."

Jane touched one of the scratches on her face. "It was a small accident."

Evie stared at her long enough to let everything sink in. "This is just great, you know that? I spend the entire day waiting around here swatting deer flies, and for what?

Somebody's fucking practical joke. I seriously don't need this." She slammed the screen door and retreated into the house.

Jane gave Cordelia the high sign, and then slipped inside. She passed through the dining room, entering the living room just as Evie threw herself onto the floral print sofa. Evie ignored Jane's presence, picking up the bottle of brandy and pouring herself another drink.

"Will you let me explain?" asked Jane.

"Why should I?"

"Because it's very important. Lives may depend on it."

"Lives? Whose life? Yours?"

"Maybe."

"Is that why you're limping?"

"It's a long story."

"Isn't everything?" She took a swallow. "Oh, what the hell. You want some?" She held up the bottle.

Jane shook her head.

"Then sit down. You're giving me a headache. Besides, I suppose it's either you or 'Gilligan's Island.'" She made a sour face at the TV set.

"Thanks." Jane pulled up a wooden captain's chair and sat down directly across from her. Out of the corner of her eye she noticed Cordelia enter the dining room and ease her large frame onto a bench near the door. Evie couldn't see her from her position on the couch.

"So," said Evie, turning off the TV set with the remote, "tell me something I don't know."

Jane smiled. In spite of everything, she liked Evie Fortnum. "Look," she said, not knowing quite how to begin. "When I talked to you the other night . . ."

"When was that?"

"At Wizards. You were in that small room at the back, near the stage door."

"Oh yeah. Yeah, I remember. Not too well, though. You understand." She held the glass to her lips and took another sip.

"You said something that started me thinking."

"Really? What?"

"Do you recall telling me that you'd been to a lawyer's office earlier in the day?"

Evie scrunched up her face in thought. "To be honest, I don't."

"You said you and Julia had each received fifty thousand dollars from Rose's estate."

She nodded.

"You also mentioned she'd willed you some of her personal possessions. Her favorite shawl, for one thing."

Evie frowned. "Where is this leading?"

"Well, that's when I got to thinking. Nobody knows any of the details of Rose's death. No one was allowed up on the third floor. I've read the police report. No mention was made of her clothing—of what she was wearing the night she died."

"So?"

"So how did you know she was wearing that shawl?"

"I . . . did I say that?"

"You said that you weren't sure you wanted to own something someone had died in."

Evie finished off the brandy, pouring herself another. The hand holding the glass was beginning to shake. "Well, it was a mistake. I must have heard it somewhere."

"There's no other explanation. You were in the attic room with her that night, weren't you, Evie? There's no use lying."

She sat up very straight. "I am not lying! I have no idea what happened to Rose. You've seriously left the planet if you think I have. Now, I think you should leave."

"And you took the ledger and the jewels. For some reason you put the ledger back in Rose's apartment, but you kept the jewels. Why?" Jane had no idea if this was true, but she had to chance it.

"I—." She began to fumble with the buttons on her dress.

"How did she die, Evie? Was it an accident? Did she *fall* down the stairs? If I give this information to the police, they may come to a very different conclusion. I guarantee you won't like talking to them. Why not try talking to me first?"

Evie gripped her glass tightly, looking at the fireplace, the ceiling, the floor—anything but Jane's eyes. "Why are you so damn interested in all of this?"

"Because I was hired to find the truth, Evie. What really happened that night? You were there. Is that why you've been drinking so heavily? A guilty conscience?"

"No!"

Jane knew she was being hard on her, but she also knew that locked somewhere inside this young woman's mind was the answer she'd been searching for. She was so close to it now. She couldn't let it slip through her fingers.

Evie got up, wobbling slightly, and walked to the window overlooking the metal dock. She kept her back to Jane. "You're not going to leave this alone, are you? Julia warned me. I should have listened. You're going to pick and pick . . ."

"Does Julia know about this?"

"She does now. That night you came to see me at Wizards? I broke down and told Freddy everything. He called Julia right away. They had this very *serious* family pow wow. You don't know what it's like, always being the center of attention. 'Poor Evie,' in trouble again. 'Hopeless Evie.' I'm always messing up. I just wanted to get away from them. From everything in my life. That's why I called Miriam. I thought I could trust her."

"Does she know the truth?"

"Hell no! I just told her I needed some space and privacy. I said I was coming up to the lodge yesterday. She's always respected that before. But then, when I got here, she was waiting for me. This family is like Velcro. I can't get away from them."

Jane could hear the desperation in her voice. "What

really did happen the night Rose died?"

Evie turned around, her eyes falling to the half filled bottle of brandy next to the couch. "What's the use? It's all going to come out sooner or later. The only thing is . . . if I tell you, you have to promise me something."

"What's that?"

"You have to let me tell Miriam in my own way. That's all I could think about today. She can't hear this from anyone else before I have my chance to explain."

"All right. Fair enough."

Evie returned unsteadily to the sofa, taking a swig of brandy directly from the bottle. Then, pausing to organize her thoughts, she tucked her legs up under herself, leaning her head on her hand. She waited another long, awkward moment and then said, "I suppose you could say it all started because of money. When I got out of prison, I was broke, with no job prospects. I knew I wanted to sing, but that doesn't pay very much, at least not at first. I found myself totally obsessing. I laid awake every night trying to figure out how I could get my hands on some serious cash—fast. I didn't want to live with my mother and Miriam any longer than necessary. I knew they loved me, but they both drove me *crazy*. I felt smothered. Constantly watched. And then, to make matters worse, they had this big break up and I had to move with Mom to her tiny apartment at the club. I thought I would die! I mean, it was like I totally couldn't breathe!"

Jane nodded. She wanted to encourage the young woman, but she didn't want to interrupt.

"It was living at the club that got me to thinking about something Julia and I once overheard. When we were kids, we discovered that a number of the bookcases in the house were really hidden accesses to some corridors which ran along the interior of the building. We used to play hide and seek in there when Rose babysat us. I don't think anyone realized we'd discovered them. It was our secret. Having to sneak around only made it more suspenseful—you know.

240

Kid stuff. Anyway, one afternoon, Julia and I were sitting behind the bookcase in the attic room, listening to Mom and Rose talk. At the time, I think Julia was probably eleven and that would make me seven. We were being very quiet because Mom was talking about Amelia Gower. We'd both seen the painting of her in the dining room many times. Julia thought she was just a rich lady, maybe a duchess or something, but I knew she was a queen. I used to beg Rose to show me pictures of her from her family's photo album. Anyway, Mom was saying something like wasn't it great that Amelia had left behind this incredible treasure. Rose agreed, adding that nobody knew what was hidden in the house. Julia and I were totally spellbound by the conversation. For months after that, it's all we talked about. We searched high and low, looking for the treasure chest, but never found a thing. Eventually, I suppose we just lost interest and went on to other games. But the thought of that treasure never entirely left my mind." She stretched out on the couch, setting the bottle of brandy on her stomach.

Jane felt a bit like a psychoanalyst. Evie's words flowed quickly now as she stared at the ceiling.

"When I moved to the club with my mother several months ago, the thought occurred to me that maybe the treasure was still there. That's when I began my systematic search. The best time was late at night. The club cleared out about ten thirty and I usually got home from my gigs around midnight. As long as I was careful, I pretty much had the place to myself. But even though I was being very thorough, I still wasn't having any luck. I began to think I'd made it all up. That the conversation between Mom and Rose never happened. I decided I needed to talk to Julia to see if she remembered anything about it. But she's always so busy.

"Even so, one night, I'd gone to her house around dinner time. She hadn't gotten home from work yet, but Freddy was there. After we got comfortable on the balcony with a cold beer, it became pretty apparent that he was seriously upset about something himself. I asked him what was wrong but he wouldn't say. Freddy's stubborn when he wants to be. He finally let it slip that he needed some money. Well, I mean, I didn't have any trouble identifying with *that*. I asked him if Julia knew what was going on and he got even more upset. That's when I told him that I was involved in something that might net me some real cash. At first he thought I was kidding, but when I didn't back down, he became interested. Julia called during all of this and said she'd be late, so he offered to take me over to Wizards. On the way, he told me he needed the money within the next couple of weeks or it would be too late. I felt so sorry for him. Freddy's an ok guy. Kind of straight, if you know what I mean, but he's been a good friend. I really wanted to help him. I wouldn't tell him anything specific, but I made a vow to redouble my efforts.

"I searched the club the next two nights until dawn. And then...everything came to a grinding halt." She stopped talking, taking several swigs from the bottle.

"What happened?" asked Jane.

"Mom...well, she came to me. She'd found out that I'd posed for a...magazine...nude. It happened right after we moved to the club. As far as I was concerned, it wasn't any big deal. To me, it just represented some quick cash. But to Saint Charlotte, well, it was more like the end of the world! She was livid! I've never seen her so mad. She threatened to call my parole officer right away and tell her all about it. Not that I cared—posing nude isn't illegal. But...then again, some drugs were involved. Not that I had anything to do with them, but they were around. Available. Somehow, Mom found out. I mean, this part of it was serious. I could be sent back to jail! So, I begged her. I pleaded for mercy. That's when she told me I had to stop all this madness—which of course included my music—and get a real job or go to college full time. I mean, I totally freaked! How could she do that to me?"

Evie laid her arm over her eyes, trying to calm down. "Three days after our conversation, she was dead. I must have been in shock for almost two weeks. When the fog cleared, Freddy came to me again. He apologized for the bad timing, but asked if I'd been able to get my hands on any cash yet. I told him I hadn't even thought about it, but he was so desperate, I promised that I'd try again. Nothing had really changed for me either. The money I might have received from my mother's will was being held until I turned thirty. Thirty! Even from the grave, she was still controlling me. Telling me I wasn't good enough. Jesus, why not just donate the money to an old folks home!" She snorted. "Miriam suggested I leave the club and move back to her place. But it was still no good. My only hope was finding that treasure."

"What about Julia? Did she receive an inheritance too?"

"Ah yes, dear Julia. Sure. But she didn't have to wait. Only problem was, Freddy said he couldn't say anything to her about needing this money. She wouldn't understand. *That* I could believe. And something told me not to press him for explanations. Anyway, I knew my access to the club was going to be severely limited once I moved out, so the next night, I decided to tackle the attic. I couldn't get up there through the passageways any more because, years before, a door had been installed with a major lock. I didn't have the key. I'd left the third floor alone because the only thing up there, other than Rose's apartment, was one of The Gower Foundation offices. It was always kept locked. But I had to at least try.

"Anyway, while I was tip-toeing down the hall in front of Rose's apartment, I heard the door open. I moved back into the shadows but not before she saw me. Except—" Evie hesitated. "She didn't think it was me. Without her glasses Rose couldn't see much, but even so, it didn't explain her behavior. See, for some reason she got it into her head that I was her grandmother, Amelia Gower.

Can you beat that? Seriously strange. I decided it was better to play along rather than explain why I was up there in the first place. She wasn't making much sense. She talked a little about Emery. Asked if she'd done the right thing in hiring a lawyer. And then she said something even more bizarre. She said she'd *called* for me—meaning Amelia. I thought she'd totally lost her marbles. I tried to put her off. Told her I didn't have the time right then to talk. But before I left, I got this idea. I asked her if she'd been taking good care of the treasure. I don't know what I expected, but after hesitating for a moment, she said that yes, she had. So, I mean, what could I do? I'm not shy. I asked to see it. But before we got any further, I heard this stupid door slam downstairs and I got freaked. I said I'd come back another night and she could show me then. I couldn't believe my ears when she agreed!"

Jane sat quietly, not wanting to force the story out of her. Yet as Evie continued to speak, Jane could hear her voice thickening. Her words were beginning to slur. It wouldn't be long before the alcohol ruined her ability to communicate. Unfortunately, they had to hurry. Jane knew she might never get a chance to have Evie all to herself again. "What happened when you went back?"

Evie took several more sips before answering, "It was three nights later. Since it was pretty late, I was surprised to find Rose still dressed. I knocked softly and then positioned myself in the darkest part of the hallway. When she came out, I asked her to show me where the treasure was. She said she needed a minute to go get her glasses, but I insisted she leave them. She went back into her apartment and reappeared a few moments later. She'd gone to get her cane and at the same time she'd tossed that silly shawl over her shoulders. Anyway, I stayed in the shadows while she unlocked the door to the attic. She wanted to talk about other things, but I demanded to see the treasure first. That's when she brought out the ledger. I got pretty pissed when I realized it was just a bunch of writing. It wasn't the kind of treasure *I* had in mind. I was feeling kind of let down, paging through it, when I noticed this red and black lacquered box sitting in the center of that old oak table. I'd never seen it there before, so I picked it up. My eyes nearly fell out of their sockets when I saw what was inside."

"The jewels," said Jane.

"Rose kept trying to explain something about how I— meaning Amelia—had left them to help her make decisions, or some such thing. I wasn't listening very carefully because I was so totally blown away over my good luck. That's when she got suspicious. Before I knew it, she was backing up, saying she had to leave. And then, before I could stop her, she tripped on one of the throw rugs and fell all the way down the stairs. I remember just standing there, holding my breath. I couldn't move. I was waiting for someone to tell me what to do. Finally, I crossed to the edge of the steps and looked down. I knew she was dead. I just had this awful sense. When I got down to her, I felt for a pulse, but there wasn't any." Her lower lip was trembling violently. She clamped a hand against her mouth, choking on her sobs. "All I could think about was getting away. There was nothing else I could do for her. I mean, it was an accident. It wasn't my fault. But I'd get blamed, you could be sure of that. So I took off. I realized later I was still holding the ledger and the jewels. As soon as I got to my room, I stowed them in my mother's attaché case. It has a lock, so no one could open it. The thing is, every night since it happened, all I can see when I'm trying to sleep is her body tumbling down those steps. How could I have been so dumb? If I hadn't insisted she take off her glasses, none of it would have happened. I loved her so much. She was like my family. Mom was dead, and now Rose. I couldn't deal with it. The only thing that made the pain go away was booze. The problem is, it just doesn't last." She began to cry. "I really loved her. I didn't mean it. I never wanted to hurt anyone. Somehow, I just screwed up. I think something's really wrong with me. Because now . . . I'm all alone."

Jane waited for a few moments and than asked, "But what about the ruby and the emerald? You put the ledger back, but why not the jewels?"

Evie grabbed a tissue from a box on the coffee table and wiped her nose. She continued to sniff as she answered, "I was going to, but then I got to thinking about how mom had shafted me over my inheritance." The self pity in her voice quickly turned to anger. "What a thing to do to your own daughter. It made me feel worthless. She couldn't trust me. Even after all the things I'd done to change my life around, even after she was *dead*, she still couldn't give an inch. Miriam agreed with the whole thing. And she was my last hope. Well, all I could say was fuck them. Fuck them all. I'd show the world what I was made of. I'd prove I could make it in the business. I just needed some time. Money was going to give me that."

"So, have you sold the jewels?"

Evie shook her head, holding the brandy bottle up to the light. It was nearly empty. "Nah. Not yet. It's not that easy."

"And what about Freddy?"

"Freddy? Oh, yeah. I just told him the deal had fallen through. Poor guy. I never told him what really happened. That is, not until the other night. It just came out. I guess I had to tell someone before I burst. He seemed . . . I don't know. Upset I guess. Sort of sad. But I know he understood. That's more than I can say for Julia. She's just like mom. Another saint."

"But does he still need money himself?"

Evie was beginning to mumble. "I s'pose. We all got our cross to bear. Maybe one of these days I'll take the cure."

"The cure?"

"Sure. I've thought about it some. A bottle of sleeping pills and a fifth of bourbon. Presto. No more pain." She finished the bottle and then let it drop to the floor.

Jane felt her blood turn cold. "Evie . . . you can't mean that. Suicide isn't an answer."

"No?"

"No!"

"Easy for you to say." Her voice was thick. She turned over and buried her head under a pillow.

Jane sat for a moment, thinking. What was her next move? She had to get Evie some help. But beyond that, she should probably talk to her father. Get a legal opinion on how she should proceed. If Evie was telling the truth, and only Evie and Rose knew for sure, Rose's death was accidental. On the other hand, it had occurred during the middle of a robbery. She could tell Mae what had happened and let her take whatever steps she thought necessary, but talking to her father still made sense. He would be flying home tonight. She could catch him at his office first thing in the morning.

Evie tried to sit up, but fell back on the couch. Jane knew she couldn't leave her here like this. She wanted to talk to Freddy right away, but first things first. Evie mustn't be left alone. Not only was her alcohol abuse at a serious stage, but if she really was suicidal, she had to get some professional help right away. Jane stood and moved over to the couch, sitting down next to her. "Evie," she said very softly, "I can't leave you here."

"Yeah," she mumbled, her head falling to one side. "I'm a fucking mess."

"Where would you like to go?"

She gave a shrug, reaching for the bottle and then realizing it was already empty.

"Miriam's house?"

"God no."

"How about Freddy and Julia's?"

She ran a hand over her eyes.

Jane could see she was crying again.

"I guess. I don't have anywhere else." She tried to focus on the grandfather clock next to the porch door.

"What time is it?"

"It's nearly five."

"Freddy teaches some class tonight. But Julia's home. Julia's always there when you don't need her. Such talent." She started to giggle.

Jane glanced at Cordelia, motioning for her to leave. She didn't want Evie to know their conversation had been overheard. "Can you get up?"

Without warning, Evie leapt to her feet, but then lost her balance and nearly fell over the coffee table. Jane caught her just in time. "Cordelia is out in the car. She'll drop you off. We'll make sure Julia is there and everything is ok. I'm going to get my own car and drive over to the U." There was no use trying to continue the conversation. Evie was too out of it.

"Good plan," she said, her voice slurred. She leaned heavily on Jane's shoulder. "Freddy to the rescue."

Cordelia held the car door open as Jane helped Evie into the back seat.

"We need to take her to Freddy and Julia's condo," Jane said, keeping her voice low. "Do you know where they live?"

Cordelia nodded. "Across from Orchestra Hall. I have a friend who lives in the same building." She climbed into the front seat and started the engine.

"I want you to make sure someone is home. Tell them she's been talking about suicide. You know what to say."

As Cordelia backed the car away from the cabin she whispered out of the corner of her mouth, "I guess we got what we came for."

Jane glanced over her shoulder at Evie. "I'd give anything if it were that simple, Cordelia. I really would."

37

Just as Mugs had promised, the old Saab was sitting in front of Cordelia's house when they arrived home. Jane repeated her instructions about taking Evie to Freddy and Julia's downtown condo. Cordelia was to make sure Julia understood the gravity of Evie's condition. Jane insisted that Cordelia not leave until she felt confident Julia could handle matters alone. In the meantime, Jane headed to the University of Minnesota to find Freddy. Not only did he need to know what was going on with his sister-in-law, but she had a few questions she wanted to put to him as well.

Since the Northrup lot was full, Jane parked her car near Coffman Memorial Union. She then walked as quickly as she could across the quadrangle to Folwell Hall. From her own days at the university, she seemed to remember the German department was on the second floor. She hoped it was still there.

As she entered the long hallway, she immediately noticed most of the small offices were empty. The only signs of life came from a room directly to her right. Inside, she could hear a radio playing softly. "Hello," she called. "Anybody home?"

Doyle startled her by appearing in the open doorway, a piece of pizza in his hand. "Ms. Lawless. What a surprise. Come in."

What the hell was he doing here?

"I was waiting for Freddy...uh, I mean Mr. Lindhurst," he said, as if answering her unspoken question. He resumed his chair, lifting his feet onto the desk top. The open pizza box rested next to him. Several discarded cans of cola littered the floor. "Can I help you?"

She stood in the doorway. "I'm looking for Freddy too."

"What a coincidence. We're both out of luck. He's teaching a class tonight."

"I know. I don't suppose you know where it's being held?"

He yawned, scratching his stomach. "Sure. Nicholson Hall. Room 201. Say, you been in some kind of fight or something?" He nodded to the scratches on her face.

Was that a smirk? "My toothbrush slipped."

"Oh," he grinned. "That can happen."

"Doesn't Freddy mind you using his office like this?"

"Nah. We're buds."

That hardly covered it.

"I'm surprised you're not over at the club tonight," observed Doyle.

"Why?"

"You didn't come in last night. I wondered where you were."

"Did you?"

"And you never came back for your soup on Monday night. Too busy, I suppose."

At his mention of Monday night, Jane felt a sudden, sharp intake of breath. What was he doing? Instinctively, she started to inch back from the door.

Calmly, Doyle took a bit of pizza. "You're one of their more faithful members I would suppose."

"Really? Thanks."

"Oh, it wasn't a compliment."

She glared at him.

"Want some pizza? Your color doesn't look so good."

"This has been fun, Doyle, but I have to run."

"Yeah, running might help." He licked his fingers.

What did he mean by that?

"If you see Freddy, tell him I'm waiting here for him."

"I'm not a messenger service."

"Ouch. Temper, temper. I stand reproved."

Maybe one of these days his jock strap would cut off circulation to his brain. Then again, maybe it already had. "I'll tell Freddy you're making good use of his office."

"You do that," he shouted after her.

Jane dragged her aching body over to Nicholson Hall. It was a lovely fall evening. Unfortunately, she didn't have time or the inclination to appreciate it. Entering through the front door, she limped up the steps to the second floor. Room 201 was directly in front of her. Sure enough, as she came nearer, she could hear Freddy's voice speaking to the class in German. She eased into the rear of the room and sat down in one of the empty seats. By the look on Freddy's face, her entrance had not gone unnoticed.

Freddy continued to lecture for a few more minutes and then told the class to take a five minute break. Jane stood as Freddy approached. She could see by his expression that he was upset.

"Why are you here?" he asked, motioning her out into the hall.

"It's Evie."

His mouth set in a grim line. "Come with me," he said, striding down the corridor to a small office. He turned and waited for her to catch up. "Let's talk in here," he said, holding the door open. "We need some privacy."

Jane hesitated. She wasn't sure following him into the room was such a smart move.

"What's wrong?" he asked, his voice impatient.

She glanced back down the hall toward his classroom. Lots of people were milling around. It was probably safe enough. Besides, if Freddy had wanted to hurt her, he'd had plenty of opportunity on their drive home from the summer lodge last night. Even though she didn't trust angelic faces, perhaps this time she should reconsider. Feeling a bit more confident, she stepped into the office and pulled up a folding chair.

Freddy sat down behind the desk.

"I'm sorry to have to get you out of class like this," Jane began, "but I think this qualifies as an emergency. I suppose I could have gone to Miriam—"

"No! No, I'm glad you came to me." He picked up a pencil and began twisting it nervously between his fingers. "Is she all right?"

"Yes. But—"

"But what?"

"Evie . . . was talking about suicide, Freddy. I'm sorry. She was alone up at the Gower summer lodge."

Angrily, his eyes examined the cluttered desk top. "I can't believe Miriam would leave her there all by herself. I explained to her how serious things were. Evie's in terrible shape. She stayed with us the night before last, but then she just disappeared. When I called Miriam, she said she had everything under control and she'd get back to me." He looked up, his expression turning to one of puzzlement. "Why were you up there again?"

"To talk to her. I know everything, Freddy. The whole story."

He held Jane's eyes for a long moment. "What are you going to do?"

"I haven't decided yet. I need to talk to my father first."

He nodded, running a hand through his blond hair. "God. It was an accident, you know. Evie never meant to hurt Rose. The fact that she had any part in it is killing her."

"I understand," said Jane, her voice turning gentle. "I like Evie a great deal. But even you have to admit, she has pretty bad judgment."

He leaned back in his chair. "That's a common malady."

"I understand you've had some problems yourself recently. Evie said you were desperate to get your hands on some cash."

"Did she?"

"Is it true?"

He took a deep breath, dropping the pencil on the desk top. "Yes. It's true."

Jane had thought hard about what Evie had told her. It seemed Freddy had first mentioned needing this cash *before* Charlotte was murdered. The fact that he still needed it after her death suggested it might not be related. Jane was betting that was the case. "I don't suppose you'd be willing to tell me why?"

"No, I wouldn't. It's no one's business but mine."

"I'm afraid the police may think otherwise."

"The police?"

She nodded, letting the threat hang in the air.

"You're going to tell them about Evie?"

"As I said before, I'm going to talk to my father about it first."

"But if you do decide to report it, would you have to mention the fact that I needed money?"

"Look, Freddy, I'm betting you had nothing to do with Charlotte Fortnum's murder. I don't believe Evie did either. Rose's death appears to be totally unrelated. I'm also betting you had nothing to do with kidnapping me the other night. If I'm wrong—"

"You're not wrong."

"Then tell me the truth! Why did you need that money?"

His brow furrowed as he considered the question. Looking up, he searched Jane's face for a long moment. Finally, he said, "Stupidity."

"Can you be more specific?"

"Oh, that's very specific. It just about covers my entire life."

253

"You know what I mean."

He gave a frustrated sigh. "Gambling on intercollegiate games is illegal, Jane, but sometimes, some of the frat houses around here organize what they call a *nightly*. The night before an event, you can put money down on your favorite team. The odds are set by the dealer—the person taking the bets. Unfortunately, I started doing this quite regularly last winter. And I won—at least initially. When my luck changed, I kept thinking it was just temporary. I got myself in pretty deep."

"How deep?"

"Right now, I owe something in excess of four thousand dollars. I've been trying to pay it off little by little, but I'm afraid I've exhausted the dealer's patience."

"Who's the dealer?"

He shook his head. "No. That's as far as I go."

"Does Julia know?"

"No! With the baby coming, it would only add to her stress." He made a valiant effort to cover up his all to apparent anxiety. Then, shrugging, he said, "As far as I can see, it's your move. If you tell the university what I've been up to, I'm in some pretty hot water. Once I get my doctorate, I'm likely to get an assistant professorship. Both Julia and I want that badly."

As they sat staring at one another, a young woman stuck her head into the room. "Mr. Lindhurst? We were all wondering when you were going to resume. Would I have time to run over to Williamson? I need to pick something up at the bookstore."

"Sure," said Freddy. "Go ahead. I'm going to cancel the rest of tonight's class. I've got an emergency."

"Oh." She glanced at Jane. As she withdrew her head she mumbled, "Sorry."

"Now," said Freddy, "where's Evie? At your house?"

Jane shook her head. "I had Cordelia take her to your condo. Evie was pretty sure Julia would be there."

"She is." He stood, starting for the door. "I want to

see her as soon as possible."

"At this point, I think she needs professional help, Freddy. Family concern isn't enough."

"I couldn't agree more." He swung into the hall and headed for his classroom. "Where did you park?" he called over his shoulder.

"Over by Coffman."

"Great. Me too. Will you help me carry some papers to my car?"

"Sure." She waited outside the room until he'd spoken to the class. A second later, he reappeared.

"Here," he said, handing her a stack of file folders. He ducked back inside and came out a second time carrying an even bigger stack. "I can't leave these here all night."

"No problem."

"I see you're still limping."

She nodded.

"Are you feeling any better?"

"Much. Thanks to you."

"Remember that before you throw my life to the dogs. Now, come on. Let's not waste any more time talking."

Together they descended the stairs and headed for the parking lot.

38

"Are you going to tell Miriam about Evie's suicide threat?" asked Jane. She led the way down the stairs to the parking lot. It was nearly dark out now. The lights from the Washington Avenue Bridge twinkled in the distance. "She might want to know."

"I suppose I could give her a call," agreed Freddy, his voice weary. "But she's tied up in one of those meetings with Mae Williams at the club again tonight. I've tried getting her out of them before. No luck." He nodded toward the north end of the lot. "My car's just over here. God, I'll be glad to grade these papers and get rid of them."

"Do you know what the meeting's about?"

"The meeting? Oh, you mean Miriam's. I think she said something about needing to choose new board members for The Gower Foundation. Eventually, Charlotte and Rose have to be replaced."

That was news. Jane thought Mae had already given her word that nothing like that would be decided until the circumstances surrounding Rose's death had been cleared up.

"It's right here," said Freddy, digging deep in his pocket. His car sat directly under one of the powerful lot lights. "Now, just a sec while I get the key." He found what he was looking for and then attempted to juggle his load while unlocking the trunk.

"Do you need some help?"

"Nope. If I can just...dammit!" Several of the folders slipped to the ground. A brisk wind instantly took the top papers and began blowing them around the lot. Freddy brought his foot down hard on one of the pages, while Jane chased two others to the side of a hill. "Just my luck," he shouted.

"We'll get them all. Don't worry."

"There's one under the wheel of that Porsche over by you. Do you see it?" He leapt to another page. "Oh Christ! Now look what I did!" The entire stack had fallen out of his arms.

Seeing his predicament, Jane immediately raced over and knelt down next to him.

"Put your knee on that group," he said. He slipped the trunk key between his teeth. "Ok, now, you stay here while I take these over to the car." He scrambled to his feet and dumped the first load into the back, returning for the next. "I'm sorry," he said, the key once again clenched in his teeth. "This isn't my day."

Jane smiled. "It's no problem." As he bent over, scraping up the next group, she noticed something which piqued her interest. "You know, you have a key on your chain that looks a lot like one of mine. My backdoor lock is kind of old. It—." She glanced up into his face. The look in his eyes told her everything.

In a single, lightning-swift movement, Freddy grabbed her right arm, forcing it behind her back. "Get up," he ordered. He let the night wind have its way with the rest of the papers.

"You broke into my house and left that music box!"

"Be quiet." He looked around to make sure they were still alone.

"You kidnapped me!"

"I said, shut up!" He dragged her over to his car.

257

The pain in her arm was excruciating. She was afraid her shoulder was going to snap.

Leaning into the trunk, he drew out a rope. "If you cooperate, this will be a lot less painful. Now, bring your other hand back here." He made a quick job of tying her up.

"What are you going to do?"

"What I should have done the other night." He forced her into the back seat. Before she knew what was happening, he'd opened the glove compartment and removed a small pistol. "Now. You have a choice. If you promise not to scream, I won't put the tape over your mouth. What's it going to be?"

The mere thought of something covering her mouth again sent a wave a panic through her system. "No, I won't scream. I promise."

"A woman of her word." He moved around to the trunk and shut it. Then, appearing with another rope, he tied her feet.

Jane tried to wiggle her hands free, but it was no use. He'd tied them too tightly.

Freddy slid behind the wheel and started the motor. He pulled quickly out of the lot. Not knowing what else to do, Jane leaned back and watched the lights of West Bank recede into the darkness. She could see that he was taking the first freeway north out of town. "Are you driving back up to the summer lodge?"

"No."

"Where then?"

"Just shut up. I don't want to talk."

"Look," she said, knowing that at this point there was little to lose, "if I'm going to die, don't I at least deserve to know why?"

He didn't speak for a long time. Finally, after leaving the worst of the city traffic behind, he said, "What do you want to know?"

"Everything!"

"Be more specific."

"Ok, why me?"

"I would think that was obvious. You were getting too close. You weren't going to let go, I could see that right from the start. The police stopped their investigation as soon as they found Emery. But you—you were a constant threat to me and my family. To my entire future. Neither you nor Charlotte left me any choice."

"What do you mean? How was I a threat?"

"Everywhere I went, you were there. When I heard on the news the other night that your father had discovered the phone call I'd made from Emery's apartment, I knew it was only a matter of time. God, I really blew that. I was trying to be too clever. When Emery burst into the club that night and threatened Charlotte, I thought I'd found the perfect solution to all my problems. So, instead of just doing the deed in the simplest way possible, I developed an elaborate plan based on Emery. One afternoon, I asked him if I could borrow his motorcycle. After a bit of hesitation, he tossed me his keys and I drove directly to the nearest hardware store. I got duplicates made of the entire set. I then had access to his apartment. The night I decided to kill Charlotte, I first went to his place and put on some of his clothes. Then I took hair from his brush in the bathroom and stuffed it in my pocket. I waited until I knew Charlotte would be leaving the club—she was so regular in her habits, you could set a clock by her comings and goings—and then I called Emery at the answering service. I told him someone was messing with his cycle. I knew that would get him out of there at the speed of light. That way, at the moment of Charlotte's death, he'd have no alibi. I thought it was a masterful plan. After Charlotte was dead, I slipped back into his apartment and returned the clothes. Thankfully, no one saw me. The only thing I never counted on was someone tracing that stupid phone call."

"But why?" asked Jane. "*Why* did you want Charlotte dead?"

He shook his head, gripping the wheel with both hands. "Have you ever known someone who was utterly certain of everything in their life?"

"No one's like that."

"Ah, that's where you're wrong. Charlotte Fortnum was the embodiment of moral certainty. She always knew with absolute conviction what was right and what was wrong. Normally, her rantings and ravings just made me tired. I simply turned her off. That is, until one day her sense of morality threatened me and my entire future." He honked at a car about to pull into his lane.

"In what way?"

"She was going to ruin me! Destroy my marriage. Take away my chances for a teaching career. Can you believe someone has that kind of power?" Looking over his shoulder, he took the next off ramp and turned onto a frontage road. "It all started last summer. One evening, much to my ill-fortune, she happened to stop into a coffee house on West Bank. I was sitting at a table in the back with one of my first year German students. Since we were talking rather . . . intimately, I didn't see Charlotte at first. But she saw us. She nearly broke down my office door the next day wanting an explanation. Naturally, I told her she was reading too much into the situation. The girl was just a friend. Nothing was going on. She didn't believe me, but since she didn't have any proof, she had to let it drop. But she did issue a rather stiff warning. She said that if she ever caught me cheating on her daughter, she would go directly to Julia with the information. She also promised she'd do everything in her power to see that Julia left me. Well, I mean, what could I do? I laughed at her. Told her she was hysterical."

"Was she wrong?"

"Wrong? What's the difference? Julia is the only woman I've ever loved. That girl meant nothing to me. Nothing. But, as my usual rotten luck would have it, Charlotte saw us together again. It was two weeks after fall quarter had begun. Late one night, I was walking Jill—that was her name—back to her dorm. We'd stopped for a last kiss under one of the doorway arches to Pillsbury Hall when Charlotte stomped by. God, she was like a bloodhound! Normally, she was always at home this time of night, but she'd recently broken up with Miriam and moved back to the club. How was I to know she was out prowling the campus looking for sin and moral corruption? Anyway, she paused right in front of us and squinted to get a better look. We both knew the jig was up. 'I'll talk to you tomorrow,' she shouted, her voice about as ominous as I've ever heard it. Then, without another word, she marched off. I told Jill on the way home that I wouldn't be able to see her again. But instead of understanding, she was furious! How could I do that to her? We loved each other. We were meant to be together. Her words sounded like the fatuous dialogue from a B movie.

"The next day, I was having lunch with Julia at the club. Just as we were being served, I glanced up and saw Charlotte charging the table like an enraged water buffalo. She demanded that I follow her to one of the conference rooms. Once we were behind closed doors, she said she now knew for certain what kind of scum I was. With her own two eyes, she'd seen me with that woman. Well, I mean, what could I say? I begged. I pleaded. I told her it was all true, but that I didn't love this girl. It had just happened—I didn't even understand it myself. I wanted out, but I didn't know how to end it. Charlotte remained implacable. Didn't I realize that, even if I *wasn't* married, sleeping with one of my students was unethical? She went on and on about unequal power relationships. I felt like I was sitting in one of those women's studies classes. And then she said the university did more than just frown on such liaisons—action could be taken against me. I sat there and let her rant and rave until finally, during one of her rare pauses, I told her I would do anything if only she wouldn't tell Julia. Her daughter was the single most important thing in my life—if I lost her, I didn't know what I'd do. My future would be ruined—and more than that, she'd be hurting Julia unnecessarily. After sweating blood for half an hour and making her every promise in the book, I got her to at least say she'd think about it. Even though I despised Charlotte Fortnum, deep down I think I trusted her fundamental compassion. We were family. I thought that meant *something*."

"But it didn't?"

He shook his head. "As the days went on, I could see the dye was cast. It was only a matter of time. And to make matters worse, Jill came to me after class one night. She threatened to go directly to Julia and tell her about our *love*, as she put it, unless I promised I would end the marriage myself. I convinced her to come with me to a motel we often used when we needed privacy. We talked for several hours." He ran a hand through his blond hair. "She just wouldn't listen to reason. I did everything I could to make her understand my position. It was only after I saw how useless my words were that I—" He stopped.

Jane waited. When he didn't go on, she asked, "What did you do?"

"Don't you see? She left me no other choice! I'm not like Emery. I don't go beating up women just for the fun of it. I had to get her to back off! I had to scare her so badly she'd never think of crossing me again. She could have ruined everything." He shook his head several times. "But there was another complication."

"What was that?"

Freddy took a deep breath. "Are you aware of the hidden corridors behind the bookcases at the club?"

"Yes."

"Well, the day Charlotte gave me her ultimatum, Doyle Benedict was behind the wall. Can you believe it? The guy was eating his lunch back there! He happens to be in the same class as Jill. After overhearing my conversation with Charlotte, he knew Jill and I were sleeping together, and he also knew Charlotte had found out and was very upset. Most importantly, he knew I'd promised never to see her again. When Jill came to class about a week later with bruises on her face and arms, he simply put two and two together."

It was all becoming clear. Here was the reason Doyle kept hanging around Freddy, taking some very unusual liberties. "And he took the opportunity to blackmail you. He knew you were the one who hurt her."

"Exactly."

"And that story you gave me about gambling—"

"It was a lie. I needed the money to pay Doyle for his silence. That guy's as thick as a brick, but he did realize one thing. A word to Charlotte about what I'd done and I was dog meat. Not only would she have spilled the beans to Julia, but I'm certain she would have gone directly to Jill and insisted she press charges against me for assault. Any future I might've looked forward to at the University of Minnesota would be over. Thankfully, Doyle wasn't too greedy. As long as I paid him regularly, he stayed off my back. I don't think he ever really understood the ramifications of what I'd done. He just saw it as *woman trouble*— and as an opportunity to make some quick bucks. Apparently, he never even considered the fact that I might have had something to do with Charlotte's murder. Then again, he and Emery were pretty good friends. Emery hated Charlotte for his own reasons. Doyle believes he's guilty."

"And after Charlotte's death?"

"It was business as usual. Doyle realized his silence was still terribly important to me. After all, he could tell Julia what he knew. It was just a hundred here and a fifty there. But when he found out Julia was going to be coming into an inheritance from her mother's estate, he upped the ante."

"To what?"

"He wants a thousand dollars by the end of next month."

"Can you pay that?"

"No. I can't and I won't." He pulled into a gas station and stopped in front of a phone booth. "I have to call Julia. Make up some excuse for why I'm going to be late. Now... don't try to scream or get anyone's attention. Remember, I *will* use this." He held up the gun for her to see and then shoved it under his belt.

As soon as he was gone, Jane tried again to wiggle free of the ropes. She'd noticed that her feet weren't tied quite as tightly as her hands. If she could just slip her foot out of her boot.... She kept her eyes glued to Freddy as she worked to free herself. As he hung up, the rope gave just a little and her foot slipped clear.

"Why won't you tell me where we're going?" she asked, resuming her former position as he got into the car.

He started the motor and returned to the frontage road. "I suppose you're right. It's not going to be a secret for much longer. We're headed up to Repentance River. Blackberry Lake to be more specific."

"My family's cabin?"

"When you mentioned the other day that you had a cabin there, I decided to drive over and take a look. It will do just fine."

"For what?"

"What I didn't have time to do the other night. Don't ask any more questions."

"But how can you just... just kill someone like that? I don't understand."

"You know, it's a funny thing." He sped onto the freeway entrance. "After Charlotte's death, I felt nothing. It was like some part of me was numb. She threatened me and my family and I had to take care of that threat. Same with Jill. I suppose you could say it was almost primal. A year ago if you'd told me I was going to... to murder someone, I'd have called you crazy. But Charlotte would never let me off the hook, not when she so clearly had the goods on me. I'd proved to her she was right. I was no good. Nothing short of her death was going to save me from such vindictiveness. I saw her at the club that morning. I tried to talk to her, but we kept getting interrupted. Even so, I could tell any further conversation was useless. That night I waited for her in the sculpture garden. We talked for a minute or two, but I could see nothing was going to change. That's when I did it. I was surprised by how little effort it took. After spreading some of Emery's hair fibers on her clothing and making sure strands of her hair were on his, I raced back to the apartment and hung his clothes back on a hanger. Then I just walked back to the club. It was so simple."

"But how could you do that to Emery? He was completely innocent."

Freddy let out a laugh. "Emery? Innocent? That guy's a walking advertisement for original sin. The entire time he was dating Evie he was beating her up. He likes that kind of game. I doubt he's ever loved another human being in his life. I don't for the life of me understand what Evie saw in him. No, Emery was the perfect choice. Talk about moral symmetry. Charlotte might even have approved." He signaled a right turn and pulled carefully off the freeway onto a deserted county road.

Jane recognized the route. She'd taken it many times herself. It took a bit longer to get to the lake, but the area was less traveled. Attempting to move her body as little as possible, she freed her other foot. Now what?

"What are you doing back there?"

"Just trying to get comfortable."

Freddy switched on the radio, finding a classical station. Vivaldi provided background music as they sped into the night. After a while he said, "No more questions?"

He seemed to want to talk. Not that he was interested in what she had to say. She was amazed that he saw no similarities between what he'd done to that young student, and what Emery had done to Evie.

"Well?"

"All right. How did you get the key to my door?"

"Easy. From your backpack. I saw you carrying it into the club one night. When I went to hang up Julia's coat, I noticed you'd left it in the coat room. So, I took a quick look. Your key chain was right in the front. I made some excuse to Julia about needing to run over to the drug store. Instead I went and had some duplicates made. Then, on the way back, I put them into the ignition of your car."

Of course, thought Jane. Why hadn't she suspected? "And the fake pipe bomb? You sent that to my father?"

"I did. I wanted to see if I could shake him. I didn't want Emery to have such a competent attorney."

So, at least about that, Emery had been right. "And the music box?"

"When I was over at Sigma Delta, I saw a bunch of them sitting next to the fireplace. When the room cleared, I just picked one up and left. I thought maybe you'd be more easily frightened. Turns out I was wrong."

"Why were you at Sigma Delta?"

"To make my weekly payment to Doyle. I hope he enjoys the extra cash. It won't be long before he meets with a small accident." He honked at a raccoon about to scurry into the road.

Jane closed her eyes and turned her head to the window. She had to think of something...fast. "How did you slip the drug into my Manhattan the other night?"

"Oh, that. I was in the bar when Doyle came in to get your drink. I'd just driven over from Wizards to pick up Julia, but she said she was running late. She suggested I go back to the condo and get some sleep. Mae would take her home later. Anyway, when Doyle came in, I told him I thought Mae needed help lifting some boxes in the food storage room. While he was gone, I put a rather heavy dose of liquid tranquilizer into your drink."

"Where did you get liquid tranquilizer?"

"Well, Miriam has never been able to swallow pills. Every medication she takes is in liquid form. Evie had

266

stolen the bottle from Miriam's nightstand. She insisted she needed it to help her sleep. I'd removed it from Evie's purse earlier that same evening. I didn't think she should be mixing it with alcohol."

"Do Evie or Julia know about...Jill?"

"Absolutely not! And they never will. Charlotte and her righteousness are the past. Julia and I are the future. That's what I have to concentrate on."

His words made her shiver. "Am I part of the past now too?"

He turned up the music. "No more talk."

"But Freddy," she said, "even though you've made some bad mistakes, you can still stop. Anytime you want! You don't have to go through with this just because you've started it. I thought...maybe...we were becoming friends. I mean, why didn't you kill me when you had the chance the other night?"

He leaned his arm across the back of the seat and turned around for a second. "I don't dislike you. That's not it at all. Actually, when it comes right down to it, I rather admire your courage. But I can't let you live. Just like Charlotte, you'd ruin everything for me. For my family. It's a question of priorities."

"Are you so *certain*?" She emphasized the last word.

"Now you're playing with me. No, I'm not certain. I'm not certain about anything. Sometimes I wonder what's wrong with me. I must have something missing inside. I could always argue either side of any given point with equal feeling. My mind can develop rationalizations at the speed of light."

"But you know they're rationalizations."

"Do I? They all seem to have relevance. Where's the truth? I can't seem to get a feel for it. Except—"

"Except what?"

"You know that houseboat I took you to? Where you slept while I finished cutting the grass? Well, that's the only place on earth I've ever been able to cut through all the crap and really...think. The most important conclusions of my life have been reached sitting on that deck. That's where I first knew I wanted to marry Julia. And later, I spent an entire night sitting in the center of the lake, figuring out what it meant to be a father. It's where I've spent my happiest hours." He shook his head. "You know, I never could go there while I was planning to murder Charlotte. I think I was afraid. I knew if I spent any time on that boat, I couldn't go through with it." His voice faltered.

"Freddy?" she asked after a long minute.

"What?"

"You never answered my question. Why didn't you kill me that night?"

"I...didn't have time. Julia was going to be getting home soon. I'd planned on putting you in the rowboat and taking you out to the center of the lake. It's very deep. I knew if I weighted your body properly, no one would ever find out what had happened. You would simply have disappeared. But all that took more time than I had."

A heavy wave of nausea passed over her. She closed her eyes and tried to concentrate on the moment. She was still alive. None of that had happened. At least, not yet. "But what about the next day?"

"Yes, I'd come back to finish it. But on my way through Brown Deer I spotted Miriam's car at the local grocery store. There was only one place she could be headed. Once again, I didn't have enough time to do it before she arrived on the scene, so I had to make a choice. I could simply leave—drive back to Minneapolis and let Miriam find you. Or I could drive up to the lodge myself and try to convince you I had nothing to do with it. The reason I decided on the latter was because once during the drive up the night before, I thought you became wakeful. I was afraid you'd seen me. I had to make sure that wasn't the case."

"And now you still have the same plan, except at a different lake."

"I mean it this time, Jane. No more talk. I've answered too many questions already." He pulled out the gun and turned around, pointing it at her. "Understood?"

She looked away.

He dropped the gun on the seat and continued driving. A few minutes later he took a sharp left onto a side road.

Jane realized they were only minutes now from Blackberry Lake. As far as she could see, she had one chance. Freddy wasn't expecting her feet to be free. If she could surprise him, kick him or knock the gun out of his hand, she might be able to get away. It was a long shot, but it was all she had. She felt the car descend to the small road which led to the cabin. Since none of the outside lights had been turned on, the property was pitch dark. She could make out a light or two across the lake, but that was it. As he came to a stop, she knew the cabin sat directly to their left. The tool shed was on the right. Once he'd turned off the headlights, she could see that the nearly full moon had risen just above the trees. It bathed the shore with its weak reflection. Depending on what happened, that might be good—or it might be very bad.

He turned off the motor and sat for a few moments in silence.

Jane hoped with all her heart that he was reconsidering what he was about to do. Even though he'd done some horrible things—and was more than capable of violence—she keenly felt his confusion. And his despair. Perhaps she could use that small reticence to her advantage. But how? The talking had stopped. Now appeared to be the time for action.

Freddy grabbed the gun and slid out of the front seat. After taking a second to get his bearings, he opened the back door and pulled Jane out. She held her feet together, pretending they were still tied. After propping her against the rear of the car, he continued to look around. As his eyes searched for the dock, Jane knew it was now or never. She wasn't going to be given lots of chances to get away. She brought her foot up swiftly into his groin. He gave a roar and dropped the gun, but didn't fall to the ground. Instinctively, she knew the blow hadn't been hard enough. Even so, she took off running toward the shed. If she could only get inside, she had the advantage of knowing the layout. Even in the dark, she was sure she could put her hand on a shears within seconds. It would take only a moment to rid herself of the rope around her wrists.

Just as she reached the door, she felt his body lunge against hers, sending her sprawling to the grass. She flipped on her back and began kicking the air wildly. She didn't have the leverage to get up. Even so, she knew she'd caught him a good one in the chest.

"You never give up, do you?" he grunted, falling on top of her and holding the gun to her temple. "Now," he said, catching his breath, "this time we're going to do it my way. No more of this shit!" When she said nothing, he yanked her to her feet. "There's a willow over there. Close to the shore. I'm going to tie you to it until I can get things organized. If you try anything else, I'll use this gun. Got it?"

She nodded.

"If you cooperate, this won't hurt. That's as much as I can promise. Now. Let's go." He grabbed her by the back of her sweater and pushed her forward. "Walk toward the tree."

She looked around at his face. The angel was still there.

"Move!"

She stumbled down the path which led to the dock. On the way she saw him pick up a rope.

"Lean into it," he ordered. "Front first." He wound the rope around her body over and over again, tying it tightly in several places. This time, he wasn't taking any chances.

The enormity of the situation was just beginning to sink in. There wasn't going to be a second chance. Her brain felt like it had short circuited, sending sparks and electrical impulses in random directions. She couldn't take it all in. Never would she see her father again. Or Cordelia. She was thirty-eight years old. Her mother had died when she was thirty-eight. Maybe this was the way it was in the Lawless family. Her mind flashed to Christine. Christine already knew what it felt like to die. At the very end, she'd said she wasn't afraid. But it wasn't like that for Jane. She hadn't had any time to prepare. She knew she was terrified.

Behind her, she could hear footsteps.

"It's time." said Freddy. His voice was soft. Almost gentle.

She ignored him, staring instead at the rising moon.

"Jane?"

"Just do it!"

Silence. "I have one last request."

A *request*? Surely he was kidding.

Another long silence. Then, coming very close to her face he said, "Tell me again why I shouldn't do this."

39

JANE turned her head very deliberately until she could see Freddy's face. "What did you say?"

"I asked you to tell me why I shouldn't go through with this."

Was she hearing him right? He seemed to be waiting for an answer. "Is this a joke?"

"No joke."

She felt her body about to explode. "Because goddammit, it's wrong! *That's* why."

"Why? I'm simply protecting myself and my family. What could be more elemental than that?"

Did he really want a polite, professorial debate? For god's sake, this was her *life* they were talking about! "Freddy, killing another human being is wrong!"

"But we do it in war all the time. As far as I'm concerned, this is war."

She exhaled slowly, trying to calm herself down. He was giving her one last chance to talk and she was damn well going to take it. "Freddy, listen to me." She had to pull it together. Her life depended on finding just the right words. She swallowed hard, noticing that her throat was as dry as chalk. "You...and Charlotte..." she began cautiously, "you disagreed over something you both felt was terribly important. Perhaps each of you had a point. But taking her life was not the solution."

"But what if she turned Julia against me! What if Julia had taken her side. I love her. We're having a child together! My marriage and my career are the two most important things in my life! Charlotte threatened both."

"Do you trust Julia's love so little that you think she'd be that easily swayed?"

He walked a few paces away. "Of course I trust her love. But you don't know her. In some ways, she was a lot like her mother. Her judgment was in question. She would have felt humiliated. I couldn't risk it."

"Yet by killing Charlotte, you've risked everything. And you've lost."

"What do you mean?"

"You're going to get caught, Freddy. If not by me, then by someone else. Remember that phone call you made from Emery's apartment? My father will use that to prove him innocent. All he needed was a crack in the prosecution's case, and this is a crack a semi could drive through. After he's acquitted, the police will go looking for someone else. It's only a matter of time. If you kill me, it will be just more blood on your hands."

"But if you're not around to talk, I might have a better chance of staying one step ahead of the police. It's all a crap shoot, you know that. Nothing is for certain."

"What about Doyle? Are you going to kill him too?"

"Doyle? Probably."

"Probably! Freddy, listen to yourself! Look where this has taken you. You beat up a young woman. Her only sin was loving you and wanting to spend her life with you. You think Emery is a complete bastard for what he did to Evie—but *you're* no different. You're just like him—a time bomb, waiting to explode. What if it's Julia next time? Have you thought of that?"

"No!"

"But it *is* possible. Freddy, think! Murder isn't going

273

to cure your problems! Where's it going to end?"

"It *will* end! And then everything will get back to normal."

Jane felt the bark scrape against the side of her face. No matter what she said, he turned it around. This was useless. He wasn't going to change his mind. The conversation was merely a way of assuaging his future guilt. He'd given his victim a fair chance to change his mind. What more could he do? She turned her face away.

"You're not saying anything." He stepped closer.

"What do you want me to say? I don't want to die! Are you waiting to see me beg?"

"No!"

"You'll regret this one day, Freddy. I guarantee it."

He turned his back to her, looking up at the clouds passing over the moon. "I don't think so."

"I'm going to make a prophecy. I'm betting my life that I'm right."

"What do you mean?"

"Very simple. You may not have felt any huge remorse about Charlotte's death, but you will about mine. And you won't be able to stand it. And later, both our murders will haunt you. I promise you on my *life* Freddy, my grave won't be a quiet one. I'll never leave you alone!"

"No more!"

"You wanted a reason to stop all this insanity, well there it is. You think you're protecting Julia and your baby, but you're only hurting them all the more. You can't keep killing people to hide what you did. And most of all, you can't hide from yourself!"

"I said no more!"

Jane could hear him walk away. "Freddy?" she called. He didn't respond. What was he doing now?

He returned a few moments later. "I have something for you." He walked around to the side of the tree.

"What?"

"It's brandy. I thought you might like some."

This was growing more ridiculous by the minute. She stared at the lake, saying nothing.

Freddy waited for a moment and then set the bottle on the ground. "I have lemonade if you'd prefer that. I'm afraid the only food I have with me is a bag of stale taco chips from yesterday's lunch."

"You're offering me a last meal?"

He shrugged. "I thought maybe—"

"I don't want anything."

"Please!"

She turned to look at him. "Why?"

"Why not?"

She couldn't take this anymore. Not another argument. He'd worn her down. She had no energy left. "All right."

"Which?"

"The lemonade." She could hear him uncap a bottle and pour some out.

He held the paper cup while she took several swallows. Then, waiting a few moments, he lifted it to her lips once again.

She finished it and then turned her head away. "What are you going to do now?" The gun was still in his belt.

"We're going to wait for a few minutes."

"Why?"

"Don't ask so many questions."

"What are you going to do to me if I do? Kill me?" This was absurd. She closed her eyes, noticing she was growing a bit light-headed. She hadn't eaten anything since lunch.

"Just be quiet now," said Freddy, sitting down on a rock.

She lowered her head against the tree trunk. In the distance, she could hear the sound of waves gently lapping against the sandy shore. Was this really happening? She felt the muscles in her legs begin to grow slack. Just like—

"Hey?"

275

"What?" He stood.

"Damn you!" she shouted. It finally dawned on her what was going on.

"Just be quiet."

"You put that tranquilizer in the lemonade."

"Shhh."

Her mind was growing fuzzy. Still, she fought with everything she had to keep herself alert. "You're really going to do it, aren't you? You're going to—." Her eyelids felt like lead weights were attached to them. She struggled to keep them open.

He brought his face very close to hers. "I promised, Jane. I said I'd do it in the most painless way possible."

"But you can't—" Her thoughts were beginning to scramble. The words simply wouldn't form in her mind. In the soft moonlight, her eyes focused one last time on his blond eyelashes.

"Just be quiet now. Don't fight it. You know, it's funny. I almost envy the peace you're going to find. Goodbye, Jane. Give my regards to Charlotte."

40

FREDDY parked his car in the underground lot and then took the elevator up to the fourteenth floor. As he entered the living room of his condo, he saw everything was quiet. Julia had left a light on for him next to the couch. He'd made good time on the way home from Repentance River. It was just after eleven.

Tossing his keys into a ceramic bowl on the kitchen counter, he headed for the bedrooms. He peeked his head into the spare room and saw that Evie was lying on the single bed, blankets piled high around her shoulders. From the sound of her breathing, he knew she was asleep. Julia had been working hard to turn the room into a nursery. He stared at the crib for a long moment before continuing down the hall.

Julia stirred as he came into their room. She opened her eyes, rubbing them for a moment, and then switched on the bedside lamp. "I'm glad you're home."

"How is she?" he asked, nodding toward the spare bedroom.

Julia took his hand and drew him down next to her on the bed. "Better. We talked for a long time. She seems to be ready to commit herself to a treatment program. I didn't want to push her. If it's not her decision, it won't work."

"What about Miriam? Did you call her?"

"No. Not yet. Evie wanted to get a reasonable night's sleep first. She's going to tell her everything in the morning."

"What do you think will happen?"

"Rose's death was an accident. I'm sure Miriam will see it that way. If Evie gives those two gem stones back, I think Miriam will have a pretty good chance of convincing Mae Williams to leave it at that. No police. Maybe this isn't the way the law looks at it, but I think Evie's suffered enough. She wants to straighten out her life. I think this time, she really means it." Julia propped her head up a bit, her eyes searching Freddy's face. "How did everything go with that student you called me about?"

"Yeah, I'm really sorry. Bad timing I guess. Actually, he's fine now. When he came to me after class, I simply couldn't say I was too busy. He'd...just broken up with a girl he's been dating for the last two years. It was pretty traumatic. And anyway, I'd only have been in the way here. Evie needed to talk to you."

She smiled at him. "You're a good man." She held his hand to her lips. "I don't know what I'd do without you. You know, before Mother died, we had a horrible argument. It was about you."

"Julia—"

"No, it's all right. But it's one of the reason's I've been so depressed lately. I hate leaving things unresolved. Mother never really wanted us to get together. That doesn't come as a shock to you, but it affected me more than I let on. But now, I think she did us a favor. She made me focus on what really matters in my life. I've been thinking a lot lately about our marriage. Don't laugh, but for a while I even worried about you and Evie."

"Evie! You didn't think—"

"No, I know you've been faithful. But, from the start, I've held back. I haven't been fair. In the back of my mind, I always wondered if Mother was right. But now I know she wasn't. I love you so much, Freddy. And I need you. You're the best thing that's ever happened to me." She kissed his fingers.

Freddy felt a spasm in his cheek.

"Is something wrong?"

He bent to give her a kiss. "Not when I'm with you."

Again, she smiled. "Are you coming to bed?"

"Not right now. I need to . . . unwind a bit. I think I'll watch some TV." Tenderly, he touched her hair.

"Do you want some company?"

"No. You need your rest." He put his hand on her stomach. "You both do."

"All right. But you won't be long."

"No, I won't." He let his eyes wash over her face. God but she was beautiful. So strong. It would be all right. He had to think that way or he couldn't go through with it. "I love you," he said, his words surprising him by their sudden fierceness.

"I know." She cocked her head. "You're in a strange mood tonight."

"Am I?" He got to his feet, turning off the light. "Now you close your eyes. I'm going to come back in here in a few minutes and I expect to find you asleep."

"But wake me when you come to bed. Promise?"

"I promise. Sweet dreams, my love." He wanted to say so much more, but instead, he just shut the door quietly and walked back down the hall.

41

Jane opened her eyes in a familiar room. Ribbon and rose wallpaper above knotty pine wainscoting. The quilt which covered her had been made by her grandmother and given to her when she was a little girl. As she tried to sit up and focus her eyes, she realized she wasn't completely awake. She'd only drifted back to consciousness a few minutes ago.

She was in her family's cabin. Freddy must have brought her inside, carrying her into one of the bedrooms. There was no other explanation. Except, why hadn't he finished the job he'd so obviously intended? A cold shiver ran through her as she thought of the last words he'd spoken. She let her head fall back against the pillow, pulling the quilt up tightly around her shoulders.

It was still pitch black outside. He'd turned on a light next to her bed. Her mind drifted as she listened to the creaking of the old cabin. Even in such familiar surroundings, she knew she wasn't safe. No one would think to look for her here. She was completely cut off. Perhaps he was still somewhere around. That thought galvanized her into action like nothing else could. She swung her feet out of bed and sat up, rubbing her temples as she tried to shake the cobwebs out of her mind.

Soundlessly, she moved into the hallway. Everything seemed quiet. As she passed each bedroom she looked inside. Nothing out of the ordinary. At last, she inched into the living room. The window next to the front door had been broken. So that's how he'd gotten in. She could see shards of glass on the floor next to a broom. He'd swept everything into a neat pile. Freddy Lindhurst was indeed a strange man. Quickly, she moved to the window and looked out. His car was gone. For the moment at least, she was safe.

Dragging herself into the kitchen, she slumped into a kitchen chair and, leaning her head on one hand, closed her eyes. What should she do now? She could call the Repentance River police. Or 911. When she opened her eyes, she noticed a piece of notebook paper which rested against a wooden bowl in the center of the table. Her name was printed on the outside. She picked it up and read:

> *You were right. I couldn't go through with it. And I can't live with myself knowing what I've done. I've made a mess of everything. Where are all those great rationalizations when you need them? I seem to be fresh out.*
>
> *Freddy*

She let the note drop to the table. Her first thought was one of relief. At least he wasn't coming back. It took a moment for the full weight of his words to sink in. Instantly, she crossed to the phone. The directories were on the counter next to it. She looked up Freddy's name in Minneapolis phone book and quickly dialed the number.

After several rings, a woman's voice answered. "Hello?"

"Julia?" asked Jane.

"Yes?" Her voice was thick with sleep.

"This is Jane Lawless. I wonder...could I talk to your husband?"

"What?" She coughed several times, trying to clear her throat. "At this hour? Do you know what time it is?"

"Actually, I don't."

There was a pause. "It's nearly 2 A.M."

"Is he there? This is kind of an emergency." She didn't want to say too much.

"Sure he's here. He came home about eleven." Her voice was full of annoyance.

Jane could hear movement. Then a soft voice called, "Freddy?"

Julia returned. "I guess he's not in the bedroom. He's probably fallen asleep out on the living room couch. Just a minute."

Jane waited, taking down a package of crackers from the cupboard. She was ravenous.

After a few seconds Julia came back on the line. Her voice sounded worried. "He's not here. I looked for a note, but there wasn't one. This isn't like him."

Jane didn't want to alarm her. After all, she didn't have positive proof of anything. "Maybe he went for a walk?"

"A walk? In the middle of the night? Look, why are you calling? You must know something! What's going on?"

"I just needed to talk to him. That's all. You don't have any idea where he might be?"

"None!"

"Ok. I'll call back in the morning."

"But—."

"Goodnight. I'm sorry I woke you." She hung up the phone before Julia could press her any further. Where could he be? As she stood staring out a window at the lake, she got an idea. The moon had moved around to the west, casting its light on the boat dock. That might be it. Sure! She had a gut feeling he'd gone to the houseboat. To think? Possibly. If he ever needed a clear head, it was now. But from the sound of his note, his intention was more ominous. Jane had a sinking feeling that Freddy was about to commit his last murder.

She immediately got on the phone to the county sheriff's office. The number rang several times before a male voice answered.

"Hello," she said quickly, "this is an emergency."

"Name?"

"What? Oh...ah, Lawless. Jane Lawless."

"Where are you located?"

"No, it's not me. I have reason to suspect someone is about to commit suicide."

"Who?"

"His name is Freddy Lindhurst. He's gone to a house-boat on Old Sawmill Lake. The east side. It's the first right off the highway as you're coming out of Brown Deer."

"All right. Why do you suspect he's about to commit suicide?"

"Why? I just know it. He's...despondent." She could tell the man wasn't buying it. "He murdered his *mother-in-law*, for chrissake."

The man snorted. "Lady, if this is a joke—"

"I'm not kidding. Have you heard of the Charlotte Fortnum murder case in Minneapolis?"

"Sorry."

"Well, it's a long story. I don't have time to explain it all right now. But you've got to believe me. You have to send someone out there right away. It's a matter of life and death." She knew she wasn't handling this well.

"Ok, calm down. Even if I wanted to send someone to Old Sawmill Lake right now, I couldn't. We're understaffed tonight. And about an hour ago there was a big barn party out near Cambridge that turned nasty. Most of my men are still there."

"But—."

"I promise I'll get someone out to that lake as soon as possible. That's the best I can do."

"Ok," she said, feeling an acute sense of defeat.

"Thanks." She dropped the receiver back on the hook. Again, she picked up the phone. She had an idea. She dialed her father's number in St. Paul.

A sleepy voice answered, "Lawless here."

"Hello Dad?"

"Jane? Is that you? For god's sake, it's the middle of the night."

"I know. Ah . . . welcome home."

"Thank you." He put his hand partially over the receiver. She could hear him tell Marilyn who was calling. "I assume you didn't call just to say hi."

"No. Actually, I have kind of a favor to ask."

"Uhm?" He didn't sound particularly receptive.

"I'm up at the cabin."

"That's wonderful, honey. But can you cut to the chase?"

"Sure." She swallowed hard. If she told him the entire story, it would take too long. If he knew the kind of danger she'd been in, he'd be hysterical. She had to make it just right. "I know who killed Charlotte Fortnum."

"Excuse me?"

"It wasn't Emery. It was Freddy Lindhurst."

"How do you know that?"

"It would take too long, but I know it for a fact. Now, here's the problem. Could you drive up here right away? I think Freddy is about seven miles away—on Old Sawmill Lake. And I think he may be about to—"

"To what?"

"Commit suicide. We've got to stop him!"

"Suicide." There was a pause. "All right. Just give me a minute. Do you have a car?"

"No."

Silence. "Then how did you get up there?"

"Freddy brought me. Actually, he kidnapped me."

"What!"

"I'm fine, Dad. Really. I thought maybe I should just start walking down the county road toward Brown Deer, but—"

284

"Absolutely not! You stay put until I get there. Do you understand?"

Hearing those words, she breathed a sigh of relief. "I do. I promise, I'll wait for you."

"Good. I'm leaving right now. There won't be any traffic, so I should be to the cabin in half an hour. Have you called the police?"

"Yes. They're sending someone out as soon as possible. But it may take them a while."

"Listen, young woman, I expect a full explanation when I get there."

"You'll have it." Something about his voice still made her feel like a teenager who'd come in after her curfew. "And Dad...thanks." She put the phone back on the hook.

A cup of tea was in order. And more crackers. When her father arrived, she needed to be physically ready for whatever the rest of the night might bring.

42

"THERE'S the turn off," announced Jane, pointing to a fork in the road. "That should take us straight to the boathouse."

Raymond braked and pulled sharply onto the unpaved path. "So, is that everything?" he asked impatiently.

"I've left out some details, but basically yes. Emery is innocent."

"Lucky for him. I wouldn't even consider representing the man after what he did to you." He glanced at his daughter, a grim expression on his face.

"So what do you think I should do about Evie?"

The car hit a deep rut. "Jesus, you'd think they'd have this road paved." He turned on his brights. "As an officer of the court, I must advise you to inform the police immediately. As your father, I can only urge you to consider your position. Should someone in the Gower family find out the truth about Rose's death, you could be in deep legal troubles for withholding evidence. Obstruction of justice. I think it's even possible you could be sued civilly."

"And if no one finds out?"

He shook his head. "Think hard, Janey. That's all I can say. But remember, whatever you decide, I'll stand behind you."

She reached for his hand. "Thanks." As she turned to look out the side window, she spotted the hill behind the boathouse. "There! It's just up over this rise."

Raymond slowed the BMW to a crawl, switching off the headlights. "No use advertising our arrival." He brought the car to a stop in a sandy patch about twenty yards from the shore. "The place looks deserted."

Jane quickly hopped out. "Look! The houseboat is gone!"

Raymond moved around the back of the car and stood next to her. He glanced at the sailboat, and then at the darkened boathouse. "What do you want to do?"

She shook her head. "I don't know." Walking a few paces toward the dock, she stopped. The moon sat low in the western sky, the lake an eerie moon crater in front of her. She listened for a second. "Why aren't we hearing a motor?"

"Maybe he's just sitting out there in the dark. It's a pretty big lake. I've fished here a couple of times."

"It's too quiet."

Suddenly, an explosion ripped the silence. Out on the water, orange and yellow flames burst into the night sky. It was like a Fourth of July celebration, only this time, with a deadly purpose.

"Get down!" shouted Raymond, grabbing her and hitting the sand just as burning debris began to fall all around them. He covered her body with his own. When the shower was over, they both sat up, watching chunks of wood burn all along the deserted beach. Neither said anything for several minutes.

Finally, Raymond slipped his arm around his daughter's shoulder. "I'm sorry, sweetheart. Looks like we were too late."

Jane was stunned. Her eyes were still fixed on what was left of the burning boat.

"He probably felt he didn't have any other choice." Raymond turned at the sound of a siren. "That must be the police. I'll run back to the road and tell them what we've found."

Jane sat for a moment longer. She felt dazed. Empty of all emotion except regret. Finally, she stood, brushing the sand off her jeans. If they could have arrived just a few minutes earlier, maybe another tragedy could have been prevented. A life for a life, that's what some would say. But that's not how she saw it. A raw feeling in the back of her throat told her she'd failed. It shouldn't have ended this way.

Picking up a stick, she walked out to the end of the dock and stood looking down at the obsidian surface of the lake. The cold, blue-ish autumn night would soon end. In a few hours, it would be light. And tomorrow, her life would slowly return to normal. Somehow, it no longer seemed enough.

"Jane?" called her father.

She turned her head. "What?"

"I'm going to speak to the police first, but they want to talk to you as well. I think we'll use the boathouse. It's unlocked. If you need me, I'll be right inside."

"Fine." She watched while he entered and turned on several lights. Two policemen followed him. Thank god he was here. She couldn't deal with the police right now. She couldn't deal with anyone. Sitting down on the wood planks, she dangled her hand in the water. It was a chilly night. She pulled her sweater more snugly around her body. As she gazed up at the stars, she listened to the sounds of the lake. In the distance, she began to pick up the faint sound of splashing. Surely a fish couldn't make that kind of noise.

She squinted into the darkness, trying to get a fix on the location. Something wasn't right. Inching back from the edge, she stared into the blackness. Suddenly, directly in front of her, a hand reached up out of the water. It looked bleached and bloodless in the pale moonlight as it seized the edge of the dock. She felt her body freeze. Before she could react, Freddy had pulled himself out of the lake and was sitting on the dock, soaking wet, his back mere inches from her. Almost as a reflex she whispered, "I don't believe it."

He turned and watched her for a moment. Then, he began shaking his hair, trying to rid it of excess water. "I don't suppose you have a towel?"

"No," she said, realizing her mouth was open. Hesitantly, she moved a bit closer, unable to stop herself from staring.

Freddy sat shivering, his arms wrapped around his chest. Through chattering teeth he said, "I suppose it would have been easier for everyone if I'd gone through with it."

Jane took off her sweater and handed it to him.

Furtively, his eyes flicked to her face. "Thanks," he said, taking it from her. "You know, I just kept thinking—maybe I can make Julia understand. Even if I go to prison for the rest of my life, if she still loved me—or if she could even *forgive* me...it would be enough." He slipped on the sweater.

"For what it's worth, I think you made the right decision."

"You do?"

She realized she wasn't frightened. Freddy looked beaten. Exhausted. She eased herself down next to him. "But you're right. Some may wish you'd taken the easy way out."

"It wasn't easy. Nothing is easy anymore." He turned his head away.

They sat for a few moments in silence. Finally Jane said, "The police are talking with my father in the boathouse. I think it's time you gave yourself up."

He took a deep breath, glancing in that direction. "I suppose so." Still, he hesitated. This time he started to cry. "I don't know how I could have let this happen. I destroyed Charlotte. And now I've destroyed not only my wife's life, but my child's. I'm too much of a coward to go through with my own death, but how can I *live* with what I've done?"

"I don't know, Freddy. I truly don't have any answers for you."

He nodded, struggling to regain his composure. "No. Of course not." He took a moment and then got to his feet, running an arm over his face. "How come you're here anyway?"

"I thought you might try something like this. I was hoping to prevent it."

"Why? You of all people should want to see me pay dearly for what I've done."

She shook her head. "It has to end somewhere. This is all such a waste."

"Jane!" called her father from an open window. "Who's that with you out there?"

Freddy's ears pricked up. "Freddy Lindhurst, sir."

"Who!"

"I'm coming right up." He turned to Jane for one final second. "I know it doesn't change anything, but . . . I'm sorry."

A cloud passed over the moon. When the dim light returned, she could see his pale, intense face framed by the indigo sky. The look of anguish in his eyes was so shattering, it twisted something deep inside her. "I know," she whispered.

He held her eyes for a long moment. Then, turning, he walked slowly down the dock toward the waiting police.

43

JANE walked quickly across the footbridge. She'd promised Dorrie she would meet her at their favorite park bench just after two. The knot in the pit of her stomach told her she'd made the right decision. No use prolonging the inevitable. Jane knew she hadn't spent a great deal of time over the last couple of days thinking about their situation. Still, she'd come to a very definite conclusion. It wouldn't take long to say what she had to say.

True to her word, Dorrie was already there, feeding the remnants of a late lunch to one of the squirrels. She turned as Jane approached. "How are you feeling?"

"Better," said Jane.

Dorrie waited until she was seated before continuing. "Miriam filled me in on some of the details. Are those scratches on your face?"

Jane nodded. "I don't really know how I got them. I was unconscious at the time." She could see Dorrie grimace. "I'm fine. Really." She glanced at the lake. Dorrie did the same. Neither wanted to start the conversation. Finally Jane said, "I understand the offer Miriam made you to sit on the Gower Board of Directors has been withdrawn."

"It has."

"I'm sorry, Dorrie. I know you wanted it."

Dorrie managed a faint smile. "It's not the end of the world." A certain depression seemed to settle over her. "Miriam was very impressed by what you did."

"Good for Miriam." She was trying not to show any bitterness, but it was a losing battle.

Dorrie took a deep breath. "I don't want to fight."

"Is that why you think I came? To pick a fight?"

She looked away. "No."

"You're going back to her, aren't you."

"To be honest Jane, I don't know." She took her sack and dumped the last bit of crumbs onto the ground. "I was hoping you'd tell me how you felt."

"I can't live like this, Dorrie." She folded her arms protectively over her chest.

"I know."

"I guess, bottom line is, I feel betrayed. Trust is a delicate thing. The fact that you didn't come to me with what was happening—and even after you'd slept together...I mean, when were you planning on telling me about it? If I hadn't heard that phone message—"

Dorrie looked down. "I'm so sorry."

"It's not enough. I care about you very much, but it's not working. I know you. You'll never be satisfied until you put your feelings for Miriam to the test."

"But if I do that, I've lost *you*."

Jane hated this. She'd never been very good at endings. "I think we've already lost each other."

Again, Dorrie turned her face away.

Jane could tell she was crying. "I'm sorry too. It's not what I wanted. I'd hoped—" She let her voice trail off. What was the point?

"I've made a mess of everything." Dorrie pulled out a tissue from the pocket of her jacket. "It's all my fault."

"I don't want to talk about whose fault it is." She just wanted this to be over.

"Can we still be friends?"

Jane closed her eyes.

"I know that's what everybody says, but I really mean it. I don't want to lose you—not totally." Tears were streaming down her face.

"Dorrie, I—"

"Don't say anything now," she sniffed. "We'll talk later. When we're both more...more stable."

Jane felt like all the blood had drained from her body. It took an effort of will just to say, "Sure. I'll call you." She stood, looking up at a flock of birds flying high overhead. They were already moving south for the winter. Funny. In the past few days, the summer warmth had finally ended. She hadn't even noticed.

"No you won't."

"What?"

"You won't call."

Jane turned and looked down at her. "Have I ever broken my word to you?"

Dorrie's mouth quivered. "No."

"I won't this time either." She wanted to run as fast as she could in any direction that would take her *away*.

"I just wish—"

"Wish what?"

"That...I was more certain." She paused. "Miriam is. She wants me to move into her house right away."

"Be careful," said Jane.

"What do you mean?"

"Just that." She wanted to say more, but it would only sound like more bitterness. "Dorrie...I wish you the best. I really do."

Gravely, she nodded.

"I'll give your regards to your Uncle Morris when I talk to him next."

"Oh?" Dorrie wiped her eyes. "Did he call?"

"He did."

"Well, at least I gave you something."

Jane crouched down, taking Dorrie's hand. "You gave

293

me a great deal. I won't ever forget that." Tenderly, she brushed a strand of hair away from her eyes. Then, before Dorrie could begin crying again, Jane got to her feet and walked quickly back across the footbridge. When she knew she was out of Dorrie's sight, she broke into a dead run.

44

"THERE you are!" erupted Cordelia, bursting into the kitchen of Jane's restaurant. "I've been waiting in your office for half an hour."

"I didn't realize we had an appointment," said Jane, leaning over one of the flat top stoves. She was tasting a new citrus sauce one of the sous chefs had made for the roast duck. "That's quite a—" She twirled her finger, "—turban."

"This old thing?" Cordelia patted the feathered, gold lamé creation into place. "Just something I threw together."

Jane remained poker-faced. "So? What's up?"

"Don't be coy. We need to talk!"

"About what?"

Cordelia tapped her foot. "I will not be kept in the dark a millisecond longer! You nearly died last night, Janey. I want the details!"

Jane grimaced. Putting a finger to her lips, she picked up her briefcase and physically hauled Cordelia out of the room. "You don't need to advertise my personal life."

Cordelia wrestled her arm out of Jane's grip. Indignantly, she straightened her paisley tunic. "I merely want to feel included, Janey. You didn't call all day. What was I to think?"

"I was in bed until one."

"I know that. I phoned your house four times this morning. Beryl was sick of hearing from me, but, stalwart friend that I am, I persisted. By the way, when did *she* get back from Peter's?"

"Just after nine. Peter brought her on his way to work. I will say this. It was great to have her back. I've missed her terribly." Jane entered her office and set the briefcase on her desk. "And it felt awfully good to sleep in my own bed again." She raised an eyebrow. "Why aren't you sitting down?"

Cordelia pointed to the clock on the wall.

"Yes? It's four. Is that significant in some way?"

"Tea time!"

"You want to go upstairs and have something to eat?"

"Smart as a whip, Janey. I've always said that about you. And I've already told Irma to save us a table in the back. The dining room isn't crowded. You can tell me everything over cucumber sandwiches, cream biscuits, Dundee cakes and Rose Pouchong. I'll settle for a simple Darjeeling if you aren't in such a bizarre mood."

"No, the Rose Pouchong is fine."

"Splendid." She flapped her elbows excitedly.

"Shall we walk up, or would you like to fly?"

Once seated in the dining room, Jane noticed Mae Williams enter the restaurant and speak briefly with the hostess.

"Looks like we're about to have company"

Cordelia looked around. "Ah. Well, the more the merrier, I always say."

As Mae approached, Jane stood. "I'm glad you could make it." She motioned her to a chair.

"I got your message. I don't have more than a couple of minutes, but I agree, we need to talk."

A waiter arrived, pen and pad in hand. "Can I get you something?" he asked Mae.

"We're having a *proper* tea," sniffed Cordelia, fluttering her eyelashes dramatically. "We've already ordered. You must join us."

Mae shook her head. "I've never cared much for tea."

"In that case," continued the waiter, "we also have a choice of several mineral waters, iced coffee, fresh lemonade—"

"Yes, the lemonade would be fine."

"Bring me one too," said Cordelia, rearranging the flowers in the center of the table.

The waiter looked at Jane.

"No thanks." She swallowed hard. "Lemonade doesn't agree with me any more."

After he was gone, Mae leaned into the table and spoke confidentially. "I want to extend to you, Jane, our deepest thanks for a job well done."

"Has Evie spoken with you then?"

"She talked to Miriam this morning. We all met together early this afternoon. There were a lot of tears and apologies. And some promises were made as well."

"Have you reached a decision yet about what you're going to do?"

"You mean, are we going to inform the police?" She paused while the waiter set her drink in front of her. "No. And, hopefully you will concur in this. Evie has made some awful mistakes for which I believe she is genuinely sorry. Right now, she needs *help*—not punishment. It's within our power to grant that. This morning, we reached an agreement. She will enter a treatment program next week. Once she's out, she will perform five hundred hours of community service. As a matter of fact, she'll be taking over Rose's job in the food storage room." She took a sip of her lemonade.

The tea finally arrived. Jane poured some for herself and then for Cordelia. "Have you talked to Julia today? I was wondering if she'd seen Freddy."

Mae gave a sober nod. "She went to the jail around

noon. Miriam talked to her briefly after she came out. I don't know what's going to happen. It's a . . . ghastly situation." She shook her head. "You know, Jane, as I look at this, Emery Gower owes you a great deal."

Cordelia snorted. "Did you hear the latest on brother Emery?"

"What?" asked Jane.

"Why dearheart, when I talked to your father around ten this morning, he mentioned that two women had just come forward to charge him with sexual assault. One he dated, the other is an employee of The Gower Foundation."

Jane whistled. "I can't say it comes as a surprise."

"Perhaps there's some justice after all," muttered Cordelia, smoothing the feathers on her turban.

Mae finished her lemonade. "Well, I've got to be off. I'm afraid I've got another appointment."

"Just one more thing," said Jane, stirring some milk into her cup. "You know that dossier you did on me? The one we talked about the night you came to my house?"

"Yes? What about it?"

"I wanted to ask you one more time. Who said I was cheap?"

Cordelia began to choke.

"Are you all right?" asked Jane, reaching around and patting her on the back.

She nodded, banging herself on the chest. "Fine," she rasped." She gave Mae a sickly smile.

"As I said before, I'm afraid our sources must remain confidential."

"But—"

"Sorry," said Mae. She smiled at Cordelia. "It was good to see both of you again. By the way, Jane, your restaurant is absolutely lovely. This is the first time I've ever been here." She took a moment to look around.

"Why don't you and your husband join me for dinner one night soon?"

Mae's expression brightened. "He'd love that. That's very kind of you."

"Good. Just call the reservation desk. They'll let me know the date and time."

Mae hesitated before leaving. "You're quite a woman, Jane. I wish it could have been under different circumstances, but I'm glad we met."

"Me too." She rose and shook Mae's hand. "We'll see you soon, then?"

"You will."

After she was gone, the waiter arrived with their sandwiches and cakes. They were arranged on a delicate, three-tiered serving plate.

"Are you sufficiently recovered to eat?" asked Jane, doing her best not to smirk.

Cordelia drummed her fingers on the table. "You did that on purpose."

"No, I just assumed you'd said it. *Cheap* is a word I can see dribbling out of your mouth. I simply wanted confirmation."

"Well now, you'll never know for sure." She closed her eyes and thrust her chin in the air.

Jane took a bite of her favorite Grasmere gingerbread. "Come on, Cordelia. Look at this spread. Blackberry and quince jam. Buttered brown bread. Anchovy crisps. Cucumber and watercress sandwiches. Brandy cream cups. Sugar thins. Fruit tarts. What more do you want?"

"Respect," said Cordelia without missing a beat.

"You always have my respect."

"Humph." She opened one eye and reached for an Orange Jumble.

Jane sat back and sighed, letting her shoulders sink. She picked up her tea cup and stared into space.

"Something wrong?"

"What? Oh, not really. I was just thinking."

"About what?"

"Oh, you know. Things. Dorrie, actually."

"What about Dorrie?"

"Well . . . I met her at Loring Park earlier this afternoon."

"Really!" Cordelia dropped her pout and began loading her plate with food.

"She'd left several messages for me over the past couple of days. I suppose she thought I was ignoring her."

Cordelia nodded, too busy eating to say very much. "Have you made any decisions?"

"I have."

"So give!"

Jane shook her head. "I just can't talk about it right now." She finished the gingerbread. "I will say this much. The last couple of days have given me quite a perspective. In a way, I think it's helped."

"Thank you Freddy Lindhurst."

Jane gave her a somewhat funereal nod.

"Sorry. Maybe we should change the subject."

"Good idea." She paused, and then lowered her voice for emphasis. "Did Dad tell you about his wedding plans?"

"No! The little rascal never said a word. I was too busy asking him about *you* to even remember."

"Well, it's official. He and Marilyn are getting married in the spring."

"That's wonderful!" Cordelia wiped her mouth with the linen napkin and held up her lemonade. "A toast."

Jane hoisted her teacup. "To young love."

Both women laughed.

"To Mugs!" said Cordelia, wiggling her eyebrows. She waited for Jane's toast.

"To . . . an unknown someone," she said at last. "I guess that tells you my decision."

Cordelia set down her glass. "I'm sorry, dearheart."

"Don't be. I wished Dorrie the best of luck with Miriam. She's going to need it."

"Ouch."

"Oh, come on," said Jane. "I'm sick of all this *angst*.

300

And besides, we never finished our toast." She elbowed Cordelia in the ribs until she once again took up her lemonade.

"Let's forget the young love crap," said Cordelia, sensing an opportunity to be picturesque. "How about this." She cleared her throat and put one hand over her chest. "To us! To bubble baths and chocolate-covered coffee beans. To feathers and fringe and flannel underwear. To Ethel Merman and Ralph Nader. To moonlight and espresso—decaffinated of course. To...oysters! To Wonder Woman and "The Wizard of Oz." To all things fat and round and rich and comforting. And most of all, to friendship and to life! May we both live it to the fullest, *wherever* it leads."

"Here here!" shouted Jane.

Across the room a man began to clap. "Great toast," he called.

Humbly, Cordelia lowered her eyes. And then—she grinned.

Selected Mysteries From Seal Press

Hallowed Murder by Ellen Hart. $8.95, 0-931188-83-0
Featuring a memorable cast of characters including Minnesota
restaurateur—and part-time sleuth—Jane Lawless, this suspenseful mystery gives an intriguing inside view of the undercurrents
of sorority and religious life. First in the series.

Vital Lies by Ellen Hart. $8.95, 1-878067-02-8 Jane Lawless
and her unpredictable sidekick, Cordelia Thorn, unravel a
gripping story of buried memories from the past that wreak
havoc on the present. Second in the series.

Stage Fright by Ellen Hart. $9.95, 1-878067-21-4 Jane Lawless
is back again and embroiled in a case of dramatic proportions. A
classically riveting page-turner in which the real performances
begin only *after* the curtain comes down. Third in the series.

Still Explosion by Mary Logue. $18.95, cloth, 1-878067-29-X
When savvy journalist Laura Malloy sets out to write a feature
on abortion, she doesn't stop to consider the consequences. But
when a bomb explodes in the local family planning clinic, Laura
plunges into an investigation that becomes increasingly sinister
and strange. First in the series.

Trouble in Transylvania by Barbara Wilson. $18.95, cloth,
1-878067-34-6 Globetrotting translator Cassandra Reilly is on
the move again. A series of chance encounters on a train to
Budapest divert Cassandra to a spa in the heart of Transylvania.
When murder strikes, Cassandra is ready to investigate with her
usual humor and aplomb. Second in the series.

Gaudí Afternoon by Barbara Wilson. $8.95, 1-878067-89-X
Amidst the dream-like architecture of Gaudí's city, this high-
spirited comic thriller introduces amateur sleuth Cassandra
Reilly as she chases people of all genders and motives. First in the
series.

SEAL PRESS, founded in 1976 to provide a forum for women
writers and feminist issues, has many other books of fiction,
non-fiction and poetry. You may order directly from us at 3131
Western Avenue, Suite 410, Seattle, Washington 98121 (add
15% of total book order for shipping and handling). Write to us
for a free catalog or if you would like to be on our mailing list.